PALMETTO CROSSING

Dan Brady

This work is dedicated to the many in the criminal justice system who place the truth above all else, and the unsung heroes working in the public sector who care for the lost and impoverished ensuring no one gets excluded from the protections of justice. It's also dedicated to the volunteers at inner city agencies, and the selfless members of the business community who contribute their love by sharing with the less fortunate.

Chapter 1

At 2:38 am, a raspberry Danish in one hand and a large travel mug in the other, Officer Michael Cady shoved his shoulder against the exit door of the Wawa gas station. Coffee aroma seeped into his nostrils, and he glanced down at the dark fluid collecting around the rim of the mug's cap. *I don't need this spilling all over my paperwork!*

He lifted the cup to his face and sipped up the overflow. Stopping to do so had allowed a delivery van to pass in front.

Had it not been for that five-second pause, Cady would have walked directly to his vehicle at the rear of the building. By doing so, he would have missed seeing the familiar rusty truck illegally parked on the grass and pointing in the wrong direction on Manatee Avenue. He shook his head. *Damn! Four hours to go, and I was hoping to get through it without more paperwork.*

Cady triggered the blue lights, checked his watch and noted it was 2:40 am. Though he could have struck the truck with a short five-iron shot, the store's exit directed vehicles into an opposite traffic flow. He had to drive four blocks before he could turn onto a street that put him back on Manatee Avenue and going in the right direction.

He parked on the grass, nose to nose and several feet in front of the truck then radioed the location and waited for the dispatcher's confirmation. He grabbed a flashlight from the console and pushed the door open. The ding, ding, ding of the opened door broke the silence of the morning.

Hot and still, the August Florida humidity clung to everything, and the intense moisture of sewer refuse from the recycled irrigation water dampened the road's edges. The odors stuck to the droplets dripping off the grass stems wetting the scraps of soiled candy wrappers, used Kleenex tissues, and newspaper sections. All was reckless debris thoughtlessly tossed out of vehicle windows or abandoned by careless garbage workers. But collectively, they were the early morning sights and smells Cady never tired of.

He slid outside, slammed the door, and waited for his body to adjust to the dampness and the odors.

Cady, a twenty-year police veteran, always wore polished shoes and a crease in his pants, the reflection of a six-year tour as an Army MP. Known as efficient and fair, he once drew ridicule for dragging a homeless person's shopping cart two miles to a local Salvation Army shelter after the individual was rushed to a hospital.

Well-liked and respected by fellow officers and community members, the brass often chose Cady to visit schools or participate in public relations events. He especially enjoyed working the midnight to eight shifts. With his daughter off to college in Gainesville, he finally could work nearly the same hours as his wife, Amy, an Intensive Care nurse at Manatee Memorial Hospital. As a night cop, he was used to surprises, but this mornings events would shoot to the front of the parade.

The lifeless person leaning against the passenger door was Cady's friend, Wally Gaslight. In the past Cady had issued Gaslight motor vehicle warnings and moving violation citations. Yet, they remained cordial and respectful friends regardless of all their encounters.

From where Cady stood, his friend appeared dead. He inhaled deeply, made the sign of the cross, and whispered, *Jeeze! Oh, c'mon, Wally.* Cady's heart pounded, his stomach soured, and he chewed against the inside wall of his mouth as he approached the passenger door.

Chapter 2

Then Gaslight stirred. Cady's first thoughts were anger toward his friend for frightening him. That quickly resolved and got replaced with relief. At first, he just stared at Gaslight slumped against the passenger door, then he noticed the horrible stench. Pointing the flashlight into the truck bed, he saw what he thought to be pieces of slaughtered animal parts oozing out a burlap potato sack. Not so unusual in these parts as fishermen often use bits leftover from dressing wild animals as bait chum.

"The volume of flies and maggots led me to believe they weren't grocery items," Cady would later joke.

A closer look revealed food scraps, pieces of human fingers, intestines, and what Cady assumed to be organs. The most startling of all was a small foot attached to a shin bone, everything exposed because a short piece of butcher's string securing the open end broke.

Cady ran a quick assessment of what he knew about his friend. In an age of developers stuffing gated communities with people from everywhere, the newcomers were a random selection of characters ranging from bankers and laborers to artists and con men. Wally Gaslight was one of the last true Floridians, a dinosaur, a real proverbial, home spun. He was slow moving, kind, humble, and loved his old rusty truck.

Gaslight was the first-person neighbors often went to for help. He fed stray animals and found homes for lost dogs and cats. Though not a solid churchgoer, he was never heard to use profanity and kept pictures of the Madonna, and various crosses and crucifixes throughout his home. Also, though not a Catholic, a set of rosary beads dangled from his windshield mirror.

Gaslight's memory of the evening would always be sketchy. He would recall Cady waking him, then being placed in the rear seat of another police car. Most upsetting was the worried stare on Cady's face while he was being driven away by the other officer. It would take several hours before Gaslight would learn the severity of his situation.

Cady's police instincts flashed alarms. He stared at the empty street, trying to think and clear his head. *Gaslight stumbled into something terrible. The right people got to get assigned to this.* Running through a list of names in his head, he scratched out some as incompetent or too insensitive. Finally, settling on two detectives in the division.

Cady turned and caught Gaslight's stir, and grin. "Wally, you're drunk," he said.

"Mr. Cady, I'm sleepin' in my truck. I knowed better thin to be drivin' drunk."

"Do you know where you are?" Cady said.

"Yes. I am at the Bucket of Blood. I'm resting cuz I gots to get back to fixin' and dressin' up the feral boar I gots hangin'.'"

The Bucket of Blood, a redneck bar in Ellenton, had been around for over eighty years. It earned its name after taking up the site of a former slaughterhouse. Cady, known and respected by almost everyone there, had to show up occasionally to quell drinking disturbances between friends and lovers. He never encountered an altercation.

Aside from finding a lot of noise and cantankerous characters, Cady figured it would never become a hangout for any serious criminal element. The patrons consisted of an older group of blue collar, decent, down-to-earth folks. The dozen or so regulars were solid enough to make it uncomfortable for any unscrupulous people to blend in. It was usually smoky, sometimes dirty, and loud on certain evenings. Cady once joked with his wife, "The Bucket of Blood is supposed to be a social club. Sometimes it like Noah's Ark, you can find two of anything there, and it may be possible to get ptomaine poisoning by just reading one of the menus stapled to the wall behind the bar."

He turned back to Gaslight who kept slurring through a story about spending part of the evening at the Bucket of Blood and stopping for a nap before heading home. "I gotta' rush n' git home n' finish the dressin' of a hog," he kept stressing.

Cady quickly surmised that several hours earlier, Gaslight started a butchering project, got distracted, and finally remembered about it, "jest now," sending him off into a state of panic.

"Mr. Cady, you knowed me. I nevah lie."

"I know you never lie, Mr. Gaslight, but lying has got nothing to do with you driving in the condition you're in."

"I haint drivin', sir. I'm stayin' here, sleepin' for a spell 'cause I gotta get back to finishing that hog."

Cady said, "Mr. Gaslight, you're on Manatee Avenue. Look around. Does any of this look like it's near the Bucket of Blood?"

Gaslight stared at the unfamiliar streetlamps, unlike any in his neighborhood. On both sides of the street were businesses, their darkened office windows exposed only the dull security lights inside. Not far ahead was the Wawa gas station, lit up enough to turn its parking lot into daylight.

"I haint drivin'. I promise. I'm just sleepin' and restin'," Gaslight said, again.

Cady said, "It's close to three o'clock in the morning, and your truck is pointing in the wrong direction on Manatee Avenue, which also happens to be a state highway."

***

As Gaslight's drunken fog lifted, Cady, every patient, allowed him time to realize that neither he nor the truck were where he thought. After discovering this, Gaslight faced turned ashen, his bloodshot eyes swelled and his bottom lip quivered uncontrollably.

"Ooh, Lord, help me! Marsha Pickering is always talkin' bout them UFO fellers she says she seen in Palmetta." Then sticking his hands out the window, he grasped one of Cady's hands between his palms as if in prayer. "Oh, Mr. Cady! What could they have done to me?"

"Wait a minute, Wally. You're taking this too far ahead right now. I'm sure once you sleep for a bit, this will be much clearer for you."

"Is it possible they stuck some pins in me? Maybe put me to sleep to do strange things to my body? Oh, Lord!"

Gaslight now became aware of the stench. "It stinks to high heavens out here! Could they have made me eatin' stuff that too upsetting to my bowels?" He jumped out of the truck and Cady stopped him.

"I'm not sure we can travel down that path right now. I've got to arrest you and have your truck towed. So, sit right here on the sidewalk. Don't move. I'll be right back."

Cady took three steps, stopped, and turned back. "Let me have the keys, Wally."

Fumbling through his overall pockets, Gaslight pulled out pieces of gum wrappers, gasoline station receipts, and spent matches. The latter stuffed away so as not to be tossed out as a fire hazard.

Stay right there, please. I'll look around for them after." Cady didn't want Gaslight to look into the truck bed or hear the conversation that was going to take place inside the cruiser.

Chapter 3

Over the radio and using call numbers only, he connected to the evening dispatcher, Ray Provencher. "Ray, is the sarge around?"

Sergeant Danny Lapointe, a thirty-year veteran, serious and honorable, got summoned to the communication room. Usually professional and cordial, but this morning Provencher noticed iciness as he relayed the mic to him.

Cady also felt Lapointe seemed unusually curt and harsh.

"This is Lapointe. What's the problem?"

Earlier that evening, Lapointe read an interdepartmental bulletin regarding Bunson Rosa, a violent sexual predator recently released from prison by mistake. Lapointe had been around long enough to read between the lines of these kinds reports. It had the smell of a major coverup. The judicial system wanted him back in prison and they wanted it done quietly. To cover up an error and keep everything under the radar and away from the press, the usual alarms sent out immediately had been slow in coming and worded cautiously.

Lapointe mused. *Got to be a lot of big asses on the line for this one. Why else would they be so quiet about it?* Throughout his years of police work, he'd seen similar situations. This one consisted of a series of lies and innuendos concerning the release of Rosa. Once reading it, Lapointe shook his head in disgust and mused. *Lawyers found a technicality in a judge's sentencing language? C'mon! Bullshit!* Rosa wasn't just a petty criminal, as the report said. Also, this perp struck close to home.

Kathleen Higgins, a neighbor, and the quiet teen who babysat Lapointe's children, was abducted and brutalized by Rosa. After twelve years, she still struggles with the effects. Lapointe's anger boiled as he thought of the anxiety and fear that is going to unfold within the Higgins family and the community if they find out this guy got released.

The convict's bus ticket showed him leaving the State Prison in Starke and heading south toward communities along the Gulf of Mexico. Lapointe feared Rosa would hide out to avoid being recaptured because he knew the Department of Prisons would eventually realize its mistake. Also, every minute he was on the street meant that young women anywhere along the West Coast of Florida were in danger of being accosted or killed.

Lapointe brought his focus back to Cady. *So, he needs homicide detectives because there is a bag with human body parts in the bed of a pick-up truck?*

"What?" Lapointe asked.

"Yes, you heard me correctly, body parts." He then asked, "Sergeant, could you see if Beaucharp and Fontaine are assigned to this?"

***

Detective Michaela Beaucharp, a New Englander half her life, reads one book a week. She's been a cop for eight years. Her father, an ecological engineer, got reassigned to Marietta, Georgia, moving the family there while Michaela was in the tenth grade. At barely five-foot eight-inches tall, Beaucharp was an outstanding athlete. Her prowess in dance was such that she was offered a promising career with the Atlanta Ballet until an accident severely tore several leg ligaments.

Disappointed and finding a bachelor's degree in American Literature unchallenging, Beaucharp opted to move back to Boston and garner a graduate degree in Criminal Justice at the prestigious Boston College. Through her graduate studies program, she opted for internships with the police division working at the Pine Street Inn, Boston's infamous homeless shelter. Once there, she worked closely with Boston's novel, *Homeless Court,* the alternative court designed to resolve misdemeanor offenses, non-violent felonies and outstanding warrants for homeless individuals who have shown a strong commitment to recovery and stability.

As Beaucharp learned, she received mentoring by some of Boston's most compassionate and professional police officers. She also assisted the counselors and case managers at the shelter, learning a great deal about the plight of the poor and homeless. She constantly tells rookies that this learning experience made her a better street cop.

Three months before graduation, she applied for a job with the Belenton Police Department and reported to the police academy four months later where she met her future police partner, and best friend, Donna Fontaine. After working various street cop assignments for five years, the department moved her into the Detective Division.

Her partner, Donna Fontaine, is a six-foot redhead with an attractive face bursting with freckles and icy blue eyes. Michaela's redneck uncle, David, a former Marine artilleryman, once said, "She's got cops' eyes. They scare the shit out of me. She could make anyone confess to being guilty of something." The daughter of a Tampa police captain with a brother in the Florida Department of Law Enforcement, she always wanted to become a police officer.

All through college she worked at the school's Safety and Security Office and took advantage of being mentored in *police work* by several retired police officers also working there. Her favorite was a retired New York sergeant, Ken Mazzie. She got paired up with him on her first college security assignment where they had to visit a rowdy group of drunk freshmen at the Student Union Hall. He was a tough-looking guy with a nose that appeared to have taken a few good punches. At first intimidated by his presence, Maizzie turned out to be a quiet, deep thinking, and sincere tutor. The first time they met would be forever etched into Fontaine's mind.

Smiling, Maizzie stuck out his hand, shook hers, and they introduced themselves.

"So, you want to be a cop," he said next.

Fontaine nodded and drawled, "My daddy serves with the Tampa PD, my brother is with the Florida Department of Law Enforcement."

Maizzie said, "A family of cops. That's a good start. You got a good idea about what the job is about."

Fontaine blushed, feeling as if she'd been bragging and waving credentials around. She hated people that did those things. "I'm sorry Mr. Mazzie.

I appear to be bragging, but I'm not really. I'm nervous and I've never done police work before, and I don't want to do something stupid."

Mazzie smiled. *"Hey kid, the name is Ken. My dad is called mister. Don't worry, we've all been on our first call. I'll tell you what my first partner, Tom King, told me on my first call. 'Kid, you're a New York cop now. You're going to come across a lot of folks you can help. Do it. Help them because you'll need the comfort it brings you because of all the bad things you'll come across.'"* Maizzie went on, *"I may sound like a social worker, but believe me, at times, it's human service work. Keep that in mind and stay as far away from the night-stick cops as much as you can. No one wants to work with those guys. They're always making trouble."*

Fontaine remembered his words and repeated them at Mazzie's eulogy ten years later at the Sarasota National Cemetery.

After earning an undergraduate and master's degree in criminal justice from the University of South Florida, she joined the department at the same time as Beaucharp. They met at the academy, and in many ways seemed to be complete opposites, yet they became the loyalist of friends.

While both are sincere and honest cops, Fontaine, sometimes, struggles with her empathy for the lost and forgotten people she happens upon in the line of duty. Beaucharp, although a sympathetic and caring individual, is more rational and pragmatic in her human transactions. They both moved up through the ranks and into the detective division at the same time.

***

Lapointe growled back. "You don't pick who you want to investigate cases. What kind of shit is that?"

"It's Wally Gaslight's truck. He's here with me right now."

"Is that the old guy from Palmetto always delivering the pork to the church barbecues?"

"Yes, and the one who brings pork to Aikin's."

"Jack Aikin, the retired New York cop? Runs the weekend barbecue at the Baptist Church on 17th Street in Sarasota?"

"That's him."

"Ah Jeeze, I know who you mean. This guy is harmless. He helped my daughter build the shelter for her 4-H sheep project. Shit, that was almost twenty years ago."

"That's what I mean, Sarge. Something ain't right here."

"I'll call the captain. We have got to keep this quiet for now. Stay there. I'm sending someone out to pick up Gaslight."

Cady said, "Sarge, I don't think he knows what's in the bed of his truck. Someone could have tossed the stuff in there, so I haven't told him. He's still drunk, and right now, he thinks aliens brought him here."

"What the—"

Cady stopped him. "I'm serious, Sarge. He is rambling on about that Marsha lady in Palmetto who always talks about seeing UFOs. He's scared to death, praying, crying, and worrying about them touching his body."

Lapointe smiled. He also understood what Cady was getting at, but blurted out angrily, "It's not your call about how things got in the back of the truck. You get that?"

"Yes, I know, Sarge. But you know Wally as well as I do."

"That's why we play this by the book. He's in the middle of a shitstorm right now."

"My thoughts exactly, Sarge."

Lapointe stopped for a moment, stared at the ceiling, and thought. "You stay by the truck and wait for the detectives. I'll get the Forensic people to the scene. Don't let anyone near it until they show up." Lapointe was silent for a moment, then shouted. "Frig it! I'll call Fontaine and Beaucharp. The captain will back me. Wait there for them, and I'll get someone to pick up Gaslight and tell them not to talk to him. Be sure you Miranda him."

"Good. I'll do that. He's still pretty drunk. If there isn't any more excitement, he may fall asleep until someone sees him. Oh, by the way. Find him a cell by himself. He's filthy and pretty ripe! Smells like the Ellenton pig farm."

Lapointe smiled. "I'll call Holding myself and have 'em move people if they have to. We'll need his clothes for evidence, he'll get a new orange jump-suit for the time being. Anything else?"

"Nope. All set at this end. I'll wait for the detectives."

Cady signed off and caught Gaslight struggling to his feet. "Mr. Cady, I gotta pee."

***

Lapointe signed off and turned toward Provencher. "Where's the list of the detectives' phone numbers?"

"It's in the top-drawer, Sarge, in a plastic folder. The yellow one is the call list."

The phone rang five times. Finally, a woman answered with a stern, heavy Southern drawl. "Fontaine! Honey, this best be important."

"It's Sergeant Lapointe, detective. Rise and shine."

"What the—"

Lapointe grinned as he heard items being knocked about and something crash to the floor, then the snap of a light switch.

"It's 3:20 am, Sarge."

"Wake your partner and head to Manatee Avenue, just west of the Wawa in the eastbound lane. Cady is waiting for you."

"Okay. What's up?"

"The scene looks wrong to him. I'm calling in Forensics so get over there with Beaucharp right now."

"Got it, Sarge."

Lapointe chuckled. "Tell your daddy I said hi."

"I will. He'll be fishing in a couple of hours."

Lapointe smiled. "The life of a retired cop. Is there anything better than that?"

"Daddy would love to have you sittin' alongside him in that Boston Whaler. You know that."

"Oh yeah, one of these days. Get on over to Manatee Avenue. And by the way, I got a feeling we should keep this one quiet until we hear otherwise."

Lapointe hung up. His next call would be to awaken Captain Bargiel, Chief of Detectives. He grinned at Provencher. "Let's rattle them a little. I love this part of the job.

Chapter 4

Donna Fontaine pulled herself to a sitting position resting against the headboard and punched the speed dial for her partner. Beaucharp picked up the phone on the second ring.

Before uttering a word, Fontaine said, "Somethin's going down on Manatee Avenue, honey. Lapointe just called me. Toss the sailor out of your bed right now. We gotta get crackin'."

Beaucharp smiled. "Sailor, huh? You ought to know! The only way to get you moving faster than a crawl is to say that the Fleet just got in at Tampa. What's up?"

"Lapointe requested us. It's media silence. I'll pick you up."

"I'm at the door now. What's keeping you?"

Fontaine grinned and hung up.

Beaucharp patted the multi-colored head purring loudly on the pillow next to her. "Sorry, Mischief, got to get going. Auntie Donna's on the way."

She rushed through some bathroom chores, checked the litter box, and then turned toward the cat. "Shoot, you're one messy guy." She doubled a plastic grocery bag, dumped in the contents, and tied a knot at the top. Mischief followed attentively supervising as Beaucharp refreshed the box.

Beaucharp quickly dressed in the clothes she'd set out the evening before. She then slid the nightstand drawer open, removed her Glock, slid a clip into the handle, checked the safety, and holstered it to her belt. On the opposite side, she placed her badge, grabbed a shoulder bag and the kitty litter trash, and rushed down the stairs. Twenty minutes after the call, she stepped out of the apartment building and Fontaine's headlights appeared at the far end of the parking lot.

Beaucharp opened the door, tossed the shoulder bag on top of Fontaine's light jacket in the back, and slid onto the seat, careful not to jar the two large coffee mugs sitting in the console. She closed the door, and Fontaine wrinkled her face. "Phew! Somethin' stinks. What you got in the bag?"

"I thought I'd bring you some lunch." She then pointed to the furthest end of the parking lot. "Stop by the dumpster near the exit. I had to clean out Mischief's litter box."

Chapter 5

After hanging up with Captain Bargiel, Lapointe checked the evening roster for someone to send for Gaslight. Tracing his finger down the list, he stopped at the name Wilson.

Harold Wilson, alias the Weasel. Overweight and lazy, and an eight-year veteran that got the name for always trying to make himself look good even if it were at the cost of making another officer look bad. He also prided himself on keeping a pristine vehicle and detested arresting drunks or street people, fearing they would soil the inside of his patrol car.

Lapointe opted to do the dispatch himself. He winked at Provencher, picked up the mic, and uttered a series of call numbers.

Wilson responded. Lapointe said, "Proceed to Manatee Avenue East to assist Cady. Retrieve a suspect and transport him to Holding. The detectives will want to interview him when he sobers up," Lapointe ordered.

Wilson asked, "What kind of suspect?"

"Wilson. It's Sergeant Lapointe." He paused, stared at the wall clock, and counted twelve seconds before Wilson responded again.

"Sarge, I'll be off duty in a couple of hours. Is there anyone else nearby?"

"I'm assigning you. Don't even read the guy his rights. It's already done. Don't speak to the suspect. Just transport him to Holding, and the duty officer will babysit."

"I'm on my way, Sarge." Wilson signed out with call numbers and the time on the twenty-four hour clock.

Provencher waited for Wilson to sign off before asking, "Sarge, you're having him pick up Gaslight?"

"Exactly. Keep quiet about this."

Provencher laughed out loud. "Cady just said the guy's filthy. Wilson's going to hate this. I wish I could be downstairs when he drops him off. Too bad it's too early for the shift change. Folks would enjoy seeing this."

Lapointe, still smiling, said, "We'll have the CATV video. Maybe we can show some of it at the division Christmas parties."

Chapter 6

Fontaine and Beaucharp were opposite enough to be a perfect team. Each the product of different education systems and diverse cultural outlooks that resulted from growing up in separate parts of the United States. While sipping at their coffee, each silently weighed their own thoughts.

Beaucharp spoke first while staring out the passenger window. "Donna, what could be so urgent that they needed us to come in this early? Something big got to be going down."

Fontaine said, "Cady is involved, and he's a good cop and capable of taking care of difficult things. You think he's in the middle of something?"

Both detectives knew the something in cop-speak could be any number of things. Something may have gone wrong with a *Shots Fired* incident, or an officer stumbled across a confusing crime scene with legal or political implications. Sometimes questionable characters needed to be dealt with to avoid issues that could complicate a District Attorney's prosecution. All the while, each tried to protect the other from their own worst feelings about what could be the worst of scenarios befalling Cady.

Beaucharp feared that Cady, although a seasoned officer, may be jammed up in a circumstance that put him over his head. Is he being forced to arrest a family member or a close friend? Is he involved in a fatal accident that has to be investigated openly? It may be an embarrassing situation they'd have to deal with using kid's gloves when it came to reports.

Fontaine worried that Cady might have come across a homicide involving a vulnerable member of the community. Once a child got killed during a drive by shooting and Cady was the first on the scene. Fontaine sat with him in his patrol car while Beaucharp did the investigation.

The man survived three tours in Bagdad, earned a Silver Star and a Purple Heart for picking up a round of shrapnel in the leg while pulling a medical team out of a burning Humvee. He unloaded dozens of M–16 magazines at insurgents while escorting Army convoys. Now, there he sat nearly weeping, while Fontaine shielded him from others at the scene. She hid behind the ploy of officer-debriefing and memorializing his statement of the event.

They drove toward Cady's blue lights and to avoid blocking a lane parked behind it, also on the grass. A set of powerful forensic lamps pointed at a rusty pickup truck and into nearby grassy areas.

Fontaine spoke first. "Holy shit! Cady, what stinks? Smells pretty near as bad as Beauchy's apartment."

Beaucharp grinned and shook her head. Cady smiled slightly, partly because of the joke and because he knew how sensitive Fontaine was to strong odors. He handed them an open jar of Vicks VapoRub. Each applied a smear under their noses over their upper lip then put on latex gloves.

Cady proceeded. "Let me fill you in, then we'll take a walk over to the truck."

The detectives nodded.

"I just walked out of the store," he pointed to the Wawa station. "I looked down Manatee Avenue and saw the truck parked in the grass and off the road, pointing in the wrong direction like it is now."

Cady described how he found someone inside the cab slumped against the passenger door. "I knew the person. At first, I thought he was dead." He stopped momentarily, choked up, took a deep breath, then shook his head. "The truck stunk, and when I threw my light into the bed, it was like a house-fly factory."

"Where is the perp now?" Fontaine asked.

"Lapointe had him transported to Holding until he could sober up. I read him his Miranda, but I think you gotta do it again when he's awake." He paused for the detectives to finish jotting notes before describing the contents in the sack inside the truck's bed. "There is an assortment of food products and body parts oozing out, including what looked like a partial leg with a foot attached."

Flood lights glared at a bulging old canvas bag. Fontaine said, "Looks like a bag we always use to get our potatoes in."

In the bed of the truck was a small leg with a foot attached. It appeared to be Caucasian and belonging to a tiny person, or a child. There also were things that looked like food scraps, pieces of body organs, and a couple of fingers slipping out of the sack.

Cady said, "At first, I thought they were just food scraps and unusable animal parts left over from a farmer's slaughtering. Then I noticed the foot and fingers. There could also be pieces of human organs as well."

The detectives peered into the bed, touching nothing. Beaucharp was the lead detective. Fontaine tapped her shoulder and then flipped her head toward the forensic people. Beaucharp nodded and said, "I'm going to talk to them. Get over to the Wawa and see if their cameras picked up anything?"

Cady flipped open his notepad, held to the light and said, "Detective, I was there at 2:30 and left about ten minutes later. It must have taken place before that."

Beaucharp then carefully circled the area next to the truck several times with Cady, each hiding their fears that the leg might belong to a child.

Chapter 7

The Wawa was empty of patrons. Jimmy Buffett's Margaritaville floated from speakers somewhere and a forty-something, premature gray cashier worked at a crossword puzzle. Her name tag said Jamie. Fontaine displayed her badge. "Hi, Jamie. Has it been quiet here this evening?"

"About an hour ago was probably the busiest. A cop was in here, and a kid came in after. Then the cop left, and another man showed up and seemed to know the kid and they left together."

Fontaine said, "You say 'a kid', how old would you say he was?"

Jamie smiled. "Well, everyone is younger than me. I guess I call everyone a kid. He may have been in his late teens, possibly early twenties."

"How about the guy that he left with?"

"I don't know. Maybe thirties, looked like a field hand coming home from a bender. Drove a green pickup."

Fontaine, still writing in her notepad, and not looking up, asked, "We need to view any videos you got for the night. Is there a manager around?"

"What's with all the blue lights out there? Is there an accident?"

"Something like that. Jamie, I just got to speak to your manager."

"He's in the office behind the beer coolers. Walk to the end of the beer case and you'll see a door. The office is behind it."

Fontaine remembered the training film in which a gas station manager, fearing a robbery was going to take place, panicked, and fired shots at someone opening the door to his back office unannounced.

"Jamie is there a way you can call him out here?"

"He might be asleep. I'll try buzzing him, and he'll think I need cashier help."

She tapped a button under the counter, and seconds later, the manager with a name tag, Joe Stowers, showed up.

He looked at Fontaine and then at Jamie and said, "What's up?"

Fontaine showed her badge, and before she could speak, Jamie said, "This officer needs to view our cameras."

Stowers looked at Fontaine. "Of course." He then turned to Jamie. "Are you going to be okay for a few minutes?"

Jamie said, "Yes."

***

The camera pointing toward the end of the lot abutting Manatee Avenue showed Gaslight's truck turning onto the street, veering in the wrong direction, and almost colliding with several vehicles, then driving off onto the grass. The camera time said 1:45 am. It also showed the shadow of someone getting out of the truck on the driver's side and walking away in the opposite direction of the store.

Fontaine said, "Sir, we're gonna need to take this tape. The forensic folks will dicker with it, might make a copy, but may not give it back to you."

Stowers said, "That's okay, officer. Do what you got to do."

"Thank you for the cooperation. They're gonna have to come get it right now and I'll have to wait here in this room."

Stowers nodded. "Of course. Would you like a coffee or a couple of donuts?"

Fontaine thought for a few seconds. "Oh, what the hey! I'm gonna have to wait for the forensic boys anyway." She reached for her wallet.

Stowers said, "Officer, please let us get them. We appreciate it when the police stop here in the evenings and early mornings. At those hours, it's comforting to know that a police car is parked in front of the store."

Fontaine phoned Beaucharp's cell and told her that a tape showed someone parking and leaving the vehicle. "According to the timer, the car's been there for almost an hour before Cady saw it. Send one of the forensic guys over to get this. I gotta wait so nothing happens to it. You know, evidentiary bullshit."

Beaucharp smiled. "Good work. I'll send someone right up. Oh, by the way, how are the Wawa donuts?"

Fontaine grinned. "Beauchy, the feller had a couple of extra, so he offered them to me rather than have to toss them out."

Gabe Sorgi, from the forensic team, came for the tape. In the meantime, Stowers put together two travel trays of coffee and an assortment of sugar, sweeteners, and creamers. He then added a bag with a variety of plain and frosted doughnuts and handed it to Sorgi. "Here, take these. They're on us."

Sorgi stared at Fontaine and pointed at everything. Fontaine said, "I'm sorry, Mr. Stowers, but we can't accept these."

Jamie, smiling, yelled from the cashier counter. "Take them. They're on us."

Fontaine shook her head and started to speak but Stowers interrupted.

"Listen, they're a courtesy. We really do appreciate having you folks around. Take them, please. It'll make us feel good."

***

They used the hood of the detective's vehicle as a table for their drinks and the bag of donuts. For twenty minutes they drank coffee, munched at the donuts, and shared information. Eventually Beaucharp turned toward the forensic team and said, "You guys need anything more from us?"

Rick Seston, the forensic sergeant, shook his head. "Nope. We're going to tape out the area, scour around a little more until the M.E. shows up for the remains. Then we'll have the truck towed to the forensic garage. You gonna wait for them?"

Fontaine looked at Beaucharp and said, "We ought to wait for the M.E. and the tow truck, just in case the driver has questions."

Beaucharp nodded.

Cady looked at his watch. "I'm going to head in; got a feeling there a lot of paperwork coming. Lapointe is going to want to talk to me." He pointed at the detectives. "I'm sure he'll want a debriefing from you two."

Fontaine said, "We gotta wait until the guy sobers up before we can talk to him. But you say you know him. We'd like to talk with you for a bit before you clock out. Will that be okay?"

"Of course, and I do know him. He'll be straight with you in the interview.

Chapter 8

After two and one-half hours of interrogation, the detectives looked at each other and shrugged. Each concluded they were looking at an innocent man. He had no idea he was carrying around a sack with human body parts.

It was close to 10 am, and the ten-by-fourteen-foot interrogation room had no windows and a metal table bolted to the concrete floor. It had a set of steel O-rings welded to the table one foot apart, used to cuff violent suspects. A two-way mirror took up almost ten feet on the longest wall. Although Gaslight was in a new orange jumpsuit, the ventilation system couldn't handle the stench of the foul body odors he carried from the clothes he was arrested in. They reeked of body filth and what was later discovered by the FDLE Forensic Laboratory in Ft. Myers to be sections of animal blood and pieces of rotting animal meat and flesh.

"Please try to explain to us, again, why Officer Cady found you asleep on Manatee Avenue?" Fontaine asked Gaslight for what seemed like the fiftieth time.

"It had to be the aliens," he said.

Beaucharp shook her head. "Mr. Gaslight, we've been all through this idea of aliens. We think you were drunk and don't remember riding to Manatee Avenue. Where are your truck keys?" He wrinkled his face. "Truck keys?"

It was Fontaine's turn. "Officer Cady couldn't find your truck keys." She didn't mention that the crime scene members spent over three hours searching the area with sophisticated metal detectors. They collected an assortment of coins, bottle caps, drug needles, and chewing gum tin foil. There were no truck keys to be found.

Beaucharp spoke again. "The tow-truck driver was going to use them to unlock the steering column. Do you remember what you did with them?"

"The aliens?" he said.

Fontaine got up from the table. "How are you gonna drive home?"

"I got extras, hidden unduh the hood, in a medal case with magnetizers holden 'em."

Both detectives knew that Gaslight was going to be released.

Beaucharp stared into Gaslight's face, pale and frightened, his puzzled eyes stared back, bloodshot, and shifting left and right in confusion and panic.

She spoke consolingly. "You may have to settle all this with a judge, Mr. Gaslight. Get hold of a lawyer or ask for help from the Public Defender's Office." When she was sure he understood what she was saying, she signaled Fontaine to meet in the hall, then pushed away from the table and stood. "Excuse us, Mr. Gaslight. We got to talk for a minute. Can we get you a cup of what is supposed to be coffee?"

Gaslight shook his head, no.

Once outside the room, Fontaine said, "Let's call the captain and get him released. After viewing the store video, we got nothing to hold him on," she continued, "besides, it won't accomplish anything keeping him any longer."

Beaucharp agreed. "Okay, but let's tell him about the bag."

Fontaine called Captain Bargiel, suggesting Gaslight be released.

When they returned to the room, Fontaine told Gaslight about the bag and the body parts in his truck. He bolted into hysteria, turned ashen, and began sweating profusely. His hands tremored uncontrollably, and he spoke with a nervous stutter. "Wa, was, was, what kind of bod, bo, body pa, par, parts?"

Beaucharp stepped in. "Mr. Gaslight, we don't know everything right now. What we can say, though, is that you've been extremely cooperative and helpful. You do understand that more people will want to talk to you about this? Later on, of course."

"Uh, uh, I, I'm in, ino, innocent!"

Fontaine, standing behind Gaslight, chewed at the inside of her mouth. Beaucharp knew how sensitive her partner could be to the plight of others.

Finally, Fontaine blurted out, "Right now, there is no serious crime, so just try to go on with your life as if none of this happened, Mr. Gaslight."

Standing out of sight of Gaslight, Beaucharp raised her dark eyebrows, rolled her eyes backward, and displayed the facial gestures that parroted a favorite axiom directed at her partner, "*Good one, Fontaine!*"

Fontaine lifted her shoulders and turned up her hand as if to demonstrate, "*What else can I say?*"

Chapter 9

Bargiel met with Captain Bird, the day commander, and brought him up to speed on the case. Bird approached Cady and asked, "Cady, they say you know this guy. Is he a flight risk?"

"No, sir. He's not a runner, and keeping him here isn't going to help the investigation."

Bird looked down at Bargiel's notes and said, "As of now, it looks like we got nothing to hold him on. You're sure he's going to hang around?"

"Yeah. I'm sure."

Bird said, "Thank you. How far along are you with your report?"

Cady flipped through several pages. "It's complete, Captain. I just got to input it into the system. That won't take me long."

Bird nodded. "Don't clock out right away, though. See if the detectives have more questions for you."

Cady nodded, and Bird left for the interrogation room. He knocked twice, then opened the door wide enough to signal Beaucharp to step into the hall.

Bird spoke quietly. "We're going to let him go. We got nothing to hold him on. Cady doesn't believe the guy is a flight risk. I'm inclined to agree."

Beaucharp pointed a thumb over her shoulder toward her partner on the other side of the door. "We don't think so either. But something is going on here and squeezing him isn't going to help."

Bird looked up and down the hall, trying to gather thoughts, then stared at Beaucharp. "Yeah. Everyone's got a gut feeling on this one. Keep Captain Bargiel and me on top of it."

Back in the room, Beaucharp leaned into Fontaine's ear and, in a low whisper, told her about the conversation with Captain Bird. Fontaine smiled, and Beaucharp turned to Gaslight and said, "Forensic found a bag of dirty clothes in the toolbox behind the cab of your truck."

Gaslight said, "That's a spare set I keep."

Fontaine said, "It looks like they were on the way to the laundry. They're keeping them as well as the clothes you were wearing. We can't release you with an orange jumpsuit, but we have a disposable white hazmat suit and moccasins. Do you want to go home in them?"

Gaslight nodded. "Yeah, that'll be fine."

Fontaine called the Forensic impound yard for the okay to release the truck. The duty officer said they had everything they needed from it, and they could be picked up anytime.

"What about the keys?" Fontaine asked.

"We found a set in a magnetic case stuck up under the rear tire well."

"Thanks. Someone's going to bring him out to get the truck."

Fontaine told Gaslight they found a set of keys for his truck, and Beaucharp called for an officer to get Gaslight a set of disposable hazmat whites and slippers and then take him to his truck.

Several minutes later, Officer Roger Dickinson from the Holding cell area rapped twice and opened the door. He immediately jumped back into the hall, inhaled loudly, and came back in. "Wow! What'd you do, Wally? It smells like you fell in a sewer."

Beaucharp said, "You know Mr. Gaslight?"

"We're neighbors of a sort. He built the rabbit hutches for my daughter's seventh grade 4-H project."

Still behind Gaslight, Fontaine signaled Dickinson to step back into the hall and followed him. Once outside, she closed the door and raised a hand to silence Dickinson before he could speak. "What do you know about this man?"

"He's a good guy. Is he being busted for drunk?"

"Look, it's pretty serious." She pointed over her shoulder, indicating Beaucharp. "We got a lot of loose ends here. We may want to talk to you a little later. That gonna be okay?"

"Sure." Then, pointing at the interrogation room, Dickinson said, "Trust me, he's a pretty solid guy regardless of what you see here."

Fontaine's brow wrinkled in worry. "Bring him back to a Holding cell for now. He'll be leaving in a hazmat suit as soon as we get someone to bring him to his truck at the forensic impound."

Dickinson smiled. Then poking fun at the stench said, "We gonna burn that jumpsuit he's wearing?"

Fontaine laughed, and the worry left her face. "Honey, we may have to torch the room!"

She turned toward the door and stopped. "Let's see if he's hungry. If he is, see if we can find him something, will you?"

Dickinson said, "If he's hungry, we'll figure out something, detective."

Fontaine opened the door and let Dickerson walk through first. Then, looking at Gaslight, she said, "Officer Dickinson's gonna take you to get dressed, and someone will see you get a ride to your truck."

Dickinson asked, "You hungry, Wally?"

"Thank you, son. I'd take a beer if you got one."

Dickinson smiled and waved toward the door, signaling Gaslight to follow him.

***

Alone in the interrogation room, Fontaine suddenly felt tired, leaned back against the wall, and watched her partner gather the notes and several pages of reference material.

Beaucharp suddenly stopped and looked up, catching her partner shaking her head and staring at the scuffed floor. She said, "What is it, Donna?"

Fontaine pulled away from the wall. "Poor bastard doesn't know if it is Tuesday or November! Lord, I hate to see people in that shape."

Beaucharp often used ancillary tasks with her hands to help fill the time needed to piece together thoughts. To many, it appeared as if she was ignoring those around her, but Fontaine knew better. Beaucharp worked some papers, aligning them and tapping their edges against the tabletop before sliding them into a folder and placing the folder into a large manila envelope.

Now focused, she said, "What are we to make of this? A bag with someone's body parts in the bed of a drunken old man's pickup truck?"

Fontaine stepped to the edge of the table. "Think about it, Michaela! Is this guy capable of doing anything despicable?"

Beaucharp shook her head. "No, I don't think so. It doesn't feel like a frame-up, either. But who misplaces body parts?"

Fontaine looked up and spoke to her image in the large one-way mirror. "Lapointe is going to call the morgue to see if they're missing bodies. He asked FDLE to contact medical schools up and down the coast. They may come up with information."

They stared and talked to each other's reflection in the mirror. "That's a good start, partner," Beaucharp said.

Fontaine brought a hand up to her chin. "This doesn't make sense. It seems that a good use for body parts would be research or medical training. Who else would have something like this lying around?"

Beaucharp pushed away from the table and picked up the manila envelope. "Maybe one of your old boyfriends. How about the guy that used to pick up roadkill?"

"He was studying to be a taxidermist."

"So, he said. When did you last hear from him?"

"He moved to South America. Brazil, I think. Besides, he's rich. His dad owns thirty car dealerships and a bank."

Beaucharp faced the door so that Fontaine wouldn't see her grinning. "Probably the South American Hannibal Lector today."

"Say what you want, but that Jimmy—"

Beaucharp turned back around, this time exposing a wide smile. "That Jimmy! How many Jimmies were there?"

"What difference does it make? Honey, the car I'm driving today is a gift from him."

"It's a rust bucket, Donna! Probably one of the cars caught in the Louisiana floods. His dad probably unloaded it onto some unsuspecting soul and was forced to take it back. You got strips of duct tape holding in the rear window from falling out."

Fontaine pulled the envelope out of Beaucharp's hand. "Minor body work's all it needs. How about we check in with Captain Bargiel?"

Beaucharp said, "We got to talk to Lapointe, too. So, let's try to get both done at the same time."

Without looking back, Fontaine rushed out the door. "Make yourself useful and get the lights."

Beaucharp smiled, hit the light switch, and hurried to catch up. *Useful!*

Fontaine brought the envelope up to her face, hiding a grin. "Yeah, I'm sick of having to carry you like an old piece of driftwood."

Beaucharp pressed her lips together tightly to keep from smiling, then suddenly burst into laughter loud enough to echo off the empty walls.

There were footsteps, and Captain Bargiel appeared at the end of the hall. "Yo, kiddies! Just the two I'm looking for. Detective Fontaine, take your partner's hand and meet me in the Green Squad Room. Tell the officers there that I'll be right in."

Fontaine smiled and looked at Beaucharp. "See what I'm talking about?"

Chapter 10

Cady, now on overtime, waited in a small conference room review-ing his report notes as Lapointe, on overtime as well, worked his way through a new box of Dunkin' Donuts. Both stopped what they were doing and chuckled when they heard the voices echoing in the empty hallway. Lapointe whispered, "Sounds like a married couple."

Beaucharp, clearly the loudest, was saying, "Yeah? At least I don't drive like a nut at four o'clock in the morning."

Fontaine said, "There's no one on the roads at this time—"

"Donna! Nuts and cops are out there!"

"Honey, please don't interrupt me. At this time of day, you can go a wee bit over the speed limit."

"Yeah, but you're supposed to slow down before you turn a corner."

"Look, it ain't my fault if you don't know how to drink coffee in a moving vehicle. I had to drive, and you notice I'm not wearing any coffee on my slacks."

They followed the smells of coffee and fresh donuts, turning into the only room with lights on. Cady was brushing powdered sugar off the front of his shirt. Lapointe waved at the counter with a coffee urn and several boxes of assorted pastries and donuts. "Grab something and sit down, detectives. The captain's going to try to be here. In the meantime, Cady's going to fill you in with what he's got."

It took Cady ten minutes to bring them up to speed on everything. They were already familiar with the bag of body parts, so he, again, described how confused and frightened Gaslight had become when he realized he was not where he was supposed to be.

Cady said he pieced together a scenario of his own. He explained, "I think on the day before, Gaslight started butchering a feral hog. He then got distracted and drove off to get something to eat at the local bar. He overdid his drinking, left the bar, climbed into his truck's passenger seat, and fell asleep." Cady concluded, "From the Wawa video, we know someone else drove the truck. Besides, he was too drunk to do it himself."

When Cady finished, the room grew silent. Beaucharp and Fontaine mulled over what they had just heard, what they saw at the scene and their interview with Gaslight. Each writing in notepads, stopping to consider and inhale more coffee.

Lapointe spoke to Cady when he saw they were finished writing. "Give me the arrest report. I'll make copies so they'll have something to review."

Beaucharp said, "Sarge, this just about a drunken arrest or is something else going on here?"

Cady said, "It isn't just an arrest. Some stuff doesn't fit here."

Lapointe said, "It's my gut, too. There's more to this than what we are seeing—"

"He woke me at 3:45 to tell me this," interrupted Captain Bargiel, leaning against the jamb of an open door. "I didn't want to disrupt the flow of anything." He stepped across the threshold. "I'm going with the sergeant's suspicion. Sometimes, all we got is a hunch."

Bargiel looked at Beaucharp and Fontaine. "What do you two think? You interrogated the guy."

Fontaine put down her pencil and looked up. "I'll be honest here. Call it a hunch or anything you want, but something is grabbing at my butt—"

Beaucharp interrupted. "There ain't a lot of butt to grab at either."

Everyone smiled except for Fontaine. She continued. "Captain, is there something buried here? I mean, are we going to find a bag of horseshit that we got to kick in the bushes later on?"

Bargiel, searching for the correct words, looked down at the scuffs on the tile floor for ten seconds. "I just looked at your case files. You're ahead of the timelines, so stay on this for a day or two. We don't know where it's going to lead."

Bargiel looked at his Timex, then at Lapointe, and pointed at the door. They had to leave. Lapointe stepped out first. Bargiel stopped at the threshold, turned, and said, "Let Birdy and me handle any of the bullshit. Just keep doing what you do. For now, we don't want anyone talking about this case except with the people from the relevant department."

***

Cady and Beaucharp quietly sat processing their thoughts until the silence got broken by Fontaine fumbling with the pastry boxes. Exasperated, Beaucharp raised her voice. "Jeeze, Donna, just grab something!"

Fontaine walked back to the table, a chocolate frosted with a bite taken out in one hand and a sugared jelly on a napkin lying across the palm of the other.

Cady looked up and said, "Thanks, I already had a couple."

"Oh, these are for me," Fontaine replied.

Beaucharp shook her head, and Cady chuckled.

Just then Lapointe reappeared in the doorway. "Detectives, who is handling the paperwork here today?"

Fontaine said, "I'll take it, Sarge. I gotta do everything else, anyway."

He dropped a large manila envelope on the oak table. "There are two copies of Cady's report and other material pertinent to the history with Cady and Gaslight."

"Yeah, give it to her. She's not driving anymore today," Beaucharp said.

Before the end of their long workday, Beaucharp and Fontaine would be subjected to surprises exploding every time they turned a corner.

Chapter 11

By 10:45, Fontaine and Beaucharp had finished speaking with forensic people who meticulously combed the crime scene and truck. They spent more than two and one-half hours interrogating Gaslight and met with Cady, Sergeant Lapointe, and Captains Bargiel and Bird. Now, they prepared to backtrack Gaslight's movements the evening before, starting with the Bucket of Blood, the last place Cady believed Gaslight was before ending up on Manatee Avenue.

On their way to central parking, Officer Wilson walked past carrying an assortment of wash rags, cleaning fluids, and deodorizers. Beaucharp didn't know that Wilson transported Gaslight to Holding earlier that morning.

"Hey, Wilson. How are they hanging?" Beaucharp yelled.

He grunted angrily and kept walking.

She turned to Fontaine.

"What's up with Wilson, and doesn't he work nights?"

"It's you," Fontaine said. "You're offensive to people. You're like a disgruntled employee."

"I'm offensive? To people?"

"You are. Honey, if the truth be told, I'm the only one who can work with you, and a couple of times, I was fixin to squeeze your jugular veins."

"Lucky me!"

"Yes. You are lucky. You should buy my lunches."

"While we're being honest here, Mademoiselle Fontaine. What was going through your head when you told Mr. Gaslight to 'just move on with his life?' What the heck was that?"

"I thought I would try a little encouraging psychology. He was pretty low."

Beaucharp laughed. "Encouraging psychology? Okay, Sigmund. You're having a hard enough time with your day job. Don't start thinking about a new career."

"You never can tell. He might think about what I said and, right now, be making plans for a new life," Fontaine said.

"I'm sure. Maybe he's home thinking about joining a Palmetto bridge club."

"Poke fun at me all you want, Beauchy. I think Mr. Gaslight is a pretty resilient guy, and I'm sure he's happy to be home after the grilling you gave him. Although, I ain't sure anyone knows how long it will take him to recover from that."

Beaucharp smiled. "Oh yeah. Gaslight's been one of my toughest. I almost had to break out the waterboard. But I agree with you about one thing. The poor man has got to be glad to return to the peace and quiet of his home."

***

Gaslight, distraught over what the police found in his truck, had a bigger shock awaiting him at home. A Crime Scene van parked on his lawn. People in white hazmat suits flowed in and out like bees gathering pollen. Several leashed police dogs sniffed and squirted on everything. The remains of a boar, now festering, hung dripping onto the dirt below.

The stench, like rotting garbage and rancid meat, filled the air all the way back to US 301. The carcass, picked over by vermin and insects for the past 36 hours, now crawled with maggots and a moving glob of brown gelatinous and green flies. Some unlucky handlers didn't pay close enough attention to their dogs and they dashed to the oozing slime and rolled around in it. Those handlers worked at trying to rinse the stench off with Gaslight's garden hose.

Although all the workers wore awkward white suits, some wore paper hats and surgical masks. Investigators working on the porch were covered head to toe in white but wore hoods with plastic facemasks. They worked silently, like mechanical appliances, poking at things inside a chest refrigerator. Someone took photos of pieces of the meat and bones, lifted them out, and placed them in plastic evidence bags. Another person wrote across the front and set the bags into a smaller refrigeration unit with FDLE stickers attached.

Gaslight found a set of soiled clothes in the laundry bin in the barn. He changed out of the white suit the police gave him into the cleanest set of dirty ones he could find. He swapped the white jailhouse slippers for the pair of old boots.

He approached the porch timidly. "I'd like to git a beer outta there if I could, sir."

Saying nothing, the suit turned to a person next to him. She peered into the chest and pointed something out.

"Wait a minute. I'll get one for you," the white suit said in a voice muffled behind the plastic facemask. Then, with a set of prongs, he lifted out a beer. Gaslight reached across and retrieved it. He wiped what may have been pieces of meat, trapped pig hair, and encrusted animal blood on the bottle's neck against his dirty shirt.

A hazmat suit approached Gaslight with a rusty meat cleaver in a plastic zip bag. "Is this yours?" he asked through a surgical mask.

Gaslight nodded. "Yes."

"We found it in the brush near the end of your driveway. Any idea how it got there?"

"No. It shoulda' have been right there." Gaslight pointed at an oak stump, stained with ages of dry blood, eight feet away. The top, severely scarred with deep crevices from the sharp objects constantly wedged into it. "I leave it there all the time."

"We gotta take this, Wally," the hazmat suit said.

"There should be the blood of wild turkey, chicken, or pig."

"I'm sure, Wally. We gotta take it because it looked like it was hidden in the brush."

Recognizing the man as a familiar church deacon, Gaslight said, "Of course. Take whatever you need here, Jim. I'd appreciate someone doing their best to see that I get things back, though."

"You recognize me? I had better not try to wear this outfit for Halloween or to knock off any gas stations."

Gaslight grinned, then walked off to be alone with his thoughts.

Sitting at a dilapidated bench under the two-hundred-year-old live oak, he watched the commotion.

Good Lord, what's going on? Somethin's gone haywire. Will things ever be the same? The detective ladies did say I'd probably get visits from more cops. I guess they're finished with me. Too bad. I like the tall skinny one.

Chapter 12

Beaucharp and Fontaine drove out of the police garage into the harsh Florida sunlight. After fumbling for sunglasses, Fontaine noticed Wilson again, still carrying cleaning rags and solutions.

"Holy shit, Beauchy. There's your boyfriend again."

Beaucharp tapped a quick toot. He flipped them the finger.

Beaucharp said, "What's really going on with that guy?"

Fontaine chuckled. "You didn't hear?"

"Hear what?"

"You gotta start paying attention to what goes on around here, partner. Wilson is the guy Lapointe sent to pick up Gaslight this morning."

Beaucharp shot a burst of laughter. "Oh man! He hates to get his car dirty. It has got to stink something awful right now. How'd you find that out?"

"Cady told me." She pinched her nose and said, "Yeah, probably smells worse than the ass of a bear."

They drove out of the lot heading for the infamous Green Bridge. It was scenic as well as the quickest way to the farming community of Ellenton and the Bucket of Blood.

Fontaine stared out the window with the passion of an artist and smiled. "I never tire of this ride. It sings to me."

The current's stubborn resistance to the wind worked in cadence with the sun turning the bay's emerald waters into an ever-changing carpet of crystal beads blinking atop the tiny crests. Nevertheless, in the futile battle pushing against the Gulf of Mexico, the wind always lost.

"This is likely the shortest way for Gaslight to get where he did after leaving the Bucket of Blood," Beaucharp said, interrupting Fontaine's yearning to spend time with her own thoughts.

The statement brought Fontaine's mind back to their mission. Before Beaucharp could finish the sentence, Fontaine reached into her shoulder bag and pulled out the large manila envelope. "Let's see what Lapointe gave us."

After gently unfolding a metal butterfly clip, she pulled out all the contents and dropped the bag between her feet. She placed the empty envelope on the console between them and spoke while reading the material.

"Gaslight worked at the tomato packing houses in Palmetto for more than forty years."

"They don't work year-round," said Beaucharp, "I think they shut down after growing season. So, what's he doing when he's out of work?"

"It looks like he spends two months every year collecting. Last year, it seems he hit the jackpot, $175 a week unemployment compensation."

"Wow! Florida really knows how to do it."

"I had to become a cop because people like Gaslight were taking all those lucrative careers with sixty days off a year. They were hogging all the good harvesting jobs in the tomato and citrus industries."

Beaucharp said, "Maybe you should've filed complaints with the Labor Board."

"I'm still thinking about it. The problem is, if I left this job, where would this leave your career?"

"My career?"

"Yeah, your career. I told your uncle, that good-looking Marine, that I would watch out for you."

"Watch out for me? Isn't that like having the fox guarding the chickens?"

"Beauchy, I keep my word. So, start getting with it. Get on the ball so that I can move on up."

Beaucharp grinned as an osprey flew across the windshield, clinging to a wriggling catch.

Fontaine went on. "It looks like the feller may supplement his earnings working on fishing boats, paid under the table, I bet, in Manatee Bay."

"Anything else?"

"He shoots boars and sells the meat to some of the small local barbecue stands."

"Any rap sheets?"

"Just traffic things. Cady issued almost all of them. Only one citation for DUI."

"Considers. His home and everything he does is in Cady's district. Any complaints against Cady? Harassments? Undue force?"

"Nothing. Hey! What's this, 'considers', thing? What kind of language is that? People usually say, figures, for something like that."

Beaucharp smiled. "What do you mean? What's wrong with it?"

"What kind of talk is that? 'Considers'?"

Beaucharp took a moment to gather the right words. "It's you people. You never really learned to speak properly."

Fontaine shot back. "Excuse me! You people. Honey, who are these, 'you people'?"

"You Southerners with your crazy way of talking."

Fontaine stared out the window, searching for a comeback. "What makes your English so special?"

"I'm from New England."

"Yeah. So?"

"We speak the King's English."

Fontaine smiled, crossed her eyes, and twirled her index finger in a circle. "Oh wow! So, we should thank some Limey King because the people of Boston have difficulty pronouncing easy words?"

Beaucharp said, "I don't even have to be looking at you, and I know you're twirling your finger. Don't change the subject when I am winning an argument."

Fontaine shook her head and grinned. "Okay, I'm going to let you win this time. Just drive the *kaah,* and slow down at the *paak* so you don't hit someone. I'll keep doing the real police work."

Fontaine went back to Cady's report and flipped through the pages quickly. She stopped and turned toward Beaucharp. "Cady's report isn't complimentary, but he didn't toss the book at Gaslight either."

"You're right. He didn't push a DUI, which might get him in trouble with the people at MADD."

Fontaine shook her head. "Wouldn't have squeezed through. The legal beagles at Morgan and Morgan would have got it tossed. No driving, no keys in the truck, no moving vehicle."

Beaucharp suddenly burst out, "Where'd his keys go?"

Fontaine said, "Whoever drove him there must have kept them."

"Why would someone drop him off on Manatee Avenue in Belenton?"

Fontaine looked down at the paperwork in her hand. "And why leave the truck parked so conspicuously? On a state highway, facing in the wrong direction?"

"Is it possible they were there by accident, looking for gas? Check how much gas was in the truck."

Fontaine shuffled through pages and pulled out a sheet. "Three-quarters of a tank. He couldn't have been trying to get to the Wawa for gas."

"Maybe the one driving was so drunk that they thought there was less gas in the tank?"

They were leaving the bridge just as Beaucharp spoke and had to stop and allow two cars to turn into a 7-Eleven gas station. They looked at each other.

Fontaine said, "You're thinking the same thing I am."

Beaucharp nodded. "Why would they drive five or six miles past the 7-Eleven looking for gas?"

They drove in silence with their thoughts. Beaucharp focused on the traffic exiting the bridge, and Fontaine watched another osprey grab something, struggle with it for a moment, and then shoot off to one of the massive streetlamps peering down at them like steel sentries guarding the bridge.

Beaucharp said, "Now we know he didn't drive to Belenton. So, we got to figure out who did. Any thoughts on that, Agatha Christie?"

Fontaine shook her head and watched another osprey lift a fish from the water. Then she said, "We got to start at the Bucket of Blood, anyway. Let's see what's on the lunch menu. I think we agreed you'd be buying."

Chapter 13

They followed Cady's directions: *Once on US 301, take the next right after the Gamble Mansion, then your next left. It's hidden at the end of a building along a gravel and crushed shells corridor. It will be squeezed in behind a strip mall behind the four-lane highway.*

The direction led them to an ugly back road, where the car collected white dust and bits of crushed shell along the bottom of the doors, rocker panels, and tire walls.

Finally, they came upon a long wooden building with the thirsty, chalky look of a place whitewashed repeatedly for too many years. At the furthest end, a flagpole supported a faded US flag hanging limply above a sagging black POW flag.

"Looks like Tobacco Road," Beaucharp said. "It's real Cracker Florida."

They slowly passed a dilapidated section with a sign, Flea Market, written sloppily on a white plank nailed unevenly to the side of the building. Beaucharp said, "Looks like my Uncle Bernie's backyard in New Hampshire before Aunt Sue made him take everything back to the dump."

"Bernie, the retired telephone lineman, dash, P.I.?" said Fontaine.

"Yeah, that's him."

Fontaine smiled. "Don't pick on Bernie. I love that old man. I'd never pick him to be a junk collector."

"It goes to show you, with proper supervision, just about any guy can be retrained and brought in line by a strong woman."

They passed a homemade trailer with metal sides supporting a hand-painted sign, *Wanted Dead or Alive Used Appliances*. A pile, more tossed in than stacked, of rusting washing machines and clothes dryers cluttered the yard. Even without a breeze, the dust kicked up by the car drifted off and stuck to the rusting metal as if the particles were delighted to get a new home. Beaucharp slowed down for a better view and several grackles stopped pecking long enough to scream at them for intruding.

"This looks like an appliance cemetery," she said.

Fontaine pointed. "They buy a lot of these from people, but most of what we see was probably discarded along the sides of the road."

Beaucharp stopped the car. "What happens to this stuff?"

Fontaine shook her head. "Boy! You Yankees are really lost. First, they yank the motors. They might be salvageable. If not, the copper winds can be pried out and sold for scrap—"

Beaucharp, still smiling, interrupted. "All that work for some scrap copper?"

Fontaine, using her finger as a gun barrel, pointed it at her temple. "Pow! Oh boy, Beauchy, I gotta just lead you by the hand."

Beaucharp began to speak but Fontaine held a hand up and said, "Be quiet now and let me finish. Aluminum pieces are recycled or sold. The rest is scrap iron or steel. A collector will swing by in a salvage truck with a retrievable claw and scoop everything up for a blanket price."

Still smiling, Beaucharp rolled down her window. "Still looking for a cheap dishwasher?"

"I'm good."

Next came an assortment of used furniture pieces that appeared to have been placed in a semblance of order. Fontaine pointed. "Someone must be coming to pick these up."

"How come this building is so long, Donna?"

"It's part of an old packing house, probably used to sort and pack vegetables or citrus for shipping oranges, or grapefruit. A lot went to the Tropicana plant nearby."

Beaucharp stopped the car again. "That had to be quite a trick because this place was here long before cardboard packaging."

Fontaine arched an index finger so Beaucharp understood that she was talking about something on the other side of the building. "A company across the river in Belenton built wooden shipping crates and flats for the growers. Supposedly, they could create any type or size of box for shipping by train and later by truck. Someone could bring measurements for tiny wooden flats to box strawberries or order a large crate to ship a piano."

Beaucharp pointed out the irregularities in the eaves along the extended roofline. "Look at it! It's about one hundred yards long and looks like it's been pieced together like a Legos set."

Fontaine turned toward her partner, squeezed her eyebrows together and shook her head. "What the heck! Did you suddenly bump your head and become Frank Lloyd Wright?"

"Just making observations. When I complete my memoirs, I don't want things misconstrued."

"Memoirs? You use big words like misconstrued in them?"

"Maybe. You'd better be careful. Maybe I'll turn you into some nefarious character. At my discretion, the Beaucharp History of Belenton doesn't have to be very complimentary of you."

Fontaine squirmed in her seat, adjusted her twisted blouse, then smiled. "Ooh. Wow. That scares me. It will probably end up a horror story embellished with ideas stolen from CSI. Maybe you'll change my name or put some warts on my nose like a witch."

"I could give you a large round butt and one leg if you want. Maybe a wooden peg like Long John Silver. That would make the narrative Frenchy or something like that. Your ancestors are Frogs, aren't they?"

Fontaine turned to her window so Beaucharp wouldn't see her grin. "Frenchy! You mean like *C'est la vie? Or Je ne sais quoi*?"

Beaucharp laughed. "Donna, what're you doing? You don't speak French."

"Of course, I know some French. You know what I said?"

Beaucharp smiled and lied. "Donna, you don't know. You may have just ordered a pizza—"

Fontaine laughed, "C'mon, Beauchy. All those words to order a pizza?"

"You didn't let me finish. You may have also added mushrooms and extra cheese."

Fontaine tapped Beaucharp lightly on the arm with her fist and said, "Beauchy, you kill me."

Beaucharp said, "I'm serious, Fontaine. You'd better be nicer to me for the sake of your posterity. With a dash of my pen, I can make you a legend—"

Fontaine stopped her. "A legend? Like Bone Mizell? John Ashley?"

Beaucharp squinted. "Bone Mizell? Who's Bone Mizell? Who's John Ashley?"

"Oh, my God. You are one lost Yankee."

Beaucharp had a way of lifting one eyebrow higher than the other when she was questioning something.

In a deep throaty burst of laughter, Fontaine pointed and said, "And look at your crooked eyebrows! Who can do that? You're like some kind of circus character from Sarasota. I heard witches can do stuff like that."

Beaucharp covered her mouth to hide the laughter and to regain her composer, she stopped the car. "Bone Mizell, or this Ashley character, whoever he is, maybe I'll make you like Lizzy Borden. Everyone can recall that lady?" Trying to keep on the subject, she said, "So, tell me, how do they end up with this funny-looking building?"

Fontaine shook her head again. "Oh, Lordy, Lordy, Lordy. What am I going to do with you? The building probably started way down at the other end, where the flagpole is. I think it was some kind of a slaughterhouse at one time."

"That's where the name Bucket of Blood comes from?"

"A good chance you're right, Beauchy. I'm seeing some of my intelligence is spreading to you. Let's finish with the building, okay?"

Fontaine continued. "I'll bet they nailed together pieces of the building as they needed more room until they could go no further. Manatee County didn't establish strict building codes until about fifty years ago."

They rolled slowly past several piles of tires and a sign advertising their sale along with stacks of rusting auto rims piled higher than their vehicle. Everything was covered in white dust and the smell of old, drying rubber and rusty metal was everywhere. The debris provided comfortable roosts for a group of feral cats, patiently staring at Fontaine and Beaucharp like spectators watching a parade pass.

A dirty gray one shot past the front of the car causing Beaucharp hit the brakes. Once safely across, it leaped up onto a vacant tire pile and joined the gallery.

"They look like The Muppets watching a ball game," Fontaine said, waving her hand toward the assembly.

Beaucharp began to experience the sense of giddiness acquired from lack of sleep. Fontaine noticed it and tried to spur on her partner's foolishness. She turned to Beaucharp and using her long fingers spread her mouth into a foolish clown-like smile, then crossed her eyes.

To avoid laughing, Beaucharp tried to not to look in her direction but to no avail. Finally, she was forced to laugh so uncontrollably that a burst of spittle shot out splattering onto the windshield.

Fontaine smiled. "You laugh much or what?"

Beaucharp's face reddened. "I'm sorry. I'm flighty because I've been up since three am." She stared out her side window fearing eye contact with Fontaine lest she create a different funny face.

Fontaine said, "I'm going to make you wear a spit mask if you can't behave." Fontaine stopped with the faces.

Beaucharp, feeling foolish, inhaled loudly, apologized for the outburst, and searched for a tissue to wipe the windshield.

Fontaine then crossed her eyes, pushed the tip of her nose up with an index finger, and said, "Beauchy, you're like a kid."

Upon seeing this Beaucharp broke into another laugh rush, recovered, and pointed to the cats. "What are they thinking right now? Looks like we're bringing them some entertainment."

Fontaine smiled. "Yeah, we better be careful with the fooling around. They'll take our tag number."

Beaucharp, still silly said, "Yeah. They may rat us out!" She stopped and looked at Fontaine. "Get it? Rat us out."

Fontaine pinched her temples. "Oh boy! I'm going to start drinking early tonight."

She pulled the overhead visor down, slid the cover off the tiny mirror, and stared at her eyes, nose, and lips. Then, drawing a tissue out of the package in Beaucharp's hand, she said, "Another day with you, Beauchy, and my face will melt."

They drove past a section with an Auto Repair sign with the heavy smell of old grease and oil-saturated soil.

"Now, that's old Florida!" Fontaine said, pointing at a homemade auto lift with steel cables attached to a hand crank, making it possible to raise two parallel platforms under a vehicle's frame. Then several rusting and smelly 55-gallon drums rested on oil drenched soil.

Beaucharp said, "If this were Jersey, those barrels would probably have bodies stuffed in them."

Fontaine said, "There used to be a lot of places like this in the area. Now, the property is being scooped up by housing developers and shopping malls."

At the end of the building the crushed shells stopped, but the road continued in dirt leading to what looked like overrun sabal palms, thistles and remnants of an abandoned citrus grove from a dozen freezes ago.

They parked next to the pole with the American flag hanging listlessly above a faded black POW flag. The building reminded Beaucharp of an old barn-like structure. It had a faded sign painted over the door that read, The Bucket of Blood Social Club.

Beaucharp said, "You want to call our location in?"

"Why not? I have to do everything."

Beaucharp grinned and started for the mic.

Fontaine slapped her hand. "Don't touch that. The way you're messing up today, you're liable to break something."

Fontaine took over the radio and uttered several call numbers. After getting a response, she gave the time in twenty-four-hour clock terms, her location, waited for confirmation, and then cleared off. She looked at Beaucharp. "There, at least it's done right." She then pointed at the flagpole. "Ever notice how lonely a flag looks when it ain't waving?"

Beaucharp nodded, thought for several seconds, then said, "What do you think we're going to find inside?"

"We're going to find people, Beauchy, and people are the same wherever you go."

Beaucharp nodded again, "Yeah. I think you're right."

"And remember, first impression is the most important. Try not to spit on anyone."

Chapter 14

Fontaine pulled the door open, and sunlight rushed in like the explosion of a camera flash. The still and tidiness surprised them. Willie Nelson's rendition of Angel Flying Too Close to the Ground flowed softly out of a speaker somewhere.

Inside was dimly lit and smelled of tobacco smoke and greasy fried pork. The floor, uneven and weary in places where the building frame settled into the sandy soil, also suffered the effects of worn-out floorboards replaced with pine slabs of various widths and depths. Some areas bowed slightly and bore the effects of food and liquor stains. Liquids spills made portions of the newer planks swell unevenly above the older ones.

A metal plaque on the wall stated it was built in 1922 for storage and converted to a slaughterhouse in 1942 to provide meat for the U.S. military and America's allies. Several brown and white photos of men and women in blood-stained aprons, standing over chopping blocks, adorned the walls on either side of the plaque.

Beaucharp pointed at it and said, "That's how it got the name."

The room had four rectangular tables with six old-fashioned folding wooden chairs at each and three small square ones. The smaller tables possessed an assortment of solid wood and traditional folding metal chairs with worn cushions.

No one was playing either of the two pinball machines, and an old-fashioned bowling machine stood idle. Several posters and photos of Cracker Florida cowboys and a locomotive hung on the walls away from the door.

Beaucharp recognized it as Cabbage Head, the first train pulling vegetables and citrus from surrounding areas to the shores of the Manatee River.

There were several Ringling Brothers Circus posters blended into a mix of photos of more white workers posing in front of long tables with produce crates. Six ceiling fans wobbled and pushed around the tobacco-soaked air without making a breeze. A central air conditioning system hummed away somewhere, doing a good job of keeping the place cool.

The Bucket of Blood, old, dark in places, and surprisingly, relatively clean, felt inviting.

The place also seemed comfortable with its scars. Beaucharp noticed a path of old gouges and tears into the floor, starting from the entrance and stopping at the end of the long bar. *I'll bet they dragged something heavy. Refrigeration units, maybe?*

To Fontaine, it had the texture of a clean, worn-out, floor of a dairy barn.

A man, at least six feet, four inches, and way past two hundred and sixty pounds, stood behind the bar in an Orange Tampa Bay tee shirt. With his arms crossed, he stood watching a news program on the flat-screen TV attached to the wall.

Beaucharp's first thought was how he reminded her of her Uncle David. *Good Lord! Those arms look like they belong to a polar bear.*

Three men and two women clustered at the bar. All, including the bartender, had drinks in front of them. Everyone turned and stared at the detectives curiously. Those sitting at the tables stopped talking and smiled warmly.

The Orange Shirt spoke first in a slow, warm, and gravelly drawl. "Howdy, ladies. If y'all Jehovah's Witnesses, please don't try to recruit anyone. Otherwise, y'all welcome to stay as long as you want."

A woman in a felt fedora seated at the furthest end of the bar said, "Hello, friends. Please come in."

The woman to her left, wearing a green tee shirt with the words *Turning Points Volunteer* and a black baseball cap with the letters TB, moved down a stool to create room for the two detectives to sit alongside each other.

Beaucharp said, "I'm Detective Beaucharp—"

Fontaine interrupted. "And I'm Detective Fontaine. We're with the Belenton PD and have some questions about something that happened last night."

"Oh, Lord!" The woman in the green tee shirt shrieked and unloaded with words in rapid-fire, machine-gun-like sentences. "Did-sum-body-have-n'-accident? Whose-hurt?"

Fontaine said, "Do any of you know Mr. Wally Gaslight?"

Chairs stirred at the tables, and people at the bar glanced at one another and hoped they weren't noticed.

The Orange Shirt said, "Is Wally hurt? If he is, we'd like to know so we can help."

Beaucharp said, "He's okay. We spoke to him earlier this morning. Did anyone see him last night?"

A voice rang out from a table cluttered with brown beer bottles. "I sat with him for a spell last night."

"What time was that?" Fontaine asked. She stretched her neck to see who said it.

A woman's voice from another table politely said, "Excuse me. You both seem like nice folks, and we respect the police no matter where they come from."

She stopped and looked around. Every head in the room bobbed in agreement. "None of us are about to say anything to get Mr. Gaslight in trouble."

This time, a brisk wave of mumbling accompanied the bobbing heads.

"We're not trying to get Mr. Gaslight in trouble," Beaucharp said. "We want to help him work out some problems he ran into last night."

"What kind of problems?" Orange Shirt asked.

Fontaine raised her hands to her chest, palms out, the universal sign of surrender. "I promise you; we are not trying to get Mr. Gaslight in trouble."

A woman at the table said, "We're sorry if we sound abrupt, but Wally Gaslight is always helping somebody. We also know that he's had some driving difficulties but has no misgivings toward the police. He'd never intentionally cause trouble."

Orange Shirt looked at Beaucharp as if he wanted to help. "There is a policeman from Belenton that stops by from time to time. Ask him." He swept his head left and right across the room, inquiring, "Anyone remember the feller's name? Quiet sort."

Felt Fedora said, "His name's Cady. Decent fellow. Changed a flat tire for me once. Didn't have to either—just a kind soul. Ask him 'bout Wally. He knows."

Fontaine said, "We know he's a good guy and wouldn't intentionally hurt anybody. We just need to know if anyone saw him last night. It is important."

Orange Shirt spoke again. "He was here for a bit last night. Was only gonna' eat but got carried away with the beer. Said he wasn't gonna' drive till he got some rest, though. People seen him sleepin' in his truck later."

"Remember what time he got here?" Beaucharp asked.

Orange Shirt said, "It was shortly after the brush fire started behind the pig farm. Check with the fire department, but I think it began around nine or 9:30."

"I saw him out there." A man in a soiled camouflage cap with the word Army embossed across the front stood and leaned heavily against a metal cane. "Wally was sound asleep, and it looked like he was about to be chauffeured. He wasn't driving. He was asleep."

"Chauffeured?" said Fontaine. "Do you mean someone else was driving? Do you remember what time that was?"

The Army hat shifted the cane to the front and leaned into it. "I'd say 'bout 12:45, maybe one o'clock. It was the Beauregard kid. He's sort of quiet. Nice kid, though." Looking at his neighbors around the table, he asked, "Don't y'all think?"

All the heads bowed in agreement.

To avoid making everyone anxious, Beaucharp left her notepad in her pocket and took mental notes. "Who is this Beauregard person? How can we get in touch with him?" she asked.

Wearing a blue tee shirt with a yellow bass leaping across the front, the lady beside the Army Hat said, "His first name is Winston. He's a nephew of Cyrus Washbee, the undertaker. He's 'bout eighteen or nineteen."

Fontaine asked, "Washbee's Funeral Home? Is that the place?" She knew about it.

"That's him," said Orange Shirt. "But that kid ain't no trouble. I've known him since he's a toddler. If he was in Wally's truck, it was only to help with something."

Beaucharp sensed the environment was turning icy. "We're not saying anyone's done something wrong." She continued, "We want to run down a few loose ends just to clear some things up."

Orange Shirt threw his hands in the air. "But this is how it starts. Something gets said, it becomes misconstrued, and situations get out of hand."

Fontaine moved to the stool in front of him. "You said that Mr. Gaslight was pretty drunk?"

Orange Shirt shook his head. "See what I mean. I didn't say he was pretty drunk." He looked around the room again at the others. "Anyone hear me say that Wally was pretty drunk last night?"

Everyone shook their heads. No.

Fontaine's shoulders dropped and her voice got scratchy. "I'm sorry. I didn't mean to sound like I was putting words in your mouth, sir. I'm like an anxious hound that gets consumed with chasing a rabbit and gets too far ahead of itself."

Orange Shirt, now feeling he'd been too abrupt, nodded. "You're okay, detective. We all say the wrong things from time to time."

Felt Fedora spoke. "For most of us here, this ain't our first rodeo. We can tell you're both nice folks, but we never had detectives show up here before, so you two kind of dropped a ton of hay on us."

Fontaine said, "Again, I apologize. But if we want to help Mr. Gaslight, we need to know some things about his schedule. Now we know he got here between 9:00 and 9:30—"

Beaucharp interrupted. "Anyone remember what he had to eat?"

Orange Shirt shuffled to the end, placed his elbows on the bar, and leaned out into the air. "He ate some fries, two hamburgers and chatted about the hog hanging in his dooryard that he'd been trying to dress all day. That's all."

Fontaine made a mental note of the time and what Gaslight ate. They now knew that he arrived at the Bucket of Blood at around nine and left at about 12:30. Probably at 1:00 am, he was seen asleep on the passenger side of his truck with a person named Winston in the driver's seat. There was a good chance that the Winston person was the figure caught by the Wawa cameras.

Beaucharp, sensing discomfort, walked over to Orange Shirt and touched his elbow. "We're not looking for dirt on Mr. Gaslight. We're just looking to fill in some lost time he can't remember. Honestly."

Orange shirt's shoulders dropped; he relaxed his arms and then spoke in a fatherly warmth. "I'm sorry, ma'am. There's no need for me to be angry. You two are just doing your jobs."

Beaucharp smiled. "We understand that this is unsettling. You're all family, and we're strangers coming in here with questions that may seem like we are accusing someone of something. That's not the case—"

"We were with Mr. Gaslight early this morning," Fontaine interrupted. "We know he's a decent guy. I'm sure he's home right now worrying over things that we can't even talk about now. In our work, we see scoundrels occasionally, and we don't mind hounding them. Wally Gaslight isn't one."

Beaucharp finally noticed the magnetic name tag, Mitchell, on the orange shirt. She turned to the people sitting along the bar, then at the tables. "We're not here trying to trick anyone. The sooner we get all the facts, the sooner Mr. Gaslight will get some comfort." She smiled at Mitchell. "My friends call me Michaela. They call my partner, ma'am—"

"It's Donna," Fontaine shouted loud enough for them to hear.

Everyone chuckled.

Fontaine asked, "Who is Marsha Pickering?" As soon as the words came out of her mouth, her intuition sent the alarm. It was a mistake.

The room grew quiet. Johnny Cash's rendition of *Ghost Riders in the Sky* had replaced Willie Nelson in the hidden speakers. Everyone at the bar looked at one another in confusion.

Green Tee-Shirt's face contorted, bringing her eyes closer together. She shot a frosty stare at Fontaine. "I'm-Marsha-Pickering. I-didn't-do-nothing-wrong. Are-you-two-lying-to-us. You-agents-from-the-Federal Government?"

Beaucharp stepped next to her and shook her head apologetically. "No, we're not lying. We brought up your name because he spoke highly of you the last time we were with Mr. Gaslight. He mentioned that you had a special experience. He worried that he might have had something similar."

"You don't have to believe me," Green Tee-Shirt shot back.

Fontaine said, "We don't believe or disbelieve you, ma'am. Mr. Gaslight mentioned your name fondly. Did you see him at all last night?"

Green Tee-Shirt, now indignant, shouted, "I ain't that kind of woman!"

Giggles erupted around the room again.

Fontaine, now red-faced, said, "I'm sorry, Miss Marsha, I wasn't trying to imply somethin' improper."

Beaucharp stepped forward. "We just wanted to follow up on Mr. Gaslight's statements. He was frightened."

Green Tee Shirt said, "I've learned to live with ridicule ever since it happened. I am not apologizing for what I saw and what happened to me."

Knowing that they'd be leaving soon, Fontaine wanted to reassure the room of their sincerity and leave in a positive light. "Folks, we ain't looking to get somebody in trouble." Then, she turned to Marsha and said, "Miss Marsha, Mr. Gaslight spoke of you with great respect."

Orange Shirt asked, "So what did Wally do? If he ain't in trouble, why are y'all cops here asking questions about him and what he'd did last night?"

Beaucharp's hand went up like a traffic cop. "As my partner said, there are a bunch of loose ends that we want to tie off. We don't want to make this any more complicated than it is. Talk to Mr. Gaslight the next time you see him. God knows he needs friends like you at this time."

Things, again, grew amicable. Trust settled in between the detectives and the patrons in the Bucket of Blood. As Fontaine and Beaucharp passed out their cards, they felt a sense of responsibility for disrupting the natural rhythm of the group. Both detectives, sensitive professionals, knew they put a crack in their little solar system.

Beaucharp would later describe it as, "*. . . we left after bringing ambiguous news about a family member and by doing so had taken away a sort of their community innocence.*"

Chapter 15

Fontaine pushed through the heavy oak door into the white-hot stillness. The bright reflection off the crushed shells stung their eyes. They donned sunglasses immediately and each footstep toward the car molested the parched, gritty powder sending tiny puffs of white clinging to their shoes and pant cuffs. A fine grit scraped against their teeth.

Beaucharp pushed the A/C to the maximum and even before the cool air began, they started writing their thoughts and debriefing each other.

The sweat on her face caused Fontaine's glasses to slip. She pushed the bar between the lenses back against the bridge of her nose.

After comparing notes, Fontaine said, "No one tried to come up with a story or an alibi for Gaslight."

Beaucharp tapped the edges of the steering wheel. "If any of them had the slightest idea about missing body parts, they hid it well. I liked everyone, especially Mitchell, the fedora lady, space traveler, and the Army Hat. They seemed sincere about their worry for Gaslight."

Fontaine said, "It's likely we'll have to come back and talk some more to these folks."

"I think you're right. At least we left on a good note. I didn't feel anyone hostile to us."

Fontaine usually hid some feelings but felt safe exposing her soft side to Beaucharp. She said, "Good people. I don't know, though. There is pain in there."

"How do you mean?"

"I don't have the words for it. They seem like a pack of lost souls."

"I think I know what you mean, Donna. It's anyone's guess what their journeys were like or what they had to leave behind."

"Yeah. Different places in the land and different places in their souls. We have to come back and visit, Beauchy. I worry about Marsha."

Beaucharp understood her partner's compassion for others. She took her glasses off and stared into Fontaine's face. "Marsha, the space lady?"

"Yes. Charlatans always take advantage of people struggling with problems like hers."

"Donna, we can drop in from time to time just in case you need to ram a boot up a charlatan's butt!"

Fontaine stared straight ahead and grinned. "That's my partner! Let's talk some more with Cady. He seems to have a handle on the place. In the meantime, let's finish what we're doing and find this kid, Winston Beauregard."

***

They spent ten minutes discussing the mysterious bag of body parts. They hoped the FBI or FDLE databases came up with some recent unusual murders, new missing person reports, or any body parts missing from contemporary crime scenes.

Beaucharp peered into her notepad and spoke without lifting her head. "DNA tests usually take at least a week. Bargeil may have to take us off the case by the end of the day, or at least until they get some solid results."

Suddenly, Fontaine reached across and tapped two quick beeps with the horn to warn a lazy squirrel that a feral cat was stalking him. The cat and squirrel scattered, then she looked at Beaucharp and winked. "The most common places where body pieces or corpses might turn up are hospitals, maybe nursing homes, med schools—"

Beaucharp interrupted. "Or funeral homes?"

Fontaine poked a long, skinny finger at her partner. "Oh yeah! You're getting it and beginning to make me proud. Let's go make friends with Winston Beauregard."

Chapter 16

The Washbee Funeral Home and Crematorium was a stately Victorian house with fifteen rooms. Built several hundred yards from the Gamble Mansion and at a time when all it took was a straight dusty road to signal progress in the county. During the Civil War, it often got searched and watched closely by the occupying federal troops.

The funeral parlor, a term used in the community for as long as anyone could remember, existed in the Washbee family for over one hundred and seventy years. Each generation cared for the property as if nurturing a rare orchid. They constantly updated the plumbing, kitchen appliances, and electrical systems.

The crematorium, completed in the early 1960s, is the only significant addition to the building. Five residential bedrooms share the second and third floors. A fully equipped kitchen and dining room occupy the rear of the first floor. Four viewing rooms—chapels, as the Washbees have always called them—are available for wakes and viewings. In addition, the small non-denominational chapel, in the far corner of the building, is available for religious services. The Washbees provide the needy, or those with no or few relatives, with memorial services at no charge.

The large front porch carried the weight of ten oak rocking chairs, a beautiful white scalloped rail from end to end, and an array of colorful plants in urns suspended from ceiling beams. If ever Victorian grace with Southern charm and dignity needed description, one would have to look no further than the Washbee Funeral Home and Crematorium.

Except for the kitchen and bathroom walls, the entire first floor was paneled with ninetieth-century solid walnut, installed at the same time American troops were staged in Ybor City enroute to do battle with the

Spanish in Cuba. Polished and maintained exquisitely for over a century, it could easily pass for a Hollywood set.

Squares of embossed metal plating, cream-colored and impeccably cared for, adorned the 14-foot ceilings. Although inoperative now, original oil lighting fixtures graced the walls alongside photos and paintings of many Washbee ancestors and friends. Each generation displays a family member in a military uniform of one sort or another. Everything got dusted twice a week.

Except for the kitchen and bathrooms, the flooring was covered with luxurious, deep wool carpets of various soft colors and brightness. The hallways had a rich blend of red and maroon, and in each of the viewing rooms, a deep rich blue-green, burnt orange, and aqua blend.

In the hallway, a stately mahogany grandfather clock chimes eloquently, reminding everyone of the hour and half-hour. It once belonged to the famous Cofield Plantation in Ellenton and, supposedly, lent to the Washbee family to hide from the Yankee foragers. It was believed that even Yankees wouldn't sink so low as to molest a place as sacred as a funeral parlor.

With all the upheaval and confusion for the wealthy families at the end of the Civil War, no one thought of coming back to collect the clock. Cyrus' great-grandfather, Orvel, didn't bother to notify anyone of its existence while all the foreclosures and bankruptcies took place as creditors chased down people collecting debts and taxes. Orvel would later tell folks *". . . it would have only ended up in the hands of a Yankee carpetbagger if anyone had said something."*

The clock's regal tolling never startled Manfred, the massive black house cat that glided about the halls like a stately owner. His purpose was to keep the unruly population of field mice in check and call upon the sorrowful and deeply distraught mourners attending in-house services. Manfred, somehow, located the most morose person, snuggled closely and purred loudly. Sometimes he would leap up onto a lap.

Today, nearly all Washbee's clients come from the area's assisted living facilities. Others are poor farm workers, and homeless people. Money slowly drizzled in. The county pays small transportation fees from the place of death to the funeral home. Sometimes, a stipend from Medicare and $255 from Social Security pay for the cremation. Also, Washbee received $50 from the county for placing an individual's ashes in a plastic-lined cardboard box or a sealed plastic urn for burial in the pauper's section of the Memphis Cemetery, a local graveyard.

Chapter 17

Their tires crunched against the crushed shells as they drove onto a parking lot where nearly everything was worn into a blinding white powder.

Beaucharp paused, rolled down her window to ensure she was capturing the whole picture, and said, "This place is unbelievable." She turned to Fontaine. "It's so neat. It reminds me of the Marine bases when we visited my Uncle David."

Several white, dusty sun-bleached sidewalks led toward the building from different directions. An assortment of ornamental plastic and ceramic wildlife figurines stared at travelers along the walkways like tiny sentinels. A variety of flora strategically drew one's eye toward the massive white Victorian building.

Beaucharp said, "This looks like a good place to pick up some body parts. What do you think?"

"That's a good point, partner. But these folks have always been philanthropists. Nothing untoward has ever come out of this place."

Beaucharp said, "Look at all the tiny creatures on the lawn."

"So that makes these folks suspicious?"

"No. Just an observation. I kind of like that stuff."

Fontaine smiled and said, "I'll pick some up for you the next time I'm at the Dollar Store."

Beaucharp chuckled under her breath, then tried to bring them both back to their purpose for being there. "Look at this place. It looks like it comes out of a Hollywood set. Is this for real, or did the Feld people build this?"

Fontaine said, "Feld? The circus and movie production company across the street from Detweiler's?"

"Yeah," said Beaucharp.

"Nope, this is for real partner, built in the nineteenth century by the Washbee family."

Beaucharp waved her hand across her image of the house. "Must be twenty rooms in there."

"Oh yeah, quite a shack. Ready to go take a look?"

Beaucharp said, "We got to call in our location. Let's see if there is anything new." She picked up the mic. "Two-nine at Washbee Funeral Home in Ellington."

A voice returned, acknowledging their location, and posting a time. "Go two-nine. Washbee Funeral Home eleven-fifteen hours."

Beaucharp asked, "Maggie, got any messages?"

"Besides Birdy saying you two, and your shenanigans, are keeping him awake nights. Oh! Wait a minute. Crime Lab says they may have something on the organs and some bones. It'll be available within the hour."

"Thanks, Maggie."

Fontaine busted in. "Some results are in. That's kinda quick, ain't they, Maggie?"

"Yeah, we don't understand that."

Beaucharp spoke. "It's got to be Fontaine causing that stuff to Birdy. I'm too busy being a cop twenty-four hours a day."

Fontaine and Beaucharp heard laughter filling the communication room. Then it stopped abruptly, and a new voice shot out at them.

"This is Captain Bird."

"Oh shit," whispered Fontaine.

Beaucharp said, "Yes, sir."

"They told you we got something new on the bones and organs?"

"Yes, sir."

"Call in as soon as you're finished with Washbee and tell Fontaine my wife wants to talk to her."

Background laughter, again, exploded. Beaucharp giggled. Fontaine grinned, blushed, and rolled her eyes.

"Yes, sir. Two-nine out," Beaucharp disconnected.

"Good job, partner," Fontaine said.

"What do you mean, good job? Evidently, you're the one with the racy reputation."

"What do you mean, racy? I'm a Baptist. Been one my whole life. How's that make me racy?"

"Don't ask me. I'm not the provocative dresser here."

"What the—"

"Don't look at me like that. You know what I'm talking about. Look how you're dressed right now."

"I'm wearing the same thing as you, a light blouse and tan slacks. What is so provocative about that?"

Beaucharp, trying to hide grin, said, "Of course, you're going to copy how I dress; you want to be successful. But you notice I don't sashay around trying to draw attention to my body."

Fontaine caught the joke and giggled as their seat belts clicked open. "You can't sashay about because you'd look like bait of some kind and the Florida wildlife might snatch you up."

As soon as the car doors slammed, Fontaine said, "I gotta pee now, Michaela."

Beaucharp said, "You can hold it."

Chapter 18

Several hours before Fontaine and Beaucharp arrived, Cyrus Washbee was confronted with a startling event. At 7:30 am, his nephew, Winston Beauregard stood nervously in his office threshold. Beauregard, usually gentle and in control, but this morning he spoke with alarm. His hands displayed the anxious twitching he hadn't experienced in many years. He wanted to discuss the events that transpired the evening before when he tried to take food scraps to Giovanelli's pig farm.

Washbee raised his voice. "Whatever made you decide to dump the bag into the bed of Mr. Gaslight's truck?" *Why am I angry? It's not his fault.*

He had never demonstrated such an outburst at Winston.

"Hattie said you gave her permission to take the van away so that she could bring the bingo things over to the nursing home. She was toting a bag of soft drinks and wouldn't even allow me to help her stack them in the van." Winston stopped and stared at the floor. "She just jumped right in. It was all I could do to pull the bag out and close the side door 'fore she drove off."

"What were you doing at the Bucket of Blood?"

Winston fidgeted from foot to foot. "I wanted to get a can of soda for the drive over to Mr. Giovanelli's."

"After Hattie took the van, why didn't you just bring the bag back home? You could have got it later."

"It was getting dark, and Mr. Gaslight pulled into the same parking spot where Hattie drove off. And you know Mr. Gaslight, he always talks." Winston smiled. "He said Hi!"

Frustrated, Washbee said, "He said, Hi, and then you threw the bag into the back of his truck?"

Winston shuffled more and broke apart. Then, tearing up, he said, "I'm terribly ashamed, Uncle Cyrus. I can never do anything right."

Washbee's icy manner softened, and he ached with the shame of having addressed his delicate nephew in such a rough manner. Now, blaming himself for not being vigilant, Washbee assumed responsibility for the mistake.

He shook his head, then said what he was sure to be a lie. "I'm sure anyone else would've done the same thing."

Unknown to Winston, or anyone else in the family, he'd got stuck in the middle of an unintended scheme that his cousin, Hattie, innocently devised. Washbee imagined the worst and was confused with Hattie's behavior. No one was aware of her motives at this time, but another disastrous circumstance occurred the day before. They were the mistakes by Washbee's nephew, Duff Bleiu, and a hospital. Unbeknown to Washbee and his nephews, these mistakes would prove miniscule in terms of the horrifying events they would later learn about.

"You don't even know what all I done," Winston said.

"You panicked and threw the bag of scraps into the back of Mr. Gaslight's truck. Is that right?"

"Yes." Washbee calmly asked Winston to sit, then reached across and touched the back of his hand. "I still don't understand why you did it."

"You know how Mr. Gaslight likes to get carried away at the bar after he eats." Washbee nodded. "So, I figured he'd be there for quite a spell. I thought I'd leave the scraps in his truck bed until Hattie returned with the van."

"That was a good idea, Winston. What happened next?"

Winston fidgeted in his seat. "Well, I smelled the smoke first, then the volunteer fire alarm shot off. I'm a member of the volunteer regiment, you know, so I rushed to the fire station down the road."

"What about the bag, Winston? What did you do with the bag?"

"It was in Mr. Gaslight's truck. Figured it'd be safe there till I got back."

Washbee nodded. "So then, what happened?"

"It turned out to be a small bush fire, but I didn't get back till after midnight. I figured that I missed Hattie but thought I'd sit in Mr. Gaslight's truck and wait a bit, just in case."

Washbee rubbed his hand nervously. "So, Winston, how is it you were driving Mr. Gaslight's truck?"

Winston fidgeted some more. "After a long while, Mr. Gaslight stumbled outside, and it looked like he was fixin' to leave. He eyeballed me, and that must have gotten him confused enough to go back around and climb into the passenger seat."

"Then what happened?"

"I said, hi, Mr. Gaslight, but he didn't seem to notice and just fell asleep with his head against the door window."

Washbee stared at Winston. "So far, you're still with the bag. How did you misplace it?" "I didn't misplace it. It was still in the truck when I left. What I did was move the truck to some other place."

"You moved the truck?" said Washbee. "Where'd you get the keys?"

"Mr. Gaslight always leaves them on the floor." Winston went on while nervously rolling one hand over the other. "You see, people were coming and going all the time and walking up to talk to Mr. Gaslight. Knowing it was his truck and all, people kept asking me, 'What's up with Gaslight?"

Fearing the conversation would become more confusing, Washbee stopped him. "Just explain it to me slowly."

Winston's hands stopped moving, and he laid them quietly, one on top of the other. "Well, sometimes they called him Wally. Sometimes they called him Mr. Gaslight."

"Okay. I mean, what happened with the truck and the bag?"

"After so much questioning and inquisitiveness by people asking about Mr. Gaslight, is inquisitiveness a real word, Uncle Cyrus?"

Washbee smiled. "Yes, inquisitiveness, is. It's a good word too."

Winston nodded. "Well, then I figured folks were getting pretty nosy. So, I decided to jest drive to Mr. Giovanelli's, place the bag in the refrigerator that he keeps in the barn, and take Mr. Gaslight home. Then I'd walk back home."

"So, the truck's at Mr. Gaslight's house?"

"No. I got confused when I left and missed a turn, then ended up crossing the bridge into Belenton."

"BELENTON!"

Winston started rolling his hands again. "Then the worst mishap of the night occurred—"

Cyrus brought his hand up like a traffic cop and stopped him. "It gets worse?" his voice rising again.

Winston lowered his head. "I crossed the bridge and turned the wrong way on Manatee Avenue. A car tooted, and the people inside it yelled and swore."

Washbee took a deep breath and exhaled slowly. "So, you're going the wrong way on Manatee Avenue? Did you have an accident? Did anyone get hurt? What happened to the truck and the bag?"

"Two or three cars came at me with the people yelling and tooting and all. I got all nervous and confused." Nearly breaking into tears again, he continued. "So, I parked alongside the road, up on the grass, clear enough of it so as not to cause trouble and left Mr. Gaslight asleep. Thought I'd leave for a bit and think about how to get Hattie to come pick me up."

"What did you do then?"

"I walked down to the corner, then went to Wawa. While getting an ice cream, I run into Bertie Howard. He gave me a ride home."

"Did you tell Bertie what you were doing in Belenton?"

"No, he didn't ask. I don't think he'll even remember it as he was all glassy-eyed like when he been taking them coxin pills."

"OxyContin," he corrected. "What about the truck?"

"Well, it wasn't going anywhere cuz I didn't want it to disappear before Hattie or someone came by to pick me up. So, I took the keys."

"Took the keys!"

"Mr. Gaslight shouldn't been drivin' drunk as he was, so I figured I'd be savin' him some problems if I took the keys."

Washbee stopped, took a few seconds to think, and then under his breath, uttered a series of volatile adjectives. Finally, he looked into Winston's face, nearly in tears, and said, "Oh Lord! You poor child of Jesus! Where are the keys? Where's the truck now?"

Washbee started struggling out of his chair and Winston began to get up to help but Washbee signaled him to stay seated.

Once alongside, Washbee said, "Don't fret. We'll pray on this. Difficult things always seem to unwind properly." He touched Winston's shoulder, smiled, started for the crematorium, then turned his head back and softly spoke. "Miss Bertha is the only thing important right now. Let's see if we can help your cousin Bleiu." He was lying one more time.

***

Winston Beauregard's incident added to Cyrus Washbee's woes. One day earlier his nephew, Duff Bleiu, the one who assumed most of the responsibilities for the cremation and distribution of the ashes came rushing past the clock, nearly tripping over Manfred and stopped abruptly in front of Washbee. He bore a striking resemblance to his mother, Ruby, Washbee's cousin who died from a toxic overdose of drugs in Baton Rouge.

"The furnace is still not working right, and Bertha Mason is next," he said, gasping for breath. "We promised her sister, Miss Julie, she would be ready in two days. She's gonna be here in an hour to discuss the services."

The clock announced the 9th hour from within its polished chestnut cabinet. Washbee looked into the face of his pocket watch, snapped the lid shut, and stuffed it back into a pocket. *It's over a hundred-eight years old and still keeping good time.* He reached across and gently touched his nephew's shoulder. "Is Olney Hazelton all set for tomorrow?"

"Yes." Bleiu looked down at his feet. "He was all alone. What if no one shows up for him?"

"I'm sure Mr. Hazelton will have friends here. Anyway, we'll be here for him."

Bleiu looked up at Washbee. "Hattie had already set a bouquet aside."

***

The plumber, Hollander Graves, built the crematorium furnace in 1960. The solid kiln-brick lined oven had a grated system ten feet long that slanted into the rear on a cast-iron frame inside a boilerplate steel rectangle. The boilerplate assembly, at one time, belonged to a section of the coal-fired furnace from a freighter in use before WWII.

The *Henry Louise*, built in the Brooklyn Navy yard in 1897, was designed to carry freight from South and Central America. It hauled its share of bananas, mangos, livestock, and giant stow-away tarantulas.

In the spring of 1940, Graves, six years a US Navy pipefitter, had just been discharged when the *Henry Louise* was on its way to the Tampa scrapyard. Graves, now anxious to return to Parrish, Florida, and begin a plumbing career, used his Navy savings to purchase a 1939 Packard pickup truck. Graves Plumbing eventually became the most innovative, successful, and honest plumbing company between Tampa Bay and Sarasota.

The well-used truck traveled the eighty-mile round trip to Tampa shipyard, collecting Navy surplus scraps of copper piping and sections of sturdy, heat-resistant steel boilerplate. The surplus material allowed Graves to pass bargain costs along to families building homes and the massive vegetable packing houses being erected by the farm co-ops. The surplus boilerplate sheets were convenient for assembling an assortment of smudge pots used when citrus growers were threatened by severe cold and frost. Graves even designed some that could be transported on trailers, pulled by tractors or horses, to various spots on the property. Other builders soon utilized the Navy scrapyard, which proved to be a bonus to every community within one hundred miles.

In 1960, Washbee asked Graves to design and build their crematorium. A propane gas flame or wood fire could perform the incineration process. The cords and tubes from the gas line could be removed if anyone chose to replace the fuel with wood. Using seasoned, dry hardwood, two cremations could occur at once with remains placed into each of the two seven-foot by twenty-inch iron chambers.

Each chamber could be slid into the kiln where at 1000 degrees it took an hour to incinerate the corpse, after which each chamber was slid out, with the help of gravity, through an iron door and allowed to cool in the brick mortuary section. Regardless of the material used in the cremation chambers, an ignitable propane line within the chimney burned off emitting smoke.

The crematorium was over sixty years old and needed work. Present funeral industry codes would not allow a replica of the existing system. If it stops working, Washbee would need to upgrade to something new.

Current pricing ran from $90,000 to $250,000. That cost would be prohibitive, given the volume of crematorium traffic. Now all they could do is keep fixing old and loose bricks and use hardwood for fuel most of the time. Getting wood fuel was not a problem as the Washbee family sat on six hundred acres of hardwood hammock.

Duff Bleiu managed most of the cremations and distribution of ashes. He also knew the crematory struggled to physically keep up, even with its slow demands. The firewall bricks were being constantly replaced. Bleiu also knew that if the system failed, present mortuary codes demanded that a new one be built, and replacement would be a significant financial undertaking. This weighed on him greatly. Then a serious incident occurred, he had to struggle with the decision he made to compensate for it never realizing the havoc he created.

***

Washbee was proud of his nephews and niece. Several days a week, Bleiu and his cousins Winston, and Hattie, also a funeral home worker, volunteered at local assisted living centers. They hosted holiday parties, bingo, and card games. Sometimes they just sat and talked with the lonely or the lost. Washbee encouraged them to participate and share holidays or special events with those without families or the ones whose family couldn't or chose not to join them.

Most of Washbee's clients came from that elderly community, many impoverished and often without family. For generations the Washbee families assumed the responsibility for those alone or too poor for other funeral homes to care for. They ensured everyone got a respectful memorial service and burial.

By the time the funeral home received elderly clients, their aged and emaciated remains had deteriorated to almost transparent tissue and bone. The incineration procedure readily consumed bodily parts efficiently, leaving only small bone segments. Once cooled, they were tamped into powder, placed into a ten-mil plastic bag, and then put into cardboard boxes. Everyone's name gets meticulously printed on the box, along with a special prayer. A numbered steel registration plate that survives the incineration is placed inside each box.

Families carried away the remains of their loved ones and placed them in homes or cemetery plots. If kept at home, difficulties arise when families move or pass away. Houses get sold, and new occupants discover funeral urns or boxes forgotten or abandoned. One can open the lid and get the number on the metal tag if the contents are not labeled. The number is registered nationally with the name of the person. Family, friends, or others can then be contacted to make people aware of the deceased's ashes.

Chapter 19

They reached the front door and Fontaine reminded Beaucharp again. "I do have to pee."

"Be quiet," Beaucharp said.

"Beauchy, just don't make me laugh again."

"Okay, stop it right now," Beaucharp scolded.

They were unaware of the earlier conversation between Washbee and Winston nor of the other important discourse between Washbee and Duff Bleiu the evening before.

It was an active business, so they walked in and were greeted by a jolt of dry, cold air.

"Look at this place!" Fontaine whispered. "It looks like the Addams Family lives here."

"Shush," Beaucharp frowned. "Am I going to have to make you wait in the car like a naughty child?"

"Look around. I mean it. It looks like a friggin' museum. Where did they come up with the colors for these carpets?"

Beaucharp grinned and said, "Remember, you're a cop. Don't steal anything."

Fontaine ran her palm along the wall. "I don't think they can even build a place like this today. Look at this paneling. Can you imagine how often you have to dust and polish it?"

"I know why something like that would strike you."

Fontaine frowned. "What do you mean?"

"That statement is coming from someone who makes her bed once a week. I don't think you even own a vacuum cleaner."

On a nineteenth-century walnut pedestal table set a drawing of a Victorian hand encased in a picture frame pointing a finger away from the wall. Beneath the framed hand, an embossed metal sign read Manager's Office.

"I guess this is where the fickle finger of fate is sending us," said Fontaine.

A voice called out. "May I help you?" It was Cyrus Washbee.

The detectives turned to find a tall, gracious-looking man in a dark suit approaching. He moved slowly, gently, as if he didn't want to awaken someone taking a nap.

Beaucharp would later recall in her notes: *He had a sincere voice*, gentle and *grandfatherly. . . slow, soft, and Southern, immediately trustworthy, and genuine.*

Fontaine, puzzled, questioned herself, *What's wrong with his face?*

Beaucharp caught it immediately and would later explain the phenomenon to her partner. "Our minds have preconceived notions," she would tell Fontaine. "It's like an incident that isn't supposed to happen. For example, a car drives by with a door missing. It's obvious that you question your senses about what you are seeing. You feel something is wrong, but because it was so unexpected, your brain can't put together what your eyes see."

Cyrus Washbee, with one missing eyebrow, and a gait slow and deliberate, had to walk sideways as if he were squeezing through a narrow door. They introduced themselves as Belenton Police detectives and asked to speak with Winston Beauregard.

Washbee believed he knew why they were there. He stopped momentarily to gather his words. Then, politely, almost paternally, asked if he could invite them into his office.

"It's important that we speak to Winston, sir," Beaucharp said.

Washbee's forehead wrinkled, and his eyes dampened. Right away, Fontaine felt the need to rush to his protection. "We just have a few questions, Mr. Washbee," she said.

"I'm afraid Winston isn't the one you want to speak with. He is innocent and only did what I asked him to do." Washbee did something he hated to do but had already done quite a bit of it that morning. He lied.

Fontaine said, "Sir, I don't think you understand. Do you know why we are here?"

"I'm sure I know why. But, again, it's all my fault."

Beaucharp said, "But sir—"

Washbee stopped her from speaking by bringing up his hand like a gentle teacher trying to quiet a noisy child. "Please, come into my office. I'll explain things the best I can."

They trailed Washbee down the hall. Behind his back, Fontaine turned toward Beaucharp. Confused, she shrugged and mouthed the words, *What's wrong with his face?*

Along the hallway, immaculately cared-for paneled walls graced with photos of soldiers in various old uniforms of what appeared to be family members in various types of formal dress, and oil landscapes of the neighboring beaches and rivers slowly moved past.

Shut up! Beaucharp mouthed back.

Washbee followed the direction ordered by the finger, stopped abruptly in front of a door with a framed sign, and lettered in Olde English Script the name Cyrus Washbee. Below, and in the standard script, was written, Director.

He held the door and stepped aside, allowing them to enter first. A large, dark cat scraped against Beaucharp's calf and raced in ahead of them.

"Oh, that's Manfred," said Washbee. "I can remove him if you want."

"He's okay. Let him stay," said Fontaine.

Central-air condensers hummed outside the window behind the mahogany desk with a neatly arranged array of papers, letter envelopes, and an orange mason jar filled with pens—the room was eloquently carpeted in beige-green wool. To the left of his desk stood a tall walnut bookshelf so well polished that light glimmered off its edges, the shelves filled with texts and heavy cardboard journal cases.

Beaucharp noted a volume of Robert Frost's Collected Poetry and a biography of Langston Hughes. Fontaine eyed Catherine Ingram's, *In the footsteps of Gandhi*, and Thoreau's, *On Walden Pond*.

The pendulum of an old banjo clock, also housed in walnut, whispered, and reflected off a full-length mirror attached to an opposite wall. In front of Washbee's desk, four cushioned captain chairs invitingly waited.

Washbee motioned toward the chairs. "Please sit down, detectives. Can I get you something to drink? It is scorching out there. Iced tea? Lemonade?"

Both declined.

Washbee nodded and, as always, waited for the guests to unconsciously rest their elbows and hands along the chair arms and quickly settle into effortless ease. Then Manfred leaped onto Fontaine's lap and began rubbing his cheeks against her chest, purring loudly, his face vibrating like a chainsaw at idle.

"I guess he likes you," Washbee said.

"We've always had cats at home," said Fontaine.

"Very well. Let me get right to the point. The material you found in Mr. Gaslight's truck ended up in there by accident."

Not realizing Washbee was only talking about Ida Foote's leg and foot, Beaucharp and Fontaine slid to the front of the chairs.

"I'm afraid this is going to be a long story, detectives. Are you sure I can't get you some refreshments?" Each shook their head.

He started with a lengthy description of how his nephews and nieces delivered food scraps to a friend's pig farm. Then, fifteen minutes into the narrative, Beaucharp stopped him when she noticed Fontaine fidgeting. She said, "Mr. Washbee, is there a lady's room nearby? My partner needs to use one."

Fontaine squinted uncomfortably. "Oh yes. We have been drinking fluids all day," she stared at Beaucharp, "I'm surprised my partner has so much control."

Washbee said, "Of course. Let me show you where it is." Everyone stood. Manfred ran out first, followed by Fontaine, Beaucharp, then slow-moving Washbee. He moved to the front again, inviting Fontaine to follow as he slid sideways-like down the hall.

"It's right there, detective." He pointed to a door next to an archway of what the detectives assumed was a memorial viewing room. He then turned to Beaucharp. "Are you sure I can't get you something?"

"I'm fine, thank you," she said.

"While your partner is in there, would you like to look around the place?" Washbee added, "It does have a few historical pieces."

Beaucharp, elated, said, "I would."

***

Manfred rushed into the bathroom ahead, unnoticed by the desperate Fontaine, until she got seated. Manfred, sitting directly in front of her, blinked several times and began dozing off into a loud purring sleep. His monotonous din made noisier with the echo from the tile walls.

Fontaine stared into his face. "What's up, Manfred? You got something going on here? Is there something you want to say before I read you your rights?"

Suddenly, her cell buzzed, and Manfred awoke. Fontaine moved too quickly pulling the phone out of her slacks, and it clumsily slid out of her hand. To prevent it from smashing onto the tiles, she quickly shoved her foot in its path, hoping to cushion the fall. The reaction, so rapid, caused her shoe to almost dislodge. The phone struck the shoe at an angle, then softly hit the floor, buzzed again, and wiggled along the tiles like a giant bug.

Manfred approached cautiously, pawing at it. The phone buzzed again and slid on the frictionless tile floor. Startled, Manfred leaped back and then cautiously approached, again touching it gently. It buzzed and crawled along the tiles one more time. Enthralled, Manfred then slapped it like a hockey puck, driving it under the bathroom sink. The phone buzzed one more time, and he ran to it, stomping and triggering the Answer button. A voice from the other end echoed.

"Fontaine? What's going on?"

Manfred slapped the phone again, pushing it further under the sink. Fontaine screamed at Manfred and frantically reached for the toilet tissue, knocking the roll off the holder. The metal cylinder pinged against the floor. The sharp noise made Manfred jump, and a white paper path unfolded as the roll traveled across the room, away from Fontaine. Thinking quickly, she stomped on the unrolled section closest to her, and the shoe fell from her foot. Nearly struck by the rolling paper, Manfred leaped aside and then dove on top of it to play. While all the time, voices shouted at the other end of the phone line.

Fontaine bent to grab the tissue under her foot, gently trying to draw in a section as if she were reeling in a fish. Then the long white sheet became a wriggling toy to Manfred. He playfully jumped on it, breaking the paper stream and leaving Fontaine with a bit of a section in her fingertips. She counted three squares. Beaucharp and Washbee, in the hallway, were puzzled by the noisy commotion.

Fontaine yelled at the phone on the floor. "I'm here. Wait a minute!"

Frantic voices ensued from the BPD Dispatch. "Fontaine, are you okay? What's going on?"

"Wait a minute! I'll be right with you." Her voice echoed.

The voice from the phone drew Manfred's attention one more time. He dove under the sink again, trying to dislodge it from the pipes. His paws smothered Fontaine's voice from the caller at the other end. They grew more concerned.

Fontaine could hear the dispatcher say, "Sounds like she's in trouble! I think we need a team."

Hearing that, Fontaine panicked. Then, shouting louder, "Maggie! I'm okay. Just wait a minute."

She heard another voice at the other end. "Call Beaucharp. Right now, call Beaucharp."

Fontaine heard Beaucharp's phone go off, then her voice.

"Beaucharp. What? Fontaine is in the bathroom. No, she's about thirty feet away. Yes, I'm sure. I'm walking over there now."

Washbee struggled to keep pace with her.

The acoustics echoed through Fontaine's phone, and the Communication Center heard Beaucharp rapping on the door and speaking.

"Hey, Donna. Everything all right in there? Station says they can't reach you."

The toilet flushed. Fontaine quickly pulled up her pants and said, "I'm okay. Be right out."

Washbee caught up to Beaucharp and said he had keys for the door. "Should I open it?" he asked.

Beaucharp nodded. "Donna, we're going to open the door. Okay?"

"Go ahead." Washbee unlocked the door and moved away, allowing Beaucharp to enter alone. Bending and crawling halfway under the bathroom sink, Fontaine yelled at the phone as she tried to pry it out of a crevice behind the vanity framework. Her blouse had pulled out of her slacks, and one shoe lay next to the toilet. Tissue paper strewed about the floor, and Manfred watched curiously, pieces of white tissue sticking to whiskers.

"Can you ever stay out of trouble?" said Beaucharp. "You look like one of those Irish Hooligans the Brits are always arresting at soccer games."

"Don't ask," said Fontaine, backing her way out from under the sink. Beaucharp spoke into her phone. "Everything is okay here. Fontaine dropped her phone and got locked in the bathroom."

"Locked in the bathroom?" the dispatcher asked.

"Yes," Beaucharp said. She then listened to their message and nodded. "It's okay. Can we call you back in five?"

The dispatcher said, "Five minutes, detective. We got some news about some of the stuff in the bag."

Fontaine stood, pushed her blouse back inside her slacks, and hobbled into the hall with a shoe in one hand. Two feet of toilet tissue attached to the other foot fluttered like the tail of a kite. Manfred ran out and playfully tackled it, rolling onto his back holding on with all four sets of claws. Washbee tried not to smile.

Humiliated, Fontaine tried to explain. Washbee listened with fatherly patience. Beaucharp, now laughing, stepped around the corner into a viewing room.

"Please, don't feel embarrassed. This isn't the first time Manfred has caused mischief." Washbee grinned and said, "This kind of place needs a little waking up once in a while."

Fontaine looked puzzled. Washbee smiled. "Waking up! Get it?"

Fontaine grinned, now aware of the shoe in her hand she attempted to put it on. Lifting her shoeless foot, she unconsciously grabbed Washbee's arm for balance, nearly toppling them both. "Oops! Oh, I'm sorry."

Still sheltered around the corner, Beaucharp leaned against a wall with her forehead bowed into her hands, trying to stifle the laughter. Then, she heard a loud monotonous hum and something warm shove against her calf. She grinned, picked up Manfred, and buried her face into his body to cover the laughter further.

Washbee and Fontaine came around the corner, surprising Beaucharp. Smiling, she looked at Washbee, then spoke to Fontaine. "What'd you do to this cat? He's traumatized."

"Yeah, about as traumatized as you could get, The Son of Sam," said Fontaine.

Beaucharp looked at Washbee. "I can go in and straighten out the bathroom, sir."

"Oh, no. Please," Washbee went on, "my nephew, Winston, will straighten it out. That tissue paper holder must have been faulty."

Beaucharp looked at Fontaine. "We have to call the precinct. I don't have a good feeling about it." Then, turning to Washbee, she said, "We may have to leave, but we'll need to come back. We're sorry to have taken up so much of your time."

"Oh, good Lord. It's no problem at all. Please come back anytime. Things I have to tell you are quite compelling, and I certainly don't want anyone to think I'm trying to be misleading."

Fontaine spoke. "Mr. Washbee, I'm sorry about all this. It was foolish, and I'm embarrassed. I can't find the words to express how ridiculous I feel."

"I'll be able to find the words for you," said Beaucharp.

"Both of you are such a delight," Washbee said. "Why don't you stop by whenever you're around? We can have lunch. I can make some sandwiches. How's that sound?"

Fontaine placed her hand on his wrist. "We'll do that, Mr. Washbee. I heard you touring the place with Beauchy; next time, I'd like one."

Washbee beamed. "We didn't get too far into a tour, but that would be wonderful. I know you are going to love my family as well."

Fontaine often took a long time to say goodbye, so Beaucharp used the interval to step out onto the porch and call the precinct. "Wow . . . That's a curveball," she said. "I'll tell Fontaine."

The dispatcher spoke again.

"Okay, we're heading right in. What time is the meeting?"

The dispatcher spoke again.

"They're waiting for us? What's that about a medal?"

The dispatcher spoke again. Beaucharp laughed.

Chapter 20

Cyrus Washbee watched the detectives drive away, their tires leaving a wake of white dust hovering in the dry air, then diffusing and falling back to the ground. He stood waving goodbye longer than necessary, hoping they would notice. Then, left alone, with the stillness of his thoughts, Washbee ventured into visiting his method of dealing with melancholy. *Take a deep breath and exhale the sadness.* His unusual gait created difficulties in performing many simple ambulatory activities. He took one-half turn with the building at his back, then another to face the door.

He opened it, and the cold air rushed past. Manfred hurried across the threshold and rubbed between Washbee's legs, nearly causing him to lose balance, then leaped onto one of the canned chairs and sat. Washbee stopped and thought, then shut the door and maneuvered onto the porch chair next to him. Then, speaking out loud, he said, "I know they'll be back. Well, someone will be back. I hope it's them. I think you liked them too, Manfred."

Manfred had a way of easing sadness. When grief was overwhelming at funeral home events, Manfred wandered about and adhered to troubled people, either on their laps or at their feet. Although never able to end their sorrow, his presence brought a subtle calm, helping people feel better. His mysticism worked for Washbee.

Washbee stroked him and smiled. "You certainly got a way about you, fatso!"

Manfred rubbed into Washbee's hand, purring loudly, then leaped onto his lap. "Okay, my friend, just a little while longer." Washbee sat with his thoughts, watching vehicles speed past. Fifteen minutes later, he placed

Manfred on a chair, struggled to his feet, and resumed his journey back to work. Manfred chased him into the building.

At his desk, unable to regain focus on work, Washbee ran his fingers across the rim of the picture frame, looking deeply into the face of a beautiful woman. She stood next to the young seaman in crisp Navy whites. Kathleen Palmer, called Katy by family and friends, while Washbee called her Rosy. He looked deeply into her face and traced his finger around the area of the bright red hair, whispering something unintelligible, then softly placed it back on the corner of his desk.

It had been eleven years since the accident, eighteen months of it consumed with Rosy in a coma. It took six months of surgeries and rehab before Washbee could move about himself. Nevertheless, his cousins from Fort Myers and Baton Rouge maintained the business in his absence.

After returning and fulfilling all the business responsibilities, he visited Rosy daily. He'd hold her hand, whisper to her, and pray. At first, he asked for a miracle, then for answers to their difficulties. After a while, the prayers eased into requests for her comfort and a loving journey to whatever would be next.

He still missed touching her face. Once, shortly after their marriage, Rosy joked that while washing her face, she noticed she had moved some of her freckles around. Washbee, a young and stoic pillar of seriousness, was stunned and lost for words. She laughed, cupped his face in her hands, pulled it toward hers, kissed him, and giggled. They both laughed. He ran this scene through his mind whenever he needed solace.

***

Back in the car, Fontaine spoke first. "I feel stupid about all this cat thing."

"At first, I thought you were injured," Beaucharp said.

"Injured?"

Beaucharp drove out onto the road and turned to Fontaine. "Well yeah! Look, you don't have to talk about it if you don't want to."

"I'm going to tell you everything. There are parts I still don't believe myself." Fontaine described the events in terms a cop would use.

First, there was Manfred, the phone call, the dropped phone, the foot protecting the phone from crashing, and the shoe coming off. Then, Manfred was chasing the phone, the toilet tissue holder breaking and rolling across the floor, and Manfred disrupted the section she was trying to reel in. By the time she finished, both were laughing. Beaucharp, unsteady with laughter, had to pull off the road and turn on the blue lights.

They settled down and Beaucharp resumed driving. Once back on the road, Beaucharp changed the subject.

"Okay, Donna, when I called back, they said things had changed. They wanted us to come in right away."

"Right away? What did they mean, things have changed?"

"Well, at first, Maggie said they had some info about the pieces in Gaslight's bag. You were in the middle of the CAT-astrophe—"

Fontaine shook her head. "'CAT-astrophe!' You're a friggin nut Beauchy."

Beaucharp went on, "Let me finish please. So, I said I would call back in five. When I called back, things had changed, again. She then said that they wanted us to come in, right away, for an important meeting."

"An important meeting? About what?"

"That's all I know, Donna. Oh, yeah! The sarge—"

"Sergeant Lapointe—"

"Yes. Let me finish. He was pleased about something and said someone should get a medal for this."

"A medal?"

"Yes, everyone was laughing in the background when she told me."

Suddenly Fontaine's mobile phone buzzed. She answered. "Fontaine. Oh, hi, Maggie. Why are you calling me on my cell? What? Really? Wait, I'm going to open the speaker for Beauchy to hear this."

Fontaine opened the speaker and turned to Beaucharp. "Michaela, better listen to this. Go ahead, Maggie."

"I'm not supposed to be saying anything. That's why I'm not using the radio, but I don't want you guys getting blindsided. Okay?"

"We didn't hear anything, Maggie," Beaucharp said.

Okay, this is a big meeting. We got people from the Attorney General's office, the Florida Department of Law Enforcement, and the FBI. It has to do with the DNA of some of the pieces in the sack. They're calling Cady back in as well."

"Wow," said Fontaine. "Who'd these body parts belong to?"

"That's all I know, Donna. Remember, be surprised when you show up."

Beaucharp said, "We got it, Maggie. Thanks for the heads up."

Fontaine broke the connection, and said, "What do you think of that, Beauchy?"

"I don't know." She smiled. "Maybe pieces of D.B. Cooper? We'll see soon enough. Lapointe seems to be happy about whoever the body pieces belong to."

Fontaine wrinkled her eyebrows. "They called Cady back in, huh? Seems like they'd call Lapointe back in as well."

The detectives contemplated in silence.

Fontaine stared into the windshield and said, "Beauchy, in the meantime, let's talk about something that has been gnawing at me for a long time."

"What's that? My analytical brilliance?"

"Can you ever get serious, Michaela?"

Beaucharp, now upset with herself for being insensitive, whispered, "Oh! I'm sorry, Donna. It's just that I can never tell when you're serious or just fooling around."

"Okay. Ready to hear me now?"

"Yes. Sorry." Beaucharp reached across and gently touched Fontaine's forearm.

"How come stuff like this never happens to you?"

"What do you mean? I do stupid things too."

"Not like me."

"Donna, you were unlucky today. It could just as well have been me in the bathroom. If you recall, I did spit all over the windshield on the way to the Bucket of Blood."

Fontaine chuckled. "Yeah, but you never seem to knock any of the canning jars off the shelf. Know what I mean?"

Beaucharp, silent for several seconds, responded. "Okay, partner. What's really up?"

Fontaine stared deeply into her partner's face. "How come I never hear you swear?"

Beaucharp squinted—the anxious expression that her brilliant mother could always provoke—then smiled. "Oh, come on! I knew it. You're playing me."

Fontaine faced the passenger window to prevent Beaucharp from seeing her grinning. "You don't swear or cuss. So how come you never utter profanity?"

"I don't use profanity because I have a vast vocabulary."

"How about the time when we got caught in the torrential rain? You said, 'It's raining like a cow pissing on flat rock'. Remember that?"

"Piss is not a swear word, Donna."

"Course it is."

"It's a bodily function. It's not profanity."

"Okay, just one time. Let me hear you say shit."

"Get out of here, Fontaine."

"Come on, Beauchy. Look at my lips, say shh, shh—."

"I'm driving, Donna. Do you know how silly you look right now? Didn't your mother ever tell you that if you make those funny faces too often, God will punish you, and your face will get stuck in one of those positions?"

"Come on. Say it. Shiii, shiiit."

"Donna, I'm driving."

"Lucky you. We're gonna have to revisit this later. It's quite upsetting to me."

Beaucharp smiled. "Upsetting? I can imagine. Probably it's enough to make you become a Democrat."

Chapter 21

They drove onto the road to Green Bridge, with Fontaine still teasing. Then, suddenly, she pointed and yelled. "Whoa! What's going on over there?"

Vehicles slowed down as motorists gawked at an ugly scene unfolding.

"Looks like he's whacking her around," said Beaucharp. "Call it in. I'll break them up."

"You're gonna want to wait for me. Looks pretty nasty."

"Call it in first."

Fontaine grabbed the radio mic and shouted their call number, "Got a code 29, Battery taking place on Green Bridge. Intervening, need transportation, stand by for EMT response."

The dispatcher responded. "You guys got a meeting!"

"We gotta do this. Some guy is beating up a woman next to the bridge. Beaucharp's pursuing now."

"Need backup?"

"Stand by. No back-up. Looks like we will need transportation, and an ambulance, though."

Beaucharp pulled the blue lights immediately and drove up onto the grass as close to the couple as possible.

"BPD. Hey, knock it off," she said, rushing through the car door, her handcuffs already out.

He was tall and lean. The Academy training kicked in, and she assessed the situation. *He's pale, got the weak-looking frame of a long-term alcoholic or someone struggling with addiction, jailhouse tattoos, grimy clothing, intoxicated or high on something. He's knocked the woman to the ground and is about to kick her.*

He saw Beaucharp moving toward him and the blue lights flashing from the vehicle behind her.

"You don't want to do that, Mister," she said.

"Oh yeah? It's none of your business. I'll be through in a minute, and we all can go on our way."

"Ain't going to happen." She kept rushing toward him. *I'm so freaking sick of bullies!*

Beaucharp slowed down and inched to within three feet of him. The stench of old beer, rancid body odor, and dirt leached out of him.

Fontaine, dashing from the car, yelled. "I called for an ambulance. Wait for me, partner."

The man scowled, then grinned and took a step forward throwing both arms out to push Beaucharp off balance. She spun quickly in kick-boxer fashion, tapping him behind the knee joint with her tiny foot. He collapsed like the bent leg of a card table, bracing his fall with one hand. Beaucharp stepped on the fingertips and slapped one ring of the handcuffs onto his wrist. Then, lifting her foot and clutching the other end of the cuffs, she quickly pulled him up.

"Up-see-daisy," she said, spinning him around and cuffing the other wrist. The whole process taking less than ten seconds.

Fontaine rushed up. "Aw, gee partner, how come you never let me have any fun?" She rushed to the woman on the ground.

The swelling and black and blue bruises disfigured her normal facial features. Blood flowed through the nostrils of a broken nose and the mouth and seeped out her ears. She tried to move, but Fontaine demanded that she stay still until an ambulance arrived. The sirens, faint at first, grew louder.

Fontaine spoke into her shoulder mic, first shouting call numbers.

"Go ahead," the dispatch said.

"It's under control here. We need transportation, Maggie."

"We got it coming, Donna. Birdy says to Mirandize the suspect and pass him on to the receiving officer. They're waiting for you guys. Do the paperwork after the meeting."

The sirens were now so loud Fontaine had to yell. "We got an injured civilian. We're gonna wait for emergency transportation, then leave."

"Copy that." She signed off just as the EMTs rushed to the injured woman, their shoulder radios alive with instructions.

"Hey, that was fast," Beaucharp pointed to the curbside.

Fontaine turned around as a patrol car pulled up. Officer Brian Wilson emerged.

"Hey Wilson, I thought you worked evenings?" Fontaine said.

"Got called in. Supposed to be my day off. Said you need some help."

Fontaine said, "Yeah. Gotta transport someone for us."

"Transported someone for Cady this morning. It took two hours to get the car clean."

Fontaine remembered. It was Wilson, Mr. Clean, who transported Gaslight earlier that day. "This one's easy. Just bring him across the bridge to central booking."

"Is he clean? I just got the stink out." He pointed to the cruiser.

"What's the holdup?" Beaucharp yelled, the prisoner wobbling, now barely able to stand.

Fontaine said, "Look, you gotta take him." Then, turning from Wilson, she shouted at Beaucharp, "Bring him over here. Now!"

Wilson watched in dismay while the prisoner groaned and cussed as Beaucharp read him his rights and inched him into the back seat. Then, unnoticed, except to Beaucharp, he filled the front of his pants with urine.

Beaucharp turned to Wilson. "See, that was easy. I seat-belted him as well. The sooner you get out of here, the quicker you can unload him."

Wilson rocketed behind the wheel, and as Fontaine and Beaucharp turned toward their car, they heard the loud, obnoxious sound of vomit splashing. First, a foul assortment of fluids and solids splashed against Wilson's side window. Then a wave spurted through the protection screen, some squeezing through and onto the front seat.

The detectives rushed to their vehicle. Grinning, Fontaine said. "Looked like old beer and hot dogs to me."

***

As Beaucharp maneuvered through the Belenton mid-day tourist traffic, Fontaine said, "All right, Michaela, let's get back to the case. What's up with Washbee's face?"

"You mean the eyebrow?"

"Oh! That's it. Have you ever been in a predicament when something was so obvious you overlooked it?"

"Yes, I have. But, to not notice someone is missing an eyebrow?" Beaucharp shook her head.

"Well, I couldn't put my finger on what was wrong with his face."

Beaucharp smiled. "It's a good thing. You might have taken a Sharpie out and tried to draw one for him. But, on the other hand, maybe you were concentrating too hard on having to go to the bathroom. Notice he limped?"

"That I did. An unusual gait, you have to admit that."

"Yes, he walks sideways like the blue crabs under the Siesta Key Pier. Maybe something to do with his vision or balance?"

Fontaine said, "Most likely an accident. We can find out." She then removed her sunglasses, turned toward Beaucharp, and pressed her eyebrows close together; a facial expression Beaucharp learned early on to mean Fontaine was extremely serious. "What'd you think of the guy? You spent more time with him."

Beaucharp, although hidden by her sunglasses, pulled one eyebrow higher than the other, thought for several seconds, then said, "I like him. Decent guy. He was anxious to tell us something. You get that?"

"I did. Said it wasn't Beauregard's fault. Said it right away."

"Yeah. He wasn't trying to hide anything."

Fontaine turned, peered through her window, took a deep breath, and released it.

Seeing her partner's frustration, Beaucharp said. "Donna, you're sort of like Counselor Troy on *Star Trek*. You're an *Empath*. You feel other people's struggles."

"No, I'm not!"

Beaucharp smiled. "You certainly are. You're touched by the struggles of Martha, the Space Lady at the Bucket of Blood. Now you're worried by what's upsetting Mr. Washbee."

"So, what if I am? We can't change who we are."

"Hey, I agree. You've got the gift of getting signaled by good people."

Fontaine nodded. "Okay, so you say it's a gift. What about you? I see you zero in on some folks."

"Yes, Donna. I can zero in on the bad people. The mysticism that triggers your empathy triggers mine for picking out nefarious characters."

Fontaine said, "That's why we're such a good team." She stared out her side window, hiding a smile. "It's mysticism, huh? Stuff like that is also why I let you think you're the boss most of the time."

Beauchmp laughed. "Let's get back to what's happening and away from the Doctor Phil business."

Fontaine turned back toward Beaucharp. "Think this meeting is a push to make a bust?"

Beaucharp shook her head. "No. Captain Bird and Bargiel aren't like that."

"What's the big deal here? Sounds like we got everyone at this meeting except the governor. Something's up, sure as hell, Beauchy."

Beaucharp slapped the steering wheel. "Oh! Maggie said Lapointe was happy about something. She said that after seeing the DNA results, he grinned and said someone deserves a medal."

Fontaine stared back out the side window at Palma Sola Bay, teeming with pleasure boats and stretches of million-dollar condominium communities, all crowding the once pristine Gulf Coast. "A medal? Could this get any weirder?"

Beaucharp, now nervously tapped without rhythm at the edges of the steering wheel. "We'll know when we get there. What will we do if they want us to bring someone in?"

"I don't know. Right now, the only one I suspect is the cat."

Beaucharp grinned. "He's the only one who's thrown up any obstructions? Tried to trip you with the toilet paper and throw off the whole investigation."

Fontaine pulled a leather bag off the floor and placed it on her lap. She fumbled inside and pulled out the yellow legal pad with the case notes. Then, waving it she said, "We got ourselves a Tolstoy novel, and we haven't even been on the case for twelve hours."

Beaucharp took the opportunity to play with Fontaine. "My, my, look how neat the notes are."

"Are we going to go through this again?"

"Through what?" "Every time I take out my case notes, you sputter. Jealousy, I guess."

"Jealousy! Come on, Donna. They have Catholic grammar school written all over them."

"Written all over them, huh? Is that supposed to be one of your Ivy League puns, a play on words, or something like that?"

"You know what I mean."

Fontaine laughed out loud. "Okay, okay. I know you're envious. Most of my grammar school teachers are still around. I can see if one of them offers remedial classes in penmanship."

"Don't spin this. Thought you said you were a Baptist?"

"I am."

"Then how come you have Catholic School penmanship?"

"I went to a parochial grammar school, St. Joseph, in Tampa. Most of my classmates were Cubans and Central Americans."

"Wasn't that a girl's school?"

"So what?"

"Just saying," Beaucharp added. "I went to a Catholic grammar school too. If you had the nuns I had, you wouldn't be so cocky today. They'd put Wyatt Earp to shame with how fast they could whip out a ruler and nail your knuckles."

"Cocky? Who's cocky?" Fontaine said.

Beaucharp smiled and said, "Don't go there, Donna. Quit while you're ahead. I also went to a Jesuit University, and those guys were like field marshals."

Fontaine brought the legal pad up to her face to conceal a smirk. "Oh, Beauchy. Wave all the credentials you want. You know I got this one. But if you want to think you're smarter than me, I'll let it go. We're 10 minutes away from our mystery meeting. Are we going to look at these beautifully written notes or what?"

"Okay, boss. You know when you're beaten."

Fontaine flipped a page. "We started early this morning with a call from Sergeant Lapointe."

"Oh boy, wake me up when we get to the section with the police work."

Ignoring the sarcasm, Fontaine read on. "He told me to pick you up, that is, if you were sober, and rush over to Manatee Avenue to meet Cady."

"Okay, we're at the crime scene."

Fontaine turned the page. "A burlap bag discovered in the truck bed. Contents turned out to be human body parts and discarded food products."

"Okay, okay. Donna, next. We had the scene scrubbed. All right, you have wonderful case notes. They're extremely meticulous and insightful; I've looked at them too. Do you see where I put a star next to things?"

"You did that?"

"Did you think it was the tooth fairy? Those are the highlight points. Just jump to them for now. We only got two more streets and then we'll have to turn into our parking lot."

"Of course. Correct as usual, Princess Michaela. Let's go to the interrogation."

"Gaslight didn't know anything about the stuff in his truck."

"He didn't even know why he was in Belenton," Beaucharp said.

Fontaine grinned and shook her head.

"What's so funny?" Beaucharp said.

"You're acting like a real detective now." Fontaine pulled her visor down and checked her face in the mirror and turned back to Beaucharp, "My style is rubbing off on you."

"Lucky me! Okay, we concluded he knew nothing about what happened the evening before. All he remembered was butchering a pig and stopping to find a place to eat. The closest place was the Bucket of Blood."

"There, we found people to verify his story." Fontaine went on. "I see little eyeball dots in the stars of each character. Very cute."

Beaucharp said, "Thank you. That visit led us to Washbee's nephew Winston Beauregard. He, supposedly, was the last one seen when he was sitting in the truck with Gaslight."

Fontaine paused and squinted again. "Wait a minute. There is a whole bunch of stuff here that's different from other cases we've had."

Beaucharp knew her partner had a special gift for discovery. Some things, innocuous at first, would eventually jump out at her. She referred to it as Fontaine's ability to stub her toe into the obvious. Something in the notes gnawed at her and Beaucharp trusted that, although presently under camouflage, it would eventually surface. At times Fontaine has even awaken her with a call in the middle of the night to share a new insight about a case.

"What do you mean?" Beaucharp asked.

"Going down the list, is there anyone we met today that you didn't like?"

"Yeah, the drunk we just busted."

"You know what I'm talking about."

Beaucharp braked to turn into a narrow street. "You're right."

Unconsciously pointing an index finger at the windshield, Fontaine said, "Some may have been struggling with demons of one sort or another, but there were no violent tendencies or hints of deviant behavior. Did you feel like anyone we met today lied?"

"Nobody was lying at the Bucket of Blood."

Fontaine sheepishly said his name. "Washbee?"

"He's no killer and he's being truthful."

Fontaine said, "He wants us to come back and have lunch with him. Not the sign of someone trying to hide something up his sleeve."

"Maybe you can fix his missing eyebrow, then."

They waited for three civilian vehicles to pass through the ticket gate, then Beaucharp waved a city parking pass at the scanner, the gate lifted, and she drove onto the first floor and into a Police Department Only space and parked.

Fontaine placed the notes back into the leather bag and unsnapped her seat belt. "What's happening? Am I wrong here? Gaslight and everyone we connect to him is innocent?"

"Looks that way, partner, doesn't it?"

"We'll look somewhere else," said Fontaine.

Once outside the car, and without notice, the 98-degree humid and salty Gulf of Mexico moisture fogged up their sunglasses. They paused to wipe them clean and listen to the gulls in the bay screaming and fighting for the discarded chunks being tossed away by those cleaning their catch at the docks.

Walking in silence at first, then bouncing ideas off each other, Winston Beauregard's name came up twice. They reached the elevator just as the ding from the opening door sounded. The casual gray headdress of the Maryknoll order gave the only indications that she was a Catholic nun. On a leather cord around her neck hung the wooden cross, hand carved for her during her missionary days in El Salvador. Always bubbly and smiling, Sister May Cronin, a community liaison from the Venice Diocese's Ministry Services, stepped out.

"Hello, detectives," she chirped.

"Hey, Sister, what's happening?" said Fontaine.

Sister Cronin slapped Fontaine a high five. "Father Fausto got an emergency call, so I'm filling in." She turned to Beaucharp. "How you doing, Michaela?" Then quickly turned back to Fontaine, gave her a deadpan wink and using her thumb like a hitchhiker, pointed at Beaucharp. "Is she behaving?"

"No, of course not," said Fontaine. "I still don't know how she made it through the Academy and probation period."

Sister Cronin smiled, placed a hand over Beaucharp's tiny wrist, and looked back at Fontaine. "Then it's good that she has you around to look after her."

Beaucharp pointed at Fontaine. "You don't want to be touching her like this. She's a Baptist, you know."

Sister Cronin, ever mischievous, said, "Well, in that case . . ." she quickly reached out, touching Fontaine's ribs with the tips of her fingers, and tickled her. ". . .Touch, touch, touch."

Fontaine giggled like a first grader and tried to swat Sister Cronin's hands, but they moved too quickly. The tickling ended in seconds. Then she pointed at Beaucharp. "You started this, Beauchy."

Beaucharp said, "Oh yeah! I'm always the blame."

Sister Cronin giggled and shook her head. "How did you two ever find each other?"

Fontaine looked at her partner. "Who knows? I got a good mind to call her mother tonight."

Beaucharp rolled her eyes. "You're going to squeal on me to my mother?"

"Just as soon I get home."

Sister Cronin looked at her watch. "Gotta go. It's always fun seeing you two." She turned to Beaucharp. "Anything else I can help you with before I say goodbye?"

Beaucharp tapped her shoulder with her fist. "You've already helped tremendously. Your touching may have anointed Donna in good way. On the other hand, she may wake up in the middle of the night spitting out pea soup."

Sister Cronin, high-fived both, and said, "I really have to fly."

They stepped into the elevator and after the door closed, Fontaine said, "Did you ever notice that she bounces when she walks?"

"Yeah, like the Flying Nun."

Fontaine threw her hands into the air. "Beauchy, honey, sometimes I think you're a lost cause. But, you know, come to think of it, I would have made a great nun."

"Oh yeah? Donna you do realize as a nun there's none of this and none of that."

They chuckled quietly, at first to themselves, and then thought back to images of their Catholic grade school and at the same time, released an outburst that rocked the elevator.

***

They rode to the second floor and crossed the skyway path into the police station. The polished granite walls and floor were bright and cool in contrast to some of the tattered 1960s ugliness of the explosive drug-infused areas several miles away. Their steps echoed off the empty walls alerting the receptionist studying a policy transcript in the bulletproof glass station.

She lifted her head, smiled, and spoke with a soft Florida drawl. "They're waiting for y'all upstairs. I'm supposed to send ya right up, conference room six."

"That's the big one," Beaucharp said.

"Yes ma'am. You two are celebrities today. But don't run up jest yet. Somebody wants to see ya first. Wait a minute, please." She punched a number into the phone console and waited for an answer. "They're here. Yes ma'am, okay." Looking at the detectives, she said, "She'll be waiting for y'all at the elevator."

Fontaine nodded. "Thanks Carol. Honey, you got any idea what this is about?"

"It's big-time detective stuff. That's all I know."

At the Police Use Only elevator, they pushed the button for the fourth floor. When the door opened, a confident looking woman in a gray pantsuit with a marathon runner's slimness stood waiting.

Displaying credentials she said, "Hello detectives. I'm Special Agent Wanda Stein."

Fontaine spoke first. "I'm Detective Donna Fontaine, and this is my partner, Detective Michaela Beaucharp." They all shook hands.

Beaucharp had a knack for noticing sincerity in people. She immediately felt Stein to be genuine but was confused why the FBI would be involved in a backwater case that wasn't even twelve hours old.

Fontaine's first impression was of Stein's muscular hands. *The result of hard gym work, or rowing, not playing golf or tennis.*

"My partner thinks she's the bright one here," said Beaucharp as she waved a hand toward Fontaine.

Stein grinned and spoke in a strong Brooklyn accent. "I know this may seem a little irregular, but once we get in that room, there'll be testosterone from floor to ceiling. You get what I'm saying?" She waited to see if they both agreed. They nodded. "The Bureau isn't trying to throw a curve here, I promise. But I'd like to talk to both of you about this case. Can we connect right after the meeting?"

Just in case her intuition was wrong, Beaucharp warned, "We can but know this. My partner and I won't pull the rug out from under anyone in the department."

Fontaine said, "We aren't a couple of Cracker Florida tootsies you're gonna play."

"I promise you. This is on the square. The Bureau isn't out to nail anyone," said Stein.

The detectives walked cautiously toward the conference room. Beaucharp reached around and tickled Fontaine's ribs as if the action came from Agent Stein. Startled, Fontaine turned with a puzzled look at Stein, then Beaucharp.

Beaucharp smiled. "Don't be manhandling my partner, Agent Stein. We're professional cops here, not pretend."

Fontaine, realizing Beaucharp touched her, looked to Stein. "See what I got to put up with? Beauchy does this to get attention. She was spitting at the inside windshield of our cruiser earlier."

Stein smiled, and a kindred spirit came to life. Within minutes, they could speak to each other in honest cop talk. Then, like the final tumbler of an impenetrable lock dropping into place, mutual trust and respect began to unfold.

Stein asked, "How long have you guys been cops?"

"About eight years," Fontaine said.

"You got a good reputation as a team," Stein said.

Fontaine spoke again. "Thank you, Beaucharp is coming along quite well."

Stein grinned and looked at Beaucharp. "Is that right, detective?"

"Oh yeah. Although, a great deal of my time is keeping Donna out of sleazy relationships."

Fontaine turned. "Sleazy relationships? What sleazy relationships?"

Stein grinned.

Beaucharp said, "The nut living in Brazil right now. Hannibal Lecter."

"Lecter?" said Stein.

Beaucharp turned toward Stein. "He used to bring home roadkill. So that's normal, huh?"

"He was a taxidermist," said Fontaine. "His name was Hollingsworth. You might have heard of his family. They're rich, own a bunch of car dealerships, and have been into banking since the turn of the century."

"Jeeze, I might have heard of them. So, they're from the Northeast?" asked Stein.

"Mississippi," laughed Beaucharp, "I think they just had a piggy bank on a family plantation."

"Beaucharp doesn't even have a steady guy," said Fontaine.

Stein was about to speak when Beaucharp interrupted. "She's jealous. Anyway, something just came to me on the elevator during a conversation with my partner. So, let's just say the person we met inspired me."

Fontaine, knowing Beaucharp was talking about Sister Cronin, looked at Stein and winked. "Like an epiphany?"

"You might call it that." Beaucharp added, "I'm thinking of becoming a nun."

Stein said, "Like Mother Teresa—"

Fontaine interrupted. "More like Sister Mary Baseball Bat."

They reached the conference room. Fontaine entered first, followed by Beaucharp and Stein.

Fontaine whispered to Beaucharp. "What the fuck is this?"

Beaucharp whispered back. "Looks like the circus has come to town. What kind of a mess did you get me into this time?"

Stein grinned to herself. *I'm going to like this assignment. Something tells me it's going to be quite a ride.*

Chapter 22

Stein was right about the testosterone. Of the sixteen people in the room, Stein, Beaucharp, and Fontaine were the only women. They sat in a row with Stein in the middle. She slid her chair two feet back from the table to avoid craning past others to view the speakers.

At introductions, each man waved titles and credentials as if they were applying for an NFL draft pick. Some told simple-minded jokes, garnering short chuckles. Fontaine introduced herself as a detective from Belenton PD, followed by Beaucharp. Stein said she was with the FBI on special assignment.

A few of the men looked at each other, shook their heads, annoyed that women were present so no locker room banter could take place.

Johnathan Hooker, a Florida's Attorney General's Office prosecutor, rose to speak first.

"I'll bet that suit cost a thousand dollars," Fontaine whispered. "Sharkskin."

"Bet he paid a hundred bucks for that haircut," Beaucharp whispered back.

"Shush," said Stein. "You don't want to miss any of this, I promise."

Hooker introduced himself, then stopped long enough to twist the cap off a small water bottle and take a sip. "Also, the Florida Attorney General's Office and I want to extend our thanks to the Belenton PD for their outstanding effort in this case. Sergeant Lapointe jumped right on it early this morning, calling in two of Florida's finest detectives . . ."

"Holy shit," said Fontaine.

"Quiet," mouthed Beaucharp. Stein lightly slapped Fontaine's shoulder.

Hooker, still talking, "...I understand they have been working since three this morning. Are the detectives here now, Captain Bird?"

"Yes, they are. We waited until they arrived."

"Raise your hands," said Hooker.

Fontaine shook her head. *Fucking asshole! We just identified ourselves.*

Beaucharp and Fontaine reluctantly brought their hands up. Surprised to find they were women, Hooker stuttered. "Oh! Ah, good job, ladies."

Grinning, Stein leaned in between and whispered. "Ladies! How'd you like that?"

Beaucharp quietly performed Fontaine's maneuver and spun her index finger in a tight circle, rolled her eyes, sighed, and said under her breath, "Ooh, baby!"

Hooker droned for another fifteen minutes and made everyone aware of where he went to college, the law firms he had worked for, and how well he knew the governor. He mentioned how overwhelming the work at the Attorney General's Office was and they consider the work Belenton PD is doing is just as vital to all the citizens of Florida. He concluded, "We're with you on this case. The Attorney General of Florida has the Belenton PD's back."

There ensued enough congratulating chatter and nodding toward the Belenton PD brass that no one noticed Fontaine as she mouthed to her partner. "What's going on?"

Stein grinned, leaned into Beaucharp's ear, and softly said, "Wait for it."

Puzzled, Beaucharp shrugged. Fontaine wrinkled her forehead and whispered, "Wait for what?"

Hooker then introduced a Florida Department of Law Enforcement spokesperson. He talked for ten minutes, exuding his department's importance, and expressing the same gratification for all the Belenton PD work. He made it a point to congratulate Police Chief Thomas King, and several commanding officers. But, unfortunately, Captains Bird and Bargiel, the two senior officers most responsible for the upper-level decisions on the case, were omitted. He then introduced a representative from the US Department of Alcohol, Tobacco, and Firearms.

The ATF man spoke for fifteen minutes and then introduced someone from the Florida Bureau of Prisons. He spoke for ten minutes and introduced someone else from an obscure state agency, who spoke for another ten minutes.

Six speakers, all from outside the department, soaked up most of the oxygen in the room.

The last speaker, stunned with no one left to introduce, turned pale, the classic deer in the headlights stare. He looked around the room and, trying to look important, raised his eyebrows, removed his glasses, picked up his notes, and tiptoed to his seat.

For nearly a minute, silence, the enemy of the parade, took over the room. Everyone stared at each other uncomfortably, then at the visiting speaker from the Attorney General's Office. Everyone waited for something to happen.

"What's going on? Somebody fart up there?" whispered Fontaine.

Stein elbowed Beaucharp and smiled. Beaucharp shook her head and smiled.

Enjoying the uneasiness of the braggarts, Captain Bird stalled for time, then got a nod from the half-smiling Chief King. His chair creaked, and Bird pushed away from the conference table and strolled over to the podium.

He unbuttoned his jacket and began. "I'm Captain Bird. Captain Bargiel and I are commanders of the Belenton PD Detective Division. We've all been invited here to catch up on some a new and vital pieces of evidence . . ."

Stein leaned in between both detectives and whispered, "Wait for it."

Fontaine and Beaucharp looked at each other, puzzled.

Bird, still speaking, ". . . we have two detectives who have been working since early this morning."

Stein leaned in again and whispered, "Wait."

The detectives looked at Stein and shrugged.

Bird went on, "... so before I bring up the new evidence, one of the detectives working the case will bring us up to date."

"There it is. It's what I was waiting for," said Stein.

Fontaine turned pale and froze as if someone dropped a snake on her lap. It took her a few seconds to regain her thoughts. She then smiled and handed the yellow legal pad with the case notes to Beaucharp. "Have at it, partner," she said.

"Me?" whispered Beaucharp.

Fontaine winked. "You got this. I'll keep an eye on things at this end."

"You owe me. Big time, you owe me."

Beaucharp grabbed the notepad. At the podium she opened with, "I'm Detective Michaela Beaucharp with the Belenton PD. My partner, Donna Fontaine, and I have been on the case since early this morning. First, we spent several hours interviewing the owner of the vehicle. From there, we tried to backtrack his movements from the day before up until the time of the arrest. So far, we have interviewed . . ." —she paused purposely using a delay technique she learned watching lawyers in courtrooms and slowly flipped through pages of the pad— "seven . . ." she stopped again, momentarily, and flipped through more pages and went on, "no, nine individuals."

"Wow! You've been busy," said the Thousand-Dollar Suit. Heads and neckties bobbed around the table. Their response, primarily to conform with the views of the expensive suit, more so than with the detectives' accomplishments.

Beaucharp glanced over at Captain Bird. He grinned and winked.

Stein whispered. "They're like bobbleheads sitting on a table, and every time the Thousand-Dollar Suit says something, someone kicks a leg of the table and they warble."

Beaucharp went on. "We had to leave an interview early to make this meeting. On the way over, my partner came up with insightful points that we want to flesh out before we can discuss them further."

"Insightful points?" asked The Thousand-Dollar Suit.

"Yes. With all crime investigations, things can unfold rapidly, as you certainly know, sir."

"Oh, we do." The bobbleheads rocked again. "Anything else you can share?"

"It was idle talk about the case in the elevator. My partner's new idea."

Fontaine turned to Stein, and whispered, "Oh shit! She's poking fun at that 'nun' thing."

Stein struggled to keep from smiling too broadly.

The Thousand-Dollar Suit had to get the last word. "We all know what you're talking about. It's like an epiphany, so to say." The heads bobbed again.

Beaucharp said, "The exact word my partner used. Discussions about our early education inspired the idea. Special Agent Stein is the one most responsible for fleshing it out. They were just thoughts and hunches we don't want to toss out right now." She gazed among the law enforcement faces knowing how angry they got when a sharp lawyer tips over their cases with a technicality. "As you all know, some lawyers use every word uttered by investigating officers to turn things around in a case and destroy a lot of good investigative police work."

Beaucharp's last line sent another wave of bobbing heads nodding around the conference table.

Beaucharp stopped speaking and ceremoniously picked up the notes like a valedictorian and slowly walked back to her seat. The content of the last sentence jumpstarted some chatter leaving a good part of the room nodding in agreement.

Captain Bargiel rose and grinned at Beaucharp. "Thank you, Detective. You and your partner are doing a great job. Let's take fifteen minutes. Then come back and discuss the information we just got from the crime lab at the Florida Department of Law Enforcement."

***

Everyone rocked and scraped their chairs away from the conference table. Loud voices and heavy footsteps echoed off the granite walls in the hallway, as people descended upon the restrooms or raced toward the elevators. Cell phones appeared out of nowhere, and people checked for voicemail and messages. Seeking more privacy for their phone calls, some moved downstairs and into a courtyard next to the soda machines, cement picnic tables, and benches.

Stein pointed at a stairway. "Let's go outside for a minute."

Fontaine and Beaucharp followed her down four flights.

"Anyone want something to drink?" Fontaine said, looking over her shoulder as she walked toward one of the soda machines.

"No, thanks," said Stein.

Beaucharp said, "I'm all set, Donna. Thanks."

Beaucharp picked out a table and sat across from Stein. Then, with Fontaine at the vending machine, she looked at Stein and said, "How'd you know Birdy was going to ask one of us to talk?"

"We spoke earlier this morning, and I figured him out right away. The guy's a straight shooter and didn't pull punches with me. Spoke highly about you two. Is there some history with your families?"

"Not with mine. Donna's dad was a Tampa cop. A captain, well respected too. But, you know, in case you're wondering, Birdy doesn't play favorites. Donna earned what she got. No one gave her this job."

"I can see how you might misunderstand what I'm saying. I wasn't implying anything. I apologize if it seemed that way."

"Well, Wanda, what are you getting at?"

"From what I see, the captain is a good guy. A real cop, if you catch my drift."

Beaucharp nodded.

Stein said, "He knew all those dudes would pat each other on the back, wave around their credentials, and name friends. He waited till all the guys zipped their flies back up to make sure that you two got some credit. He put his ass out there when he called one of you to talk. What if you guys were sitting on your hands through all this? Things would have turned bad for him. He took a chance, and you knocked it out of the park for the department."

Beaucharp turned toward her and said, "Hey, sorry, Wanda, if I insulted you with that nepotism shit."

Stein's eyebrows lifted, and she stared into Beaucharp's face. "*Shit!* They told me you didn't swear."

"What! You did some homework?"

Stein nodded. "Got to. It's special stuff we do, and it's meticulous work. People can get hurt if we make the wrong decisions or if the ball gets passed to the wrong players."

Beaucharp smiled, shook her head and said, "I can't believe it. Where'd you go to school?"

Stein laughed. "PS 49 and Erasmus High in Brooklyn, then Brandeis outside Boston."

Fontaine appeared, sipping at the excess soda seeping along the top ridge of the diet drink can.

Stein said, "It's dripping. Did it explode when you opened it?"

"Just a little. I think it gets shaken up when it rolls down the chute."

Beaucharp chided. "Okay, Wanda. We got to stop talking about her. She's back."

Fontaine sat next to Beaucharp. "So, what's happening, Stein? What you doing here?"

"I can't say anything until the disclosure of the new evidence we're getting at this meeting. I hope the boys stop kissing each other's ass long enough for us to get on with this."

The loud stomping of footsteps, all rushing toward the elevators, disrupted their conversation. Beaucharp pointed to the stairway. "Let's get back," she looked at Stein, "I got to keep Fontaine moving, or she'll fall asleep."

"I'm taking my drink back in with me," Fontaine said.

Chapter 23

Back in the conference room, everyone took their same seats. Chief King's was empty, and Captain Bird stood at the podium. With everyone seated, he began. "We got the rush results from the Florida Department of Law enforcement's Crime Lab. The Attorney General, and the FBI are aware of some findings."

Beaucharp whispered to Stein, "I still don't get it. Why are they all here?"

Stein said nothing.

Bird, still talking, said, "... the contents of the sack consisted of human body parts . . ."—everyone in the room knew that—". . . there were several pieces of organs, fingertips, and a thumb, and a severed leg part consisting of a small shinbone with a foot attached."

"Maybe check out where Beauchy was cooking last," Fontaine joked under her breath.

Bird kept talking, ". . . the forensic people tell us there are three different DNA samples among the group. Before anyone asks, the vehicle owner's DNA wasn't among them."

The ATF agent raised his hand. Bird acknowledged him.

"Any matches?"

Bird took a deep breath. "Yes. One consequential match, and that's why we're here." He turned to Sergeant Lapointe. "Sergeant, would you debrief us, please?"

Bird stepped to the side. Lapointe approached the podium, carrying an oversized manila folder. After placing it on the pedestal and unfolding the flaps, he awkwardly removed several sheets of paper, some with numerous graphs of various colors. Others were legal documents bearing the seals of various Florida state agencies. Icy, stoic, and surprisingly sprite for having worked the evening before. He peered out into the crowd through unfashionable horn-rimmed trifocal glasses, bushy gray eyebrows rubbed against the frame. He began without looking at the material taken from the envelope.

"The DNA gathered from the blood and tissue samples taken from the pieces of human organs, several fingertips, and a thumb belong to the known felon, Bunson Rosa."

Lapointe paused and watched a few state agency people squirm uncomfortably, then resumed. "For those who have never heard of him, I will enlighten you. Rosa was a violent sexual predator. He was ruthless and cruel. After terrorizing the Belenton community for several months, BPD apprehended him by a stroke of luck and dogged detective work. The arrest was controversial, as was the trial . . ."

Lapointe explained that many legal technicalities arose and provoked nasty arguments between Rosa's lawyers and the District Attorney. Throughout the trial, the Belenton Herald, TV stations and even bloggers wreaked havoc on the Manatee County judicial system.

Eventually, prosecutors and his defense reached a compromise, and Rosa earned a twenty-five year sentence. That created more mayhem when the media pack got wind of the sentencing. It had taken the Manatee County judicial system several years to regain its public respect and balance. Recently, lawyers for Rosa discovered a technicality in the judge's sentencing language that they were trying to use as a wedge.

Amid the appeal's mayhem and confusion, Rosa was released from Florida State Prison in Starke by mistake. It was a clerical error involving another inmate whose name closely resembled Bunson Rosa's.

It was a controversial trial, a controversial sentence, and now, a controversial release from prison. Many segments of the Florida Legal System respected for integrity, were left tainted in Rosa's wake. Their reputations, once pristine and wholesome as the beaches of Siesta Key, suddenly appeared corrupt and filthy like the red tide areas reeking of flies and dead sea life, the debris so nasty the gulls wouldn't even eat there.

Beaucharp noticed that several minutes into Lapointe's narrative Chief King quietly returned to the conference room, took his seat, and passed a note to Captain Bird. They whispered.

Lapointe continued, "The news of his release will vault the Manatee County legal system back into the news. The shock to local law enforcement and the State District Attorney's office is going to be overwhelming."

"I get it now," Beaucharp whispered. "Everyone is running for cover. Looks like the Chief just picked something up too. He's whispering to Birdy."

"Yes," said Stein. "Before this hits the media, everyone is getting a heads up."

Lapointe, still talking, ". . . also, within the sack was a section of a leg with a foot attached. Forensic says it wasn't long from being severed and belonged to a small female between ninety and one-hundred years old . . ."

"Sure your old boyfriend is still in Brazil?" whispered Beaucharp.

"Shush," said Stein.

Lapointe read from a separate blue sheet of paper. "A small segment of blood had DNA belonging to a woman. A different woman than the one the leg belongs to. The only match we have currently is for Rosa."

Lapointe stopped, allowing everyone to discuss what he just unloaded on them. Loud chatter rocked the room for several minutes. Frowns and nervous tics wrinkled the faces of some, uneasy smiles on others.

Fontaine took a breath and sighed. "CYA. All these people are here looking for a way to cover their ass and the ass of their departments."

Beaucharp turned to Stein. "You already know about this, Wanda?"

Stein said, "I did. The Bureau is the one that performed all the tests. They're allowing the State Labs to take credit for it. The Belenton Police Chief and division commanders have already gotten notified. It happens all the time. It's not new to any of the brass."

Fontaine looked at Stein. "Honey, how'd this material get to Quantico, be tested, and come back here in six, maybe eight hours?"

Stein said, "We use the USF Medical Lab. An open grant from the FBI, NSA and CIA allows us twenty-four-hour access to all their lab facilities. We use their staff or, if need be, fly our own in. With the right equipment, a quick DNA test takes only a few hours."

"So, Wanda, you're here because the FBI did some legwork, so they want to be part of the show?" Beaucharp asked.

Stein looked to Fontaine, then to Beaucharp, and whispered. "There's more to it than that, Michaela. They're worried that something bigger has taken place. Larger than just the killing of a brutal perp. I am authorized to explain it all to both of you. Trust me. Captains Bird and Bargiel already know what I'm doing here. They'll debrief the Chief, and he'll decide who else should know what's going on."

"For now, let's listen to what the boys are saying," said Fontaine.

All three nodded.

A wild feeding frenzy of words broke as every department spokesperson added their contempt for the media and all the sleazy lawyers they could think of.

Fontaine said, "I don't get it. More than half of them here were lawyers in firms making lots of money proudly defending people like Rosa. What happened?"

Stein said, "They left with substantial reputations and plenty of money to contribute to political parties. That gets them the attention of the dragons of influence. They're hoping to gain cushy judgeships, or appointments to high-level agencies or even important cabinet seats."

"*Power* is the unsung hero here," Beaucharp said.

Captain Bird passed Lapointe the note he got from the Chief. The noise in the room thickened. Egos crashed into one another as everyone tried to push their ideas to the front.

Lapointe read the note, stepped away from the podium, looked around the room, and caught Stein's attention. He motioned for her and the detectives to step outside. They quietly left and waited in the hall. Lapointe whispered something to Bargiel as he passed, stepped outside, and walked over to the women. "You guys gotta get to Interrogation. Rodriquez, from Narcotics, is waiting for you."

"After the meeting?" asked Fontaine.

"No, right now. I gotta go along too."

"Any idea what this is about, Sarge?" Beaucharp asked.

"The perp you busted on the bridge three hours ago."

"The perp? He wasn't carrying. What's Narcotics want with him?" said Fontaine.

Beaucharp, showing little humor, spoke through a clenched jaw. "Let's go."

Rodriquez filled her in on the plan. "We're going to relieve my partner. He should have wound him up. So, you'll prance in, play the role until he gets agitated, then the sergeant will relieve you."

"Got it," said Beaucharp.

"Okay, everyone behind the mirror," said Lapointe.

"The ADA is there now," said Rodriquez.

"The ADA?" Stein asked.

"We wanna play this by the book," Lapointe said.

Everyone nodded.

Rodriquez walked them down the hall to the soundproof room with the one-way mirror and waited for them to enter. Everyone introduced themselves to Assistant District Attorney Marci Grover. She pointed toward the one-way mirror and placed her index finger to her lips, not to hush anyone but for her concentration.

Chapter 24

Rodriquez entered the interrogation room, scowled, and looked at his partner. "They need you in the evidence lab, David." He continued, "Something about a DUI arrest last Wednesday."

David Dione spent the past twenty minutes antagonizing Labbe intentionally to keep him off balance. He frowned. "Ah shit. You going to be okay here? Labbe and I are like cousins at this point."

Labbe yelled at Dione. "Up your ass!"

Rodriquez pulled a chair away from the table and dropped onto it. "I'm all set. It's only paperwork to fill out. It may be a while, so they're gonna find someone to fill in till you get back."

Dione left and shuffled into the observation room. After a quick round of nods and quiet introductions, they watched Beaucharp enter the interrogation room and fall into an empty chair. She pulled out a handkerchief and wiped the tabletop in front of her.

Across, with his left hand cuffed to a metal ring, Morris Labbe's face reddened, and his purple neck veins bulged behind the crude jailhouse tattoo ink. "What is she doing here?"

"My partner had to leave. Detective Beaucharp was around. We thought she might come in to help," said Rodriquez.

"I remember you," Beaucharp said. "You made me break a fingernail."

"Detective, Mr. Labbe says that it was a misunderstanding he was having with his friend. You butted in and made things worse."

Labbe rocked back into his chair and squinted, his bloodshot eyes bulging like red grapes. "I'm filing charges too. There wasn't any reason for you to brutalize me."

Beaucharp looked at Rodriquez. "I didn't even want to stop. My partner made me." Then she turned to Labbe. "You made me miss a hair appointment."

"You need more than a haircut to do something with that face."

Beaucharp looked at the jailhouse tattoos up and down his arms and across his hands and knuckles. Some were faded, barely blue dots, perhaps vague ideas, all self-made. One oddity jumped out. On his left forearm, he attempted to inscribe MOM. However, he wrote it while looking down his arm toward the back of his hand. When viewed with his hands on the table, his endearment read, 'WOW'.

Beaucharp pointed. "What the hell is that on your arm? What does WOW mean?"

"It's MOM. What are ya, stupid?"

"Your mother's name is WOW?"

"You asshole, you're looking at it upside down."

Beaucharp bowed her lips downward into an upside-down smile, and mockingly tapped her index finger against a temple. She said to Rodriquez, "It's such an easy word to spell. How do you screw that up?"

Labbe slammed his free palm against the metal table. The loud thud was absorbed immediately into the specially textured wallboard.

Rodriquez, struggling to keep from smiling, turned to Labbe. "Morris, do you want me to snap the cuff back on your free hand?" Then he looked at Beaucharp. "This won't take long, detective. It's regulation. When we talk to him, we need two detectives in the room," he lied.

Beaucharp said, "Okay, what do you want me to do? Whew! Is that him that smells so bad?"

"What fuckin' kind of shit is this?" Labbe screamed and pointed at Beaucharp. "How did an asshole like that ever become a cop? Belenton got to be hard up or she's been riding someone. Maybe daddy put a lot of money in someone's campaign?"

Beaucharp dove at the opportunity. "How did you become such a sissy? I knocked you down and threw the cuffs on like you were a little girl. My partner thought you were going to cry."

Labbe raised his free hand to slam the table again, stopped, and looked at Rodriquez. "You know you're lucky. I would've started on you right after I finished with that slut."

Beaucharp said, "Don't talk like that about my partner." Behind the two-way mirror, Stein smiled and elbowed Fontaine. Turning to Rodriquez, Beaucharp asked, "What am I doing here, detective?"

"Come on now. Both of you," Rodriquez said, "Let's get this crap done with." Then, he changed the tone and appeared saddened. With his forehead wrinkled and his eyebrows stitched together he stared at Labbe. "You know, we wanna eat sometime. Right?"

Labbe nodded.

Pointing at Labbe, Beaucharp said, "Why don't you call me back after he's taken a bath?"

Labbe wriggled at his chain. "You skinny little bitch. I won't be locked up forever. I'll get out and break your fuckin' neck like a wooden match."

Still behind the mirror, Lapointe smiled and whispered, "Good job." He quietly stepped from the room.

There was a rap on the interrogation room door, it opened, and Lapointe stuck his head in. "Everything okay in here?"

"Get this little bitch out of here before I kill her," Labbe shouted.

Looking at Beaucharp, Lapointe said, "Detective, I think you got a call."

"We got to have two detectives here, Sarge." Then tilting her head toward Labbe, she said, "This little girl might get upset."

Labbe's nostrils flared and quivered, his face reddened again, and he jerked at the wrist cuffed to the table.

"Do you mind if I take her place, Angel? How about you, Mr. Labbe?" Lapointe asked.

Labbe quieted and nodded.

Rodriquez turned to Beaucharp, "Do you mind, detective?"

"Who was the call from, Sarge?" Beaucharp asked.

"Begonia, aah, Begonia something?"

"Oh, great! Ruby Begonia, my stylist. She must have an opening this afternoon. I have to make it. You guys don't mind?"

"I'll cover for you, detective," said Lapointe.

Lapointe stepped in and closed the door. Beaucharp stood, walked to the door, cracked it slightly, closed it again, and turned toward Labbe. "If I have to come back, make sure he takes a bath in bleach." Then she left, and once outside, her voice echoed in the hallway. "Hey McKenzie, you ever hear of anyone with a mother by the name of WOW?"

"That little bitch. I'll kill her," Labbe bellowed.

Lapointe didn't speak for half a minute, hoping the silence filling the room made it seem much longer. Then, he looked at Labbe and said, "I could use a coffee now. How about you?"

Labbe said, "How about a soda?"

Trying to look confused, Rodriquez raised his eyebrows. "Sarge, we're in the middle of something."

Lapointe looked at Labbe, then back to Rodriquez, took a deep breath, and sighed. Then Lapointe stared at Labbe and, in a fatherly manner, as if consoling a child that had just taken a spill from a bicycle, said, "It was pretty noisy in here. We need some kind of break." Then, still looking at Labbe, Lapointe asked Rodriquez, "We got anything in the vending machines out there? I'll go get something."

"I think it is only Diet Coke," Rodriquez said.

"Diet Coke okay?" Lapointe asked Labbe.

Labbe said, "Yeah."

Rodriquez slid away from the table. "Let me go get them, Sarge. I need a break myself after that woman."

Lapointe nodded, rolled his eyes in disgust, and shrugged his shoulders at Labbe.

Labbe shook his head and shrugged back.

"Bitch!" Labbe said.

Rodriquez approached the door, stopped, then turned and asked Labbe, "Are you gonna be okay?"

Labbe's bobbed his head. "Yeah."

***

Beaucharp joined everyone behind the mirror. "How'd I do?"

ADA Grover smiled and waved her hands at the sides of her head as if she were trying to get someone's attention in a crowd. "We've never met, but I hate your guts."

"So how long should this take?" Fontaine asked.

Grover turned to all three. "Pretty soon Lapointe is going to find Labbe's connection to Rosa, and if we're lucky, we can learn where the rest of him is."

"What if he can't make this work?" asked Beaucharp.

Fontaine smiled. "Well, at least we had a good show."

Stein said, "Right now, this guy's gotta be afraid some of the boys on the inside will find out a tiny lady cop took him down. It will make him look like a soft touch. So, if nothing else, he's sweating that piece out."

Fontaine peered into the mirror. "Lapointe is gonna get him to talk about his issue with Rosa. Word will get around that he took on Bunson Rosa, the miserable bastard—"

Stein interrupted. "Then he can deny the small lady cop thing. He can say she maced him, or both detectives kicked him around because he was too drunk to protect himself."

***

Alone with Labbe, Lapointe engaged in small talk. "So, where you from, Morris?"

"Polk County Correctional by Lakeland."

Poor bastard's been in jail so much he's institutionalized. "No, I mean, where'd you come from *originally?*"

"Pittsburgh."

"Oh Jeeze. I was in Pittsburg almost fifty years ago. Everything is on a hill."

Labbe looked down at the table. "It's damn cold in the winter, too."

Lapointe rubbed his hands together, describing how he used to keep them warm. "Oh yeah, I remember that. So, how'd you end up in Florida?"

"Transferred here from West Virginia."

"What happened in West Virginia?"

"Not much."

Lapointe knew better, having already read Labbe's rap sheet. In West Virginia, he was serving his third prison stretch. He did four years in Pennsylvania for a gas station robbery in Scranton, then six more years for a botched grocery store robbery in Hershey. Four months after that release, he attempted to rob a woman at an ATM in Charleston, West Virginia. She was a New York City police detective on vacation. He acquired two permanently bent fingers on his left hand as a result of that arrest.

While serving the sentence, he ratted out the prison drug dealer to get two and one-half years shaved off his time. After he testified, and for his protection, they transferred him to the prison in Lakeland. The procedure is a common practice used throughout every prison system in the United States.

Labbe concluded. ". . . I was transferred here for my last three years so I could start a new life."

"It's too bad you run into this bad luck. What'd you do to the detective to make her single you out?"

"What do you mean?"

"Well, why'd she want to arrest you? You're a pretty big guy. How come she didn't just drive past? Did you flip her the bird or something?"

Rodriquez returned but waited outside the door for two minutes before knocking and stepping in with three soft drinks.

"Let me pay," Lapointe said.

"It's okay, Sarge. I got them." While passing out the sodas, he asked, "So, we getting anywhere here?"

Lapointe said, "We were just going to talk about the arrest."

Labbe looked at Rodriquez and opened the can. "The bitch busted me for no reason." With his free hand, he took a deep swig and set the can on the table, still clutching it. "She wanted to show off in front of the tall, good-looking cop."

Behind the two-way glass, Beaucharp shook her head. Stein smiled and elbowed Fontaine again.

Lapointe raised his eyebrows. "Do you mean her partner, Detective Fontaine?"

"Yeah. I was having a discussion with my girlfriend, and they pulled over and started pushing me around."

"Your girlfriend is in the hospital, Morris," Rodriquez said. He paused to see Labbe's reaction. "There was more than just a discussion taking place."

Labbe took another drink, ignoring Rodriquez, and glared at Lapointe. "Okay. You want something from me, don't you?"

"How come you haven't lawyered up?" Lapointe asked.

"What for? I just bitch-slapped her. I'll be out of County in six months."

"She's in the hospital right now. Did you know that?" Rodriquez said, controlling his patience.

"They took her off in an ambulance," Lapointe said.

Rodriquez rocked in his chair. "The judge isn't going to look at this as a simple assault."

"Are you guys saying I should lawyer up now?"

Lapointe slowly lifted his can, took a sip, and set it back down. "I'm saying, I'm surprised that you didn't."

Labbe gulped another drink. "I've been down these roads before. I get a *Public Pretender,* oh excuse me, Defender, and things are stretched out for months before I even get a chance to go to court." He stopped and ran his finger around the edge of the can, pushing the excess liquid into the triangle-shaped hole on the top. "I can end up sitting in County for eighteen months before I get a trial. If I play it out, the judge will give me another year. Nine months after that, I'll be out on good behavior."

Lapointe said, "Well, we may be able to help you with a couple of charges if you are straight with us."

Labbe, still holding his drink, leaned back into his chair. "I just told you about how this is going to unfold. So why should I do anything to help you?"

Casually rocking in his chair, Rodriquez suddenly let the legs hit the floor with a thud. He stared into Labbe's face and said, "Let's be honest here, Labbe. The detectives got you by the short hairs, you know that. So, what are we gonna do here—"

Lapointe's chair scratched against the tile as he slid it away from the table. "Morris, why don't you just lawyer up? Maybe you can get a better deal."

Labbe burst out, "Fuckin' prima donna little bitch."

"Well, whatever." Rodriquez added, "You're going to do some time. It's anyone's guess what the judge will do."

Again, Lapointe lifted his can to his lips, stopped, and placed it back on the table. "Morris, what do you think the boys in lockup will think about you getting nailed by a lady cop who's only five-foot-eight?"

Labbe took his hand off the can. "How are they going to know who arrested me?"

Lapointe slowly shook his head from side to side. "Belenton isn't a big town, and you're going to be in County for a while. You just said that. How many people do you think you'll run into who know most of the cops in town? The detectives who arrested you are quite popular. I'll bet both of them have friends in lockup—"

"I'd say at least a dozen," Rodriguez interrupted. "Getting arrested by Detective Beaucharp doesn't make you look like much of a tough guy, does it?"

Lapointe leaned forward. "You can't stop the news about this bust from getting around. Can you imagine how long the line will be with suitors auditioning to become your new jail house fiancé? And, you know how well news travels throughout the system, and it's anyone's guess where a judge could send you next. We think you're going to do some time for your girlfriend's condition. You could become quite popular in your new joint after County."

Rodriquez said, "Morris, no one wants to put you in that kind of a situation. So, let's get straight here so we can figure out a way to move this along."

Labbe's face, now reddened like it was ready to burst, shouted, "Fuckin' prima donna little bitch."

Lapointe was waiting for Rodriquez to set Labbe up for the shot. "Rosa was a turd. No one cares about him. I'd like to hear how things went with you and him."

"What about him?" Labbe said.

Beaucharp spoke as she wrote in a small notepad, "I've already asked FDLE's Special Victims Unit to send feelers out to counties on the Gulf Coast."

"They also have a protocol with hospitals. I'm waiting to hear if we can get a hit from one of them," Fontaine added.

Grover placed her glasses back on and turned toward Fontaine. "You guys are a couple of steps ahead of me. You and your partner work this any way you see fit. The Feds seem as close to this as we are, so stay close to Stein. I'm not sure how long we can keep her."

"Keep her?" Fontaine went on, "Can we get any money for her right now?"

Beaucharp said, "How about we keep her for a little while? I would like her to be able to see how the department uses Fontaine as a bad example."

Stein softly fisted Beaucharp's shoulder and smiled.

Chapter 25

Grover knew that Beaucharp and Fontaine had been working the case for almost fourteen hours. She asked to review their case notes and flipped through Beaucharp's first. "These are outstanding. They're complete and comprehensible, detective."

"Thank you."

Grover looked at Fontaine while still holding Beaucharp's notes. "I'm going to assume that yours are as good. Make copies and leave them in Admin. Keep your own sets and log out. Go home and get some sleep."

Fontaine said. "What about the report?"

"You have good case notes. Do the report tomorrow and—"

Beaucharp interrupted, "Captains Bird and Bargiel like our reports submitted daily."

Grover stared at the floor, momentarily thinking, then said, "I'll talk with the captains and get someone in Admin type up the report. Get some sleep. Something tells me tomorrow will be an early call and another long day."

Beaucharp said, "Just so you know, Fontaine's notes are usually written in crayon. For a long time, we were unsure about allowing her to handle any sharp utensils."

Grover grinned. She turned to Stein. "I have to call the Tampa Bureau as soon as I leave here. Can I ask them to keep you on the case?"

"Of course."

Looking at the detectives and then back to Agent Stein, she joked. "You have an unblemished record at the Bureau. So, you're not afraid of getting corrupted hanging around these two?"

"No problem. I can whip them into shape."

The detectives left Grover and Stein. Beaucharp stopped her partner in the hall and said, "Take off, Donna. I'll make the copies and take a squad car home. You'll get your notes back tomorrow morning."

"You're sure, partner?"

"I'm sure. Grover is right. Tomorrow is going to be another early one."

Fontaine walked away, her footsteps echoing in the empty hallway. Beaucharp sauntered in the other direction toward the Admin and summed up the events of the day in her head.

We haven't even been on the case for a full day and have already gathered a cast large enough for an Agatha Christa novel. The story comes with the antiquated Washbee, and his home with the unusual cat. What a setting! I'm almost afraid of what might show up tomorrow.

On her drive home Fontaine's thoughts hurtled through her head. *This Bunson Rosa evidence on Labbe's clothes? Within Gaslight's bag of oddities, an old leg, Rosa pieces chopped like someone was getting ready to toss them in a stew, discarded food, and the DNA of another woman. Another woman? We have a missing victim. How about the folks at the Bucket of Blood? She smiled. It's like a freaking train wreck.*

***

Fontaine hit Beaucharp's number from her cell. It rang two times.

"What's up, partner? Forget something."

"Beauchy, we got another victim out there. We didn't see this coming."

"Yup. You're right Donna. Something else we're going to have to piece together tomorrow."

"Beauchy, hold on. Guess who's calling me now? It's Stein."

Fontaine switched to the incoming call. "Yo! Agent Stein. We got a mystery victim, don't we?"

Stein said, "Yeah. Something to think about tomorrow. I just asked the Bureau to start a broader missing person's search."

"Good job. Wanda. Nice to see my federal tax dollars working efficiently. I got Beaucharp on the line, we'll talk tomorrow?"

"You bet. See you in the *am*." Fontaine dropped Stein's line and resumed the conversation with Beaucharp.

"Stein's asking for a deeper Bureau search."

"See you in the morning, Donna. Stay away from the navy bars tonight, going to need you on your game tomorrow."

Fontaine grinned. "See you tomorrow. Don't forget to pick me up or there won't be anyone to carry you for the day."

Beaucharp hung up and went back to bouncing ideas around in her head. *The extra DNA? It's a woman. Who is it? One of the women at the Bucket of Blood? Anybody in Washbee's family? I hope not, but the chips are going to have to fall where they may.*

She was still pondering ideas when she drove out of the Police Only gate. Her thoughts moved on to Agent Stein, and she quickly dismissed anything foul about her being on the case. *Stein is competent and caring. She'll learn more about the case when we fill her in with our details tomorrow. She might see something we're missing.*

A traffic light stopped Beaucharp at the intersection to turn onto Green Bridge. She stared at her notebook in the passenger seat, then spoke out loud. "The sooner Stein meets Washbee, the better. She'll snap us out of it if we're being overly biased toward Washbee's family."

She toyed with the idea of stopping by Washbee's on her way home but changed her mind. *I better get some sleep.*

Chapter 26

On the evening before the morning Winston told Washbee about the episode with Gaslight's truck, and Washbee met Fontaine and Beaucharp, he was reviewing administrative duties of the funeral home. He discovered a bombshell. Among the stacks of daily mail came various pieces of literature from hospitals, doctors' offices, Social Security Administration, and letters from family and friends of the deceased that the Washbee Funeral Home and Crematorium had served. Washbee always looked at the personal letters first and responded with handwritten notes.

The mail also brought numerous advertisements about funeral home accessories and modern embalming implements. Washbee screened these junk envelopes and stacked them in a pile eventually to be tossed in the recycling. The humidity caused the glue from the flap of one letter to fuse to a large advertisement envelope, adding weight to the document. Assuming the extra weight could portend an item of importance, Washbee didn't discard it immediately.

Washbee found the hidden letter. It was addressed to the Washbee Funeral Home and Crematorium from the Tingston Wolfe Memorial Hospital in Ellenton. Enclosed was an apology from the Director of Orthopedic Surgery.

Dear Cyrus:

I apologize for the late arrival of the limb from Ms. Ida C. Foote. Removal of her leg was a last-ditch effort to control the effects of gangrene poisoning. Unfortunately, Ida passed away several hours after surgery. Ida Foote's remains were retrieved late that afternoon while the leg remained in the hospital lab.

An administrative snafu, like those frequented upon us in our Navy days! Dr. Michaels, the pathologist, picked up the mistake. We traced it to Ida Foote, 96, of Belenton. I trust you'll find a way to unite it with Ms. Foote.

Best regards, Larry

P.S. Stop by when you get a chance. Carol and I miss seeing the kids.

Washbee grinned and allowed his thoughts to take him back to when he and now Dr. Lawrence Burns were teenage gunnery mates on the Navy destroyer Ben Richard Bronstein. Because they grew up with Washbee and his wife since they were toddlers, Dr. Burns and his wife always referred to nephews Duff Bleiu, Winston Beauregard, and niece Hattie Winslow as the kids just the same as if they were Washbee's own children.

The letter was dated three days after Ida Foote's cremation. Puzzled, Washbee went in search of nephew Duff Bleiu, his crematory operator.

Bleiu, outside stacking cordwood into the bin that fed the crematory incinerator, got startled and jumped when Washbee poked his head out the door.

"Did we get a Tingston Memorial package, Duff? It should have arrived a couple of days ago."

Bleiu nodded, stopped working, and slowly removed and folded his leather gloves, using the time to develop a response. "Uncle Cyrus, I was going to talk to you about that."

"Duff! Do we have the package?"

"It's a complicated story, Uncle Cyrus. I should come in to talk about it."

"Okay. Wash up and meet me in the office."

Washbee shuffled his way back to the office and was, again, studying the letter when Duff Bleiu showed up.

"Come on in Duff, and close the door, please."

Before he could shut the door behind him, Manfred rushed in. Bleiu chose the seat across the desk facing Washbee. Manfred walked in a tight circle once, then leaped onto Bleiu's lap and began purring loudly.

Washbee spoke first. "Please, tell me the whole story about the package and where it is now."

"Well, the piece arrived late," said Bleiu.

"What do you mean, the piece arrived late?"

"Miss Ida's leg."

"Miss Ida's leg? Miss Ida was cremated on Wednesday. Wasn't it placed in the box with her?"

Bleiu, unable to always develop a cognitive response immediately, lowered his head, staring at his belt buckle. He usually needed to create a narrative and then a summarization to respond to difficult questions. Washbee reached across the desk and softly patted the back of Bleiu's hand.

Bleiu said, "Actually, it wasn't with Miss Ida."

Washbee took a deep breath and exhaled slowly.

Bleiu went on. "Miss Collette, you know the lady who looked after her from time to time? She was there when Miss Ida died."

Sensitive to Bleiu's challenges, Washbee's eyes dampened as he struggled not to say his thoughts out loud. *Oh! Poor Duff.* "Okay, Duff, try not to get off track here. There's nothing to be nervous about." Washbee was lying.

"Well, Miss Collette said Miss Ida had diabetes, really bad, and was in a coma when they brought her to the hospital, and doctors had to chop off her leg cause gangrene had already set in by that time. She died anyway."

"Duff. Son. Pick up your head, please."

Duff, now with watery eyes, looked at Washbee.

"Where is Ida Foote's leg now?"

"It's in a bag with the scraps for Mr. Giovanelli's pigs."

Washbee went numb. He couldn't think of what to say, and everything went still as if the universe stopped, the entirety of it suspended in mid-air. Manfred's purring filled the stillness until interrupted by the hallway clock chiming the half-hour. Later, Washbee would tell the detectives that he could hear his food digest at that moment.

Dropping from Washbee's hand, the letter floated to the desktop. "We need to understand this a little better, Duff. Why is Miss Ida Foote's leg in the bag with the scraps for Mr. Giovanelli?"

Bleiu's head bowed again, and an anxious facial tic twisted his lips and caused him to lift his eyebrows simultaneously. He then stumbled over his words as his fears of letting down his uncle grew.

Unable to reach across the table and hug him, Washbee smiled and said, "Duff, no matter what happened, no one has gotten hurt."

Bleiu looked up at his uncle cautiously. Manfred rubbed against his cheek and purred.

"It's okay, Duff. We'll figure it all out, I promise." Washbee knew the statement was also a lie. So, he then slowed the discussion tempo to let Bleiu recount everything with as little interruption as possible.

Bleiu continued. "Well, you know how stubborn Miss Ida was."

"She got around pretty well for a ninety-six-year-old living alone," said Washbee.

Bleiu nodded. "Yes, she lived in the same house she was born in."

Washbee leaned back into his chair. "People visited every day. Didn't they?"

"Church folks and friends. They made sure she ate and kept clean, things like that. No one realized she was ignoring the meds she was supposed to be taking."

Washbee paused and thought for a little while. "Easy to see how that can happen, Duff. She was quite independent and could be ornery. If someone challenged her, she might not let 'em back into her home."

Bleiu buried his face into his hands. "This is awful, Uncle Cyrus."

"I'm sorry, Duff. I know it is. But you're doing a good job here."

He lifted his head and looked at Washbee. "Well, Miss Foote got rushed to the hospital when a visitor found her asleep in the chair. She was watching Oprah. Isn't that something?"

"Yeah, she loved Oprah. Please go on. How'd you get the leg?"

"I'm guessing that as a last-ditch attempt to save her, they whacked off the leg and placed it in the special refrigerator they set aside for such things."

"Okay. So, what were we doing with it if Miss Foote was cremated three days ago?"

Tears welled up in Bleiu's eyes. "Someone at the hospital forgot to include the leg when we picked her up. So, when Miss Collette told me about the chopped-off leg and how Miss Foote died, it upset me terribly."

"Of course, it would, Duff. You're a good person, and we all loved Miss Ida."

Washbee opened a drawer to retrieve a box of tissues, like he'd done countless times for family mourners, and passed it over to Bleiu. "Take your time, son."

Bleiu, still sobbing loudly, said, "I'm sorry, Uncle Cyrus. I got upset, really bad. But you know Miss Maureen, that nurse from Boston, well, she got an orderly, and placed Miss Foote onto our gurney." Bleiu pulled at the tissues three at a time and blowing his nose in two sharp bursts, the first one frightening the cat.

Washbee, unable to watch Bleiu in such pain, struggled out of his chair and squeezed into the seat next to him. Softly patting Bleiu's elbow, Washbee said, "This has got to be painful, Duff. We can talk about it later."

"No, Uncle Cyrus! I have to tell you because I don't know if I was right or wrong."

"Duff, you did what you thought was right."

"The leg showed up two days later, in a box of dry ice, wrapped in paper like the stuff you see at the butchers."

"Why didn't you incinerate it then?"

"You know how tiny Miss Ida was. It looked a little larger than a turkey leg."

Bleiu's bottom lip quivered, and he wept again. "Uncle Cyrus, you know the incinerator is old, and I struggle to get the bricks back together every time. So, I didn't want to fire it up for just one leg."

"I know you're trying to do the right thing here. What were you going to do with the leg?"

"I was waiting for the next person to be cremated so I could toss the leg inside the empty tray we used if we were cremating two. That way, I could keep Miss Ida's ashes from getting mixed up."

"So, what did you do with the leg in the meantime?"

"I left it wrapped in the paper from the hospital and stuffed it into the big refrigerator where we keep cadavers and the scraps for Mr. Giovanelli's pigs."

Bleiu then went off on another narrative. "You know, Mr. Giovanelli gathers scraps from some of the nursing homes to feed the wild hogs he raises. Well, we told him we sometimes have leftovers from our dinners and scraps from catered events at funeral receptions. No use in letting that stuff

Chapter 28

Beaucharp reached across to open the door for Fontaine because both her hands held coffee travel mugs. The smell of fresh coffee rushed in as two long arms pushed the mugs through to Beaucharp and she placed them into the slots of the center console.

Fontaine took the seat after tossing Beaucharp's shoulder bag into the back. "How'd you sleep?"

"Pretty good." Beaucharp enjoyed testing her partner's gullibility so to have some fun she thought she'd joke about her dream. "Except for a ranting Canadian carrying on this morning."

"You got neighbors from Canada? Snowbirds?"

"We'll talk about it later."

"Oh yeah! I'm thinking this hot guy with a mustache?"

"Pretty close," Beaucharp smiled.

"Dark eyes and a lot of hockey trophies?"

"Wow! You know your Canadians, don't you?"

Beaucharp stopped at the parking lot exit, took a loud sip of coffee, then turned onto the street and said, "How we gonna work Washbee into this?"

Fontaine raised her eyebrows. "I don't know. Wait a minute. What do you mean?"

"Okay, let me put it another way. Do you think Washbee killed Rosa?"

Fontaine laughed. "Of course not. He walks about one-quarter-of-a-mile-an-hour. He'd have trouble swatting flies. How could he get into a brawl with anyone?"

"How about Mr. Gaslight?"

Fontaine said, "Course not."

"Anyone in the Bucket of Blood strikes you as the perp?"

"No. I think we've been over this yesterday. Oh! I know where you're going now."

Beaucharp, now silent, slowed down and drove to the side of the road, hit the blue lights, and stopped. She shifted into Park and looked at her partner.

Fontaine knew that something serious was gnawing at her. Beaucharp kept weighty things from cluttering her thinking by addressing them as quickly as possible. Sometimes it meant tearing the scab off a painful wound and examining it. Once, she woke Fontaine and dragged her to an old cemetery at 3 am. Approaching the entrance, they noticed a familiar white Ford Escort. It belonged to a man who filed a missing person's report on his girlfriend. Beaucharp hit the blue lights as soon as they were spotted, and the man ran off into the brush.

Immediately, Fontaine called for assistance. Within minutes, two Florida Highway Patrol teams showed up with K-9s. They apprehended the man an hour later.

Their inquiry began after Sargent Lapointe smelled something funny about the missing person report. He whispered his concerns to Fontaine and Beaucharp, so they backtracked the man's movements on the days previous to filing the report. They discovered he lied about places he'd been when questioned.

In his initial report, he stated that he and his girlfriend argued, and she left right after. When she didn't come home for two days, he called the police and reported her missing. He told the detectives he was too upset to go to work and spent several days at home, waiting for his girlfriend to call or return.

From an anonymous tip, they learned he purchased items at a local Ace Hardware. The detectives retrieved a copy of a receipt for a shovel and grass seed. The purchases raised alarms with Beaucharp.

The next evening, she awoke at 2:00 am from a sound sleep. Why would a condo dweller need a shovel and grass seed? She got up and re-examined her notes, then on a hunch, woke up Fontaine and drove to the Old Parrish Cemetery.

The cemetery was secluded. First established when Parrish was originally called Oak Hill Plantation in 1867. It sat at the end of a dusty, unkempt road. Seldom used today, it contained the burial site of former slaves, community members, and pioneers from the mid-nineteenth century. Within its boundaries, a massive granite monument memorializes the names of the Confederate veterans interred there. The suspect grew up in that secluded section of Parrish. He knew the place was barely used anymore.

Under cover of darkness and in the early morning hours, the sandy soil would make it easy to bury the remains of his former girlfriend then reseed the area with the fast-growing grass.

Fontaine rolled the scenario around in her head. *The cemetery idea worked out. Beaucharp woke me and we pulled it off.* When it was all over Beaucharp said, "I had to move on it. Thanks for trusting me, Donna."

***

"Trusting me." Those words stuck with Fontaine. After that incident Fontaine always respected her judgment, no matter how weird.

She asked, "What's up, Michaela? Something is gnawing at ya."

"I'm thinking about what new evidence might have come up that could not wait until eight this morning."

"You think they got the person involved? The case is barely twenty-four hours old."

"No. They wouldn't order us in on overtime for that. So why did they keep Lapointe on the case yesterday? It was all overtime for him," Beaucharp said.

"There has to be something going here," Fontaine paused, lifted the travel mug for a sip—the coffee was too hot—and placed it back inside the console slot. "I think it's more than the Brass at the Attorney General's Office covering their asses."

"What could it be?"

"Wait a minute, Michaela! This nasty Rosa character has been like a chicken bone in the judicial system's throat. Maybe they want an end to this once and for all—"

Beaucharp interrupted. "Yeah! They want it to end right now. Get Rosa out of the news!"

"They want to nail someone, cut a deal with them, and wrap up the case?" Fontaine asked.

Beaucharp said, "All those people are looking for a way to protect their agency." She took a sip of coffee and held onto the mug. "Birdy, Bargiel, and King are giving us full rein to act on this and the state boys are going balls to the walls to rush this. They even asked for help from the Feebs. That's not frickin' normal for them. That's how Stein got put on the case. Think she's part of it?"

Fontaine shook her head. "No. She's too smart for that shit. Anyway, we're up to our asses in this now. I'm not worried. Lapointe, Birdy, and Bargiel got our backs."

Beaucharp pulled the lid off her travel mug and blew across the top, then took another sip. "You're right. There's been a lot of politics in the middle of this. The state boys are leaving us alone. That's unusual because they love to get their pictures in the papers and their names in the local newscasts. It's like they're pushing us and the Belenton PD out front."

Fontaine thought and drummed her fingers on the dashboard. "Yeah! We're like Laurel and Hardy in the French Foreign Legion. The colonel asked for volunteers, and everyone in the regiment took a step back, leaving those two out front."

Beaucharp laughed and stared out her side window, watching the eastern sky gather the crimson streaks of a Florida dawn. Silently, each tried to piece together and measure what had transpired during the last twenty-four hours. They knew as soon as something looked like it was going to break, it would be then when a whole bunch of neckties would try to rush to the front of the cameras to take bows.

Fontaine broke the silence. "You ever had DNA crime reports come back so soon from the labs?"

"Not really."

The conversation lasted twelve minutes, and much of what Beaucharp called "detective meat" got addressed. They needed to connect with Stein as soon as possible. Fontaine dialed her mobile. It went right to Voicemail. "Wanda, it's Fontaine, the one who keeps Beaucharp out of trouble. Call me when you get this."

"Nothing more we can do," Beaucharp said.

Fontaine's phone chirped as they drove through the police parking gate.

"It's Stein," said Fontaine before hitting the talk button and turning on the speaker.

"What's up?" Stein asked.

Fontaine answered, "We've been called in early again. When is a good time for us to connect?"

"I'll see you in the conference room." They heard her ask someone, "What conference room is this? Four? I'll see you guys in conference room four. I got some donuts."

***

Stein stood waiting in front of conference room four with a half-eaten donut and a Styrofoam coffee cup. The front of her blouse had a slight dusting of powdered sugar. Fontaine touched the powdery section with an index finger and said, "You eat much?"

Stein said, "Oh shit! I got to fix this. Walk with me to the loo."

Fontaine rolled her eyes and said, "Oh, my! To the loo! Honey, what are we freaking Brits now?"

Stein laughed and spilled droplets of coffee onto the granite floor.

"Knock it off, Donna!" Beaucharp said. She looked at Stein and asked, "What are you doing here?"

Stein stopped at a water fountain, handed Beaucharp the donut and coffee, then wet a napkin, and wiped the sugar away. "This will do it." She kept the napkin and took the donut and coffee back. "At 6, I got a call from the Tampa Office that said someone was panicking at the state level. I think they want me here to be sure the Bureau doesn't take a hit for anything that goes wrong."

"Beaucharp got a call around the same time, then she called me. I've never seen so many fireworks go off with a case. This is like a shit-tornado," Fontaine said.

"Boy, I'd like to see one of them," said a grinning Beaucharp.

Stein waved them back toward the conference room. "The hotel is right across the street, so I came right over. I knew a bunch of cops would be around, along with a few neckties, so I figured I'd grab a couple of dozens of these,"—she tossed the last piece of a powdered donut into her mouth—"from Belenton Donuts on 14th Street."

They followed Stein into the room and Fontaine left for the counter with the donuts. Looking back over her shoulder she said, "At least you went to a classy place for these, Stein. Get us some good seats and I'll get us a couple of good ones before they all disappear."

Stein followed Beaucharp to the front row.

Fontaine arrived with three jelly donuts and offered one to Stein. "Our favorites," she said.

Stein declined, grinned, and winked at Beaucharp. Beaucharp took one, shook her head, and smiled.

"Did she tell you about her new Canadian friend?" Fontaine asked.

Embarrassed and red-faced, Beaucharp laughed, remembering she forgot to let Fontaine know that she was joking, and her encounter was a figment in a dream.

Stein winked and said, "A Canadian, Michaela! Ooh-La-La! 'Qui Parte Quebecois'?"

Fontaine said, "Oh, I think he's a real froggy with a mustache and hockey trophies up the gazoo."

Beaucharp said, "You guys are getting this blown out of shape. I'll fill you in after this meeting. But, believe me, it's nothing like she's carrying on about. And Fontaine, the word is 'wazoo' not gazoo."

"What? No, mustache?" said Fontaine.

Stein chided in, "C'mon! A Frenchie with no mustache! Dump him before this goes too far."

Beaucharp said, "You two are crazy. So, I'm recommending counseling, I mean, the real nutso-facto stuff for both of you when this case is over."

"Why are you waiting, Beauchy?" Fontaine looked at Stein, "If we're that nutty, call the guys with the nets to come in and scoop us up right now, honey."

"I can't just yet." She smiled. "This whole case may head south and turn into a train wreck. If that happens, I gotta have someone to blame."

Stein laughed and looked at both. "Were you guys separated at birth? I can't think of any two people in the world more deserving of each other."

Beaucharp grinned and said, "How about you, Stein? How'd you get here? Who'd you piss off at the Bureau?"

Stein smiled.

Fontaine inhaled a second donut, brushed the grains of sugar off her blouse and before Stein could answer said, "You know anything about what's going on here today?"

"All I know is that they found some more evidence. My Bureau source says it was discovered by accident. Something got mislabeled and ended up in forensic."

The conference room hosted a large oval table that seated thirty. All the seats were taken at 7:10, leaving five people standing next to a wall.

Captain Bird stood up at his seat and bellowed, "Listen up." The room quieted. "New evidence has surfaced, and we think that there is a good chance that our detectives can make an arrest today. Also, anything spoken about in this room is information only for those present. This is serious. We are a relatively small unit so if any of this gets out, we won't have to go far to find out who leaked it." Bird then nodded to someone standing.

At the signal, ADA Grover, holding a tan folder, stepped away from the wall and walked to the podium and dropped the folder on top and said, "We don't know why, but this gag order is coming straight out of the Governor's Office. If someone pulls the pin, we're all going up. So, we're offering this caveat. All police units, including profilers and forensic people must stay. Any other associated elements can leave right now."

Those present knew it could be the most complicated case to ever develop in modern Manatee County. Everyone wanted to be part of it, the true professionals out of a sense of duty, others for the notoriety and the sake of their careers. No one left the room.

Fontaine turned to Beaucharp and whispered. "What the hell did you do?"

Stein smiled, and Beaucharp said, "What do you mean?"

"What kind of fuck-story are we in the middle of here?"

Beaucharp said, "The kind we both live for, partner."

Stein spoke in a low whisper, almost under her breath. "This bullshit happens all the time at the federal level. The evidence they found must be directly connected to someone you questioned."

Beaucharp scribbled quickly on her notepad and shoved it in front of Fontaine. *What new evidence? Who's it connected to?*

Grover left and resumed her spot by the wall and Lieutenant Tom English from the FDLE Crime Lab came the podium and introduced himself. "A meat cleaver was picked up at a site the Florida Department of Law Enforcement was surveying yesterday."

Beaucharp pulled her pad back and wrote, *Gotta be Gaslight's place,* and slid it back to Fontaine.

Stein could read Beaucharp's scribbling each time.

English continued, "It was grabbed by accident and almost discarded. For some reason, it got mixed in with the forensic organic material scheduled for DNA testing. Since the technician had it in front of him, he tested the blood samples. Some of the blood DNA belonged to Rosa, and some blood DNA matched the unknown female blood discovered with the body parts.

We also got another set of prints."

A noisy buzz echoed around the room. English allowed it to continue for a bit then said, "Okay! At ease, everyone. The cleaver was amid some wild shrubbery along US 301. It could have been dropped there by mistake or placed in hiding. But, right off the top, it is a good contender for the murder weapon used on Rosa."

English went on. "Okay. We got Rosa's blood and someone else's prints and blood. The Belenton detectives and a member of the FBI will follow up on this today. They'll be debriefed on the situation. Keep to your schedules just in case this all runs into a dead end."

Chapter 29

Beaucharp looked around the room, then to Stein and Fontaine. "Wait here for me. I got to go to the can, and I'm sure Lapointe will want to talk to us." She smiled and pointed at Stein. "You're in charge."

Stein smiled. "You mean the loo?"

Fontaine said to Stein, "Don't try to figure out that Yankee language. I'll see if there are any donuts left."

As Beaucharp started for the door, Sergeant Lapointe waved her over. She approached close enough to point her thumb over her shoulder and mouthed, "I got to run to the ladies for a minute."

"Go ahead. I'll wait for you. It'll only take a minute." Lapointe then signaled Stein and Fontaine to wait for him in the room. They acknowledged and watched him step out the door. Lapointe, waiting in the hallway, nodding at familiar people scurrying out. Each eager to get back to their phones and emails and check for any changes within their divisions that might have happened while they were cloistered.

A noisy hand-drier roared, and seconds later, Beaucharp walked out in time to see Captain Bird and Chief King approach Lapointe. King leaned close and whispered something. Bird, silent, raised an anxious eyebrow and waited for a response from Lapointe. Lapointe signaled with a nod. Bird smiled, and both officers walked off toward the Police Only Elevator.

Beaucharp approached Lapointe. "What's up, Sarge? I thought you were supposed to be off last night."

"I got an early call and came in for a couple of hours. How well do you two trust Agent Stein?"

Beaucharp understood what he was asking her and Fontaine. She paused, then looked into Lapointe's eyes. "We trust her. She's on our side."

Lapointe shrugged, inhaled deeply, looked at all three, and said, "Now that you all know what is going on, no one will hold it against anyone who decides to step away."

Beaucharp and Fontaine agreed to ride it out to the end. Stein pointed at the two detectives. "I'm in. Someone's got to keep an eye on these two."

Fontaine pointed her thumb at Stein. "If she wants any action, she gotta finish this and get back to Tampa before the fleet returns."

Stein and Beaucharp laughed. Lapointe looked puzzled.

"It's a private joke, Sarge. It has something to do with how Fontaine and Stein worked their way through college," Beaucharp said.

Finally getting the joke, Lapointe grinned, winked at Beaucharp, and turned to Fontaine. "What did you do with all the tuition money your daddy sent you?"

Fontaine said, "That's another story. Y'all are going to have to wait for my memoirs."

The conference room door opened without a knock. Lieutenant Patroine, a notorious sneak and precinct gossip, rushed in.

"We're just leaving, Lieutenant," said Lapointe.

"What's going on? I was supposed to have this room five minutes ago."

"You should have knocked. I didn't realize someone had already scheduled it. We could have grabbed another."

Patroine's only qualification for his lieutenant bar came from marrying the daughter of a city commissioner. That alone didn't endear him to many in the department. Also, he constantly attempted to push his weight by exerting rank over those with a lesser grade. "These rooms are supposed to be signed for. Their intended use is supposed to be stated in writing."

Lapointe, tired and irritated, said, "The room is all yours, Lieutenant. We're sorry if we caused you any delay."

The four stood to leave while Patroine kept ranting. "Well, who will sign for the room? You all have been here for at least fifteen minutes."

Lapointe's suspicions were confirmed. Patroine was outside, trying to listen. Because of his arrogance and inability to maintain confidentiality, he was rarely allowed in on significant department transactions.

"Lieutenant, you got the room now," Lapointe said.

Patroine waved his arms as if frustrated. "Well, I don't think it works that easily. There has to be documentation for the use of these rooms."

Lapointe looked toward the women and said, "I'll meet you in the hall."

Stein, Beaucharp, and Fontaine walked out. Lapointe hit the speed dial on his phone. Patroine watched nervously.

The caller answered. "Captain Bird."

"Got a problem. Someone wants to know why we are using a conference room."

"Who has the problem?" "Lieutenant Patroine."

Bird appreciated Lapointe's professionalism, always addressing rank respectfully, seldom discourteously speaking of senior officers by their last name only.

Bird was also familiar with the lieutenant's self-importance and understood what was happening. "Put him on. I'll take care of it."

"Don't keep him on for too long. I got to sign out in ten minutes."

"Put him on."

It took less than fifteen seconds to resolve the issue. A red-faced Patroine returned the phone to Lapointe and said, "Why didn't you tell me the captain okayed the room?"

Lapointe took his phone and left the room to ensure that no further discussion on the matter would ensue. In the hall and out of earshot of Patroine, Fontaine asked, "How did it go with Labbe last night? They were supposed to take him to Rosa's campsite."

Lapointe said, "They didn't go. Labbe got skittery all of a sudden. Rodriquez and Dion are taking him this morning."

Beaucharp said, "We got an interview to complete with Mr. Washbee and his nephew. We'll be in the neighborhood, so we ought to check on them."

Lapointe said, "I don't know what they're gonna find out there. They may ask for you guys. I'd suggest you each take a pair of Timberlines in case they need help searching in the palmettos or along the old railroad bed."

As Beaucharp, Stein, and Fontaine started to leave, Lapointe stopped and turned back around. "Oh! I almost forgot. Your reports for yesterday—"

"Oh shit!" Fontaine threw her hands in the air. "We forgot."

"Birdy had the clerks type them using your notes. He knew you were going to have another hectic day. So, before you sign out today, check to see if they are all right. If they work for you, initial them."

Beaucharp said, "Tell the captain thanks."

Stein said, "Whose car are we taking?"

"What are you driving?" Beaucharp asked.

"A Bureau Escort SUV. One of the small four-doors. It's tiny and spunky."

"Spunky, huh? That'll do," said Fontaine. "But I would've preferred one of those big and roomy black ones I see you guys in."

Stein said, "It'll have to do. I'm not high enough up the food chain for a classy Suburban."

***

Stein had boots in her car. Fontaine and Beaucharp retrieved theirs from a squad car trunk and changed into them right away. As they were leaving, Fontaine rushed toward the police parking area. "I got shotgun!" She shouted like an excited child.

They were going to visit Washbee right away and wanted to debrief Stein before leaving the parking lot. "If we miss something, look at our notes," Beaucharp said.

"Beauchy makes fun of mine because I write so special," Fontaine said.

"Special, as compared to what?" Stein asked.

"Some Yankee barmaids, I guess," said Fontaine.

Stein and Beaucharp grinned.

After the fifteen-minute debriefing about their visit to the Bucket of Blood and then Washbee, Beaucharp asked, "Making any sense, Wanda?"

Stein looked at Fontaine. "The whole thing seems like a controlled crash! But it does make sense."

Fontaine said, "If you have questions or new ideas, speak up."

Beaucharp spoke from the back seat. "She's right. We got ideas, but we're open to your suggestions."

Stein scanned through the pages. "You scratched out, as offenders, any of the people you've met so far."

The detectives nodded.

"I get that this Washbee person has more he wants to talk about."

Fontaine said, "Yes. He had more to say, but we had to rush away for that big meeting yesterday."

Stein stared off into the distance, keeping her thoughts to herself. Beaucharp and Fontaine respected the silence. They acted the same way when they had to make critical decisions dangerously close to crucial areas of an investigation.

Stein finally spoke. "Will it upset the rapport you have with Washbee if I show up?"

Fontaine glanced up and down Stein like a carnival barker trying to guess her weight.

"I don't know, Beauchy. What do you think?"

"Oh yeah. She's got an honest face. I think we can pull it off with her."

Stein clicked her seat belt. "You guys got no choice. I'm driving. Point me in the right direction."

Chapter 30

Traffic moved slowly over Green Bridge, giving them time to enjoy the harbor wildlife, and watch a small flotilla of charter boats and shrimp trawlers with long foaming wakes snaking behind them. The boats led parades of gulls and osprey down the Manatee River meandering out into Palma Sola bay and then the Gulf of Mexico.

Stein pointed out Fontaine's window. "Those birds are having a great time. They trying to pick up scraps?"

Fontaine smiled. "Yes. Fishing boats travel out to the Gulf and back every day and the birds always seem to know what time to show up."

From the back seat, Beaucharp said. "I wonder which one sets the alarm clock?"

Fontaine turned her visor down and flipped its mirror open to view Beaucharp. Sure that Beaucharp could see the stare, she raised a sarcastic eyebrow. "They develop a kinship with the boat crews. Sometimes deckhands shove ship scraps and leftovers aside and dole them out as they slip crosses the bay."

Beaucharp, now, regretting the annoying remark said, "Commercial fishing is hard work. I have family living in Gloucester, right on Cape Ann, and they've been fishermen for generations."

"They're the farmers of the sea," said Stein. "Any type of farm work is grueling. John Kenneth Galbraith once said, 'After you grow up on a farm, any kind of work you do after is easy.'"

An osprey clutching a large fish shot past and soared to the top of a colossal steel streetlight. Others, already perched, tore at food, paying no attention to the action around them. Pelicans glided alongside the car like fighter escorts traveling at the same speed.

Stein said, "What a beautiful place. Some people vacation in these parts and once they get back home, they talk about seeing this stuff for the rest of the year. You guys get to see this every day."

Beaucharp and Fontaine agreed in silence. The tires' rhythm against the asphalt partook in a spellbinding combination of a symphony, and a canvas of billowing white clouds in flawless blue skies, everything juxtaposed against the serene emerald of Palma Sola Bay.

Stein roused them. "Tell me what I do once I get over the bridge."

From the back seat, Beaucharp tapped Stein's shoulder. "As soon as you leave the bridge, take a right. We want to take you past the Bucket of Blood to get a feel for that place. We may have to go back and interview some of those folks again."

Stein nodded.

Beaucharp's phone chirped. "Shoot!"

She scrambled through her bag, found it, and tapped the answer key. "Beaucharp . . . What? What next? Can you say that again? I'm going to put the phone on speaker." She pointed the phone toward the front seat.

"Detective, this is Mona from Central Dispatch. You guys have to go to US 301 North. Meet with detectives Rodriquez and Dione directly in front of the Palmetto Crossing mile marker. They'll be waiting with a prisoner."

"That's about a half-mile past Wally Gaslight's house," Fontaine whispered.

"Is the perp giving them trouble?" Beaucharp asked.

"Negative. A dog is running around with a human skull. Get this! They say the skull has something sticking out of its mouth. The dog keeps circling playfully, and they can't pursue and still maintain the status of the prisoner."

"What about Animal Control, Mona?" Fontaine said.

"Negative. They're stuck at a site in Lakewood Ranch. There's an alligator in the hallway of the elementary school. Rodriquez and Dione are waiting for you guys."

Fontaine said, "Tell them ten minutes."

"Ten-four. Ten minutes ETA US 301, Palmetto Crossing." The dispatcher, forgetting she was using a phone, automatically uttered call numbers to sign off.

Fontaine instructed Stein. "Still take the first right off the bridge. That'll put us right on US 301 North. They should be about six miles up the road."

Stein smiled and looked at Fontaine. "Don't mind me. I'm going to talk out loud to myself. First, there is a bag with human body parts mixed with table scraps. Some pieces belong to one of Florida's most notorious predators. A skeletal piece belonging to a woman in her nineties or possibly older. An alligator lost in an elementary school and a dog running around with a human skull with something sticking out of its mouth. Quite a slice of paradise you got here. It's beginning to sound like Jurassic Park."

Beaucharp said, "Sure is."

Stein went on. "A culture shock moving here from New England, Beaucharp?"

Beaucharp replied, "Oh yeah. It's like tiptoeing through the tulips for Fontaine, though. I think there may be something in the water."

Fontaine said, "You guys are a couple of slickers. It's good I'm here because I think both of you are liable to panic at the sound of the bullfrogs farting in the middle of the night."

Beaucharp laughed. "Good Lord! Was that what that noise was?"

"Okay. We're on US 301 North," Stein said.

Fontaine pointed. "Keep going straight, and we'll see them. I'm still trying to picture a dog playing with a human skull."

"Shoot!" Beaucharp yelled. "You got forensic gloves in here, Wanda?"

"You'll find a box in the console between us."

Fontaine fetched a pair for each, stuffed three extra sets into her breast pockets, turned to Beaucharp and said, "Just in case."

"Someone's gotta handle the skull," Beaucharp said.

Fontaine asked, "Where are your evidence bags, Wanda?"

Stein pointed with her thumb over her shoulder. "In the trunk."

They drove ten minutes and spotted the blue lights of the unmarked cruiser, protected by an area coned off and an orange Men Working sign. The detectives were on their phones, standing at the rear of the vehicle.

Later, the report said they flagged down a passing Florida Highway Department maintenance truck and commandeered several traffic cones and two orange 'men working' signs.

Stein flipped on her blue lights and squeezed between the cones pulling up behind the detectives. "I'm going to leave the vehicle running to keep the air on."

Fontaine, noticing Labbe in the back seat, turned to Michaela. "Looks like your boyfriend's here."

"Damn! He's going to be angry seeing me. You got any disguises in the trunk, Wanda?"

Stein said, "Just the standard US Government issue of eyeglasses with a big nose, Groucho Marx-type eyebrows, and mustache."

Beaucharp said, "I'll take my chances."

Fontaine waited for the last car door to close with a thump, then said, "What's up, Angel?"

"You met my partner, David Dione?" He pointed to the man leaning against the car in the New York Mets tee shirt. A badge dangled from a lanyard draped around his neck.

"Yes, we all met yesterday," Fontaine said.

After everyone shook hands, Beaucharp said, "You got a dog running loose here?"

"You didn't get the latest piece of news?" Dione asked.

Stein said, "You're kidding! There's more?" She rolled her eyes. "How much crazier can it get?"

Suddenly, from the squad car came a loud stomping and pounding against the door. It was Labbe carrying on in the back seat.

"Excuse me," Rodriquez said, then walked to the side of the car and exchanged words with Labbe. Labbe then turned his head to face them through the rear window and smiled. Rodriquez returned.

"What's going on?" Fontaine asked.

"Labbe saw his favorite detective," He pointed to Beaucharp, "and wanted to share a few words with me."

Stein asked, "How'd you quiet him down?"

"I told him that the ADA might believe his story about the use of excessive force during his arrest and sent Beaucharp out to apologize."

Beaucharp looked at Labbe. "What did he say to that?"

"He's still upset with his arrest yesterday, and how you treated him during the interrogation. He uttered a few adjectives in upper and lower case. The bottom line, he isn't accepting your apology, and, using his own words, 'You're going to have to live with the problem you created'."

Beaucharp spun around so as not to let Labbe see her laugh. Then Labbe, like an angry dog seeing its tormentor, began thrashing again.

Starting toward the vehicle, Dione suddenly stopped and looked back over his shoulder. "I'll talk to him." He stopped next to Labbe and said something. Labbe turned around toward the detectives and smiled again. Dione shook his head, then walked back to the detectives.

Stein asked, "What now?"

Dione said, "He's pissed now because he thought Beachamp was laughing at him. I said he upset her, and she turned away because she didn't want him to see her cry."

A smiling Labbe stared back through the rear window.

"I can't believe someone could be so stupid," Fontaine said.

"It gets better." Dione grinned, then turned to stare into an open field. "He wants us to tell the detective that he's not a fool. He's been in four prisons and in lots of jails in three states. He knows the law and, again, using his own words, 'I've got her on this one'."

Now impatient, Stein said, "Okay! Let's get on with it. What's all this about a dog playing with a skull?"

Dione said, "There's more than a skull out here. About sixty feet in front of the car is what's left of a human corpse. We called it in and are waiting for forensic."

While Dione spoke, sirens sounded in the distance. "Is that them?" Stein asked.

"I think so. We called just minutes before you arrived," said Rodriquez.

Dione resumed the narrative. Labbe couldn't remember the exact spot. We found it when we came across a bunch of vultures and flies. It stunk like putrid meat left out in the sun. So, we left Labbe in the car and walked up to see what was happening. He hasn't seen what's in the culvert yet, and we called for someone to take him back to County."

"Where's the dog?" Fontaine asked.

and he ran up to her feet and sat, still clutching the ball. Fontaine bent down and scooped him up.

He folded into her arms as if he had known her his whole life.

"He won't drop that ball, will he?" Stein said.

"Why? You want it back?" Fontaine kidded.

Beaucharp said, "He'd better hold on to it. If he drops it, he's apt to lick your face."

Suddenly, Fontaine shot off, running toward the car. "Oh, shit, he stinks! Unlock the doors, Wanda."

Stein clicked the unlock door button on her spare key fob and yelled, "It's open now! Sure you want him inside?"

Stein grinned. Beaucharp shook her head and yelled, "Meet you at the forensic tent."

Chapter 32

With the puppy safely inside the SUV, Fontaine rushed to join her partners. By the time she arrived, orange blower hoses were pointing into the culvert, and Beaucharp and Stein wore a new set of forensic gloves. Beaucharp held open the forensic bag with their old, discarded gloves and the skull, and Fontaine peeled hers off and tossed them in. Stein held a new pair out for Fontaine. "The Forensic folks gave us these."

Fontaine examined the ditch cautiously, wrinkled her face, and immediately put on the new set of gloves.

Beaucharp pointed at the equipment. "The place was full of flies, maggots, and various crawling insects. After the photo people finished, they had to ventilate for the stench and blow some insects away."

The corpse lay in a storm culvert about six feet deep and almost twice as wide, its slanted sides overgrown with weeds and stubble. The bottom had been flattened like someone had used it for a temporary home. An assortment of food wrappers, beer cans, various clothing pieces, fire ashes, and the remnants of a tattered suitcase with wheels and a handle were scattered about.

Tipping her head toward the Forensic people, Stein said, "They think animals tore everything apart."

Amid the trash and rags were pieces of internal organs that appeared to have been viciously torn out. Beaucharp would write in her notes that the scene: *. . . had the characteristics of a deer killed and mutilated by wolves or coyotes that had been scared off before they could finish . . . unmistakable portions of the human rib cage, part of a pelvis, and one arm . . . a leg had been torn from the torso, gnawed severely, and dragged about thirty feet away. The pit stunk like a dead animal left to decay, bloat, and explode in the Florida* *heat. Blood that insects or wild animals hadn't sopped up gelled and stuck to the ground and the surrounding grass on the edges.*

They watched the Forensic teams move clumsily in their white hazmat suits, trying, methodically, to separate pieces of body parts and place each one into its own evidence bag. Previously, each piece of material, bone fragment, skeletal section, and organ had a numbered tag placed next to it, then photographed from several angles. They were gathering the pieces and putting them into bags with a photo number affixed. The process, meticulously done in case a crime scene image had to be replicated in a forensic lab.

Dione approached and signaled them to follow him to the cars. Beaucharp handed the bag with the skull and used gloves to a forensic team member. Then, walking away, she stopped and turned. "Let's hope this is all part of the same person." A head in the white hazmat suit nodded.

Beaucharp caught up with the others in time to hear Dione say, "The Forensic people brought us a cooler with cold water."

The detectives quietly followed Dione, each trying to wrap their minds around what could make sense of the horrifying scene. Dione's car, parked in front of Stein's, blocked the view of the FBI SUV. When they reached it, Fontaine remembered the puppy and shouted. "Oh shit! What about the dog?"

Rodriguez stepped from behind the SUV with the puppy on a makeshift leash. "You forgot to lock the car, so we took him out and gave him some water. He's a cute little guy but stinks badly. What you going to do with him?"

"Gonna hand him over to Animal Control if they ever show up," said Beaucharp.

"Wait a minute," Fontaine said. "He's my dog."

"You gonna keep him?" Stein asked.

"Might!"

Rodriquez said, "It's a smart one. I think he's a blue tick, and they're pretty gentle."

Fontaine looked at Stein, then at Beaucharp. "I'm serious. I might keep him. Growing up, we always had a dog in the house."

"You're working a bunch of crazy hours, Donna. You can't leave him home alone all day," said Beaucharp.

"Give him to your dad, Donna," Rodriguez said.

"You know my dad?"

"He was my little league coach. Now he's my nephew's coach."

"Did you grow up in Tampa, Angel?" Beaucharp asked.

"Yes, and I still have family in Pinellas and Hillsborough County. Puerto Ricans are big on family things so we go to every first communion, confirmation, and wedding. That also includes sporting events whenever family member's children participate. Colleen and I go to dance recitals and athletic events at least twice a month."

"My dad is retired now," Fontaine said. "But he loved coaching little league."

Rodriquez said, "John, uh. . . Captain Fontaine was one of my references for the Belenton PD. When he found out I wanted to become a cop, he told me to use his name as a character reference on my application. Shall I call and see if he wants a dog?"

Fontaine said, "I'll talk to him, Angel. I think you're onto something, though."

Beaucharp grabbed three bottles of water from Dione's car and passed one to Stein and Fontaine, and said, "We gotta stay hydrated."

"So, where's Labbe?" Fontaine asked after taking a long, deep swallow.

Dione grinned. "Once you three went after the dog, we took him for a stroll to the storm culvert and asked him if this is where Rosa was camping when—"

Rodriquez interrupted. "He saw the mess in the ditch and came undone. I've never seen anyone fall apart that fast. He swore he didn't do it. He collapsed to his knees and started crying and praying to Jesus. We had to take him back to the car and call for a pick-up. He's now in a suite at the County Hilton."

Dione said, "Wilson showed up. What is it with that guy? He sounded like he wanted Labbe to take a bath before he would let him in the car."

Beaucharp and Fontaine started laughing. Rodriquez and Dione looked puzzled, then Stein said, "Wilson is terrified of these two. They have been sticking him with lousy cab fares for a couple of days now."

Rodriquez and Dione grinned. They knew of Wilson and read between the lines.

"So, you guys are with Narcotics and Vice," said Fontaine.

Dione answered. "That's the title. Mostly narcotics, though. A lot of the stuff we do is working with the feds. Agent Stein knows what we're talking about."

Stein nodded. "So, they'll be taking you off the case now."

"Yes," Rodriquez said. "It wasn't our case. Labbe knew us from other busts and thought he could use us to work out a deal."

Dione said, "We'll probably have to testify in court on some of this and sit through a few depositions."

Rodriquez turned to Dione. "As a matter of fact, we have to check with the Forensic people right now. If they don't need us anymore, we'll call in and get out of here.

So, who gets the stinky dog? Keep the leash."

Fontaine said, "We'll take him for now. I'm going to call my dad. That was a good idea."

Beaucharp turned to Dione and said, "I'll walk over with you and see if they need us here." She turned and crouched as if taking a catcher's position behind home plate, faced the puppy, and said, "Stinky, you're in charge till I get back."

Fontaine looked at Stein. "If we can get out of here, we'll bring him to the Palmetto shelter. It's just up the road, and they'll take care of him until I get things straightened out."

Stein said, "Good idea. They'll bathe and brush him out."

Beaucharp returned right away. "We got cleared to leave, but they want copies of our reports. Just the portions that pertain to what we did here."

Stein and Fontaine looked at each other, and Fontaine said, "Man, you can tell it's a special one. Everyone wants a good paper trail."

Beaucharp said, "Let's be thankful that we're just the grunts."

Rodriquez and Dione shook hands, thanked them, and left.

Stein turned to her partners and said, "Okay, let's saddle up, guys. We got to take Cujo to the shelter and head over to the Washbee place. I can't even imagine what I'll find there."

Chapter 33

Beaucharp rode shotgun this time, while Fontaine sat in the rear seat with her new friend and the windows open. Stein pointed to her radio. "Michaela, tune us into your call center, please. We'll use it to log out of here."

Beaucharp said, "I'll use my phone. It might be easier." She hit the speed dial and after three rings the dispatch picked it up.

"Mona, it's me," Beaucharp said. "We're leaving US 301 Ellenton, enroute to Palmetto animal shelter, then Washbee Funeral Home."

"Still, with Stein and Fontaine?"

"Yes. Any messages, Mona?"

"Nope. How'd you make out with the dog?"

"Things went well. Fontaine's got a new boyfriend now."

Mona smiled and said, "We'll stay in touch." She then hung up.

Almost immediately, they saw the sign for the Palmetto Animal Shelter. Stein followed the arrows into a horseshoe crushed-shell driveway. "You people ever hear of asphalt here?" she said.

Fontaine said, "Pull up to the front door, Wanda."

A lady shot out the door as soon as the car stopped. "That space is for emergency drop-off," she shouted.

Fontaine jumped out with the dog. "It's okay, Mira. I want to drop someone off for a little while."

The woman smiled. "Oh! It's you, Donna. What-cha got there, honey?"

"I want to leave this guy here for a while. We don't have any time for paperwork. Can you take care of him for me?"

"Of course. What's his name?"

"Ain't got one right now. I'm gonna give him to my dad. Can you give him a bath and get him shined up? I'll swing by later to talk. Will that be okay?"

"Sure. We'll take good care of him." Mira waved to Beaucharp and Stein and took the leash from Fontaine.

The puppy, tail wagging uncontrollably, raced ahead of Mira through the door, acting more like a traveling adventurer than an orphan.

Beaucharp said, "Look how happy he is. Where does he think he's going?"

Stein said, "He's smarter than we think. The little bozo landed on the lap of luxury. Once he leaves here, he won't have to wrestle with cadaver pieces. He'll have only the best soup-bones money can buy."

"Dumping him off was pretty easy," Beaucharp said.

Fontaine stared out the window and grinned. "There were a few guys I would have liked to have unloaded that easily."

Beaucharp laughed. "Yeah! Dump them off at some Useless-Guy Door in an empty warehouse somewhere."

Stein nodded. "Yeah, but sometimes, just dropping them off isn't enough."

"I know what you mean, Wanda," Fontaine said. "It would also be nice if we could ask for our money back, damaged goods or something like that."

Beaucharp pointed. "When you get out of the driveway, turn left, and we'll be able to reach the funeral home much quicker than going back out on US 301."

Stein drove on and said, "What next? This is like Pee Wee's Great Adventure."

Fontaine tapped Stein's shoulder. "Pee Wee's from Sarasota, and oh boy! Honey, you ain't seen nothing yet."

Chapter 34

In 10 minutes, they were driving onto the white, dusty Washbee Funeral Home and Crematorium parking lot. Stein stared at the Victorian building. "Look at this place! Is it for real? It looks like a movie set."

Fontaine said, "That's what Beauchy said the first time she saw it. It's the real deal."

"Wait till you get inside. It's like a combination museum and an affluent antique shop," said Beaucharp.

"I can't wait," Stein said and parked next to a massive live oak, hoping it would cast enough shade to allow the inside of the car to suffer less from the midday sun.

"I read your reports of the last meeting with Washbee. Should we have called in advance? These guys can get pretty busy, and I don't think we want to hang around." Stein stopped in the middle of a sentence. "You knew he would not be busy, and he's not a flight risk. Right?"

Fontaine said, "If you think this building is one-of-a-kind, wait until you meet Mr. Washbee."

Beaucharp patted Stein's shoulder. "And it's not a run-of-the-mill funeral home, either."

While gathering her thoughts, Stein placed both hands together in front of her face as if she were getting ready to pray. She then spread them apart like she was bragging about the size of a fish. "Nothing that happens from here on in will surprise me. If you say he is green with two heads, I'll believe it. I won't be surprised if he walks sideways like a crab."

Fontaine and Beaucharp looked at each other.

Beaucharp said, "Oh, my gosh! Wanda, Mr. Washbee has ambulatory issues. He drags one leg."

"Jeeze! I'm sorry. No way I was trying to poke fun at anyone. I didn't know, honestly."

Fontaine said, "Of course, you didn't know, and we're not worried about your motives. He also has some facial issues. He's missing an eyebrow. We're bringing these things up now, so you won't be as shocked as we were."

"Wanda," Beaucharp stared into Stein's face. "The guy's a darling of a man. One of a kind, you're going to like him."

Stein pulled the keys out of the ignition. "Well, you two got honest faces. I'm going to take your word on this."

As they walked toward the building, white puffs of shell dust lifted and fell against their boots and pants cuffs. Fontaine looked down at her feet, shook her head and said, "It's as dry as a popcorn fart out here!"

Stein shook her head. "Where the hell do you guys get this stuff? Popcorn fart?"

Beaucharp said, "Around here, everyone acts like my partner. I really mean it when I say there may be something in the water."

When they reached the front steps, Fontaine stopped and turned to Stein. "Just watch out for the cat."

Stein looked at Beaucharp, questioning with her raised eyebrows.

Beaucharp shook her head and smiled. "The old cat is lovable beyond words."

"Yeah? Beelzebub, if you ask me," said Fontaine.

Stein started up the steps first, stopped at the landing, and turned to the detectives. "I never know what's going to happen with you two. When I ring the doorbell, will it sound like a lady screaming in a 1930s horror movie?"

Stein's illusion went unrequited. She started for the bell, and suddenly the door swung open. A surprising gust of cold air tore into her face. Impulsively, her classical mind summoned up a poetic quirk. *Escaping cold air, kamikaze-like attacking the heat!*

Washbee, standing on the other side of the threshold smiling, welcomed them. Once inside, he said, "Oh, it is so nice to see you two again, and you brought a friend along. How nice, another police officer?"

Stein said, "It's hard to understand what something like that could be like. There were no economic cushions for families. Can you imagine the fears parents had to contend with? How courageous were the people like Olney to journey out into the world on their own, some barely teenagers?"

"Indeed," Washbee said. "He roamed the United States as a hobo traveling in boxcars, finding work on CCC jobs, in migrant farm camps in California, and on cattle ranches in Montana and Wyoming. World War II broke out and, being only four-foot-eleven inches tall, he couldn't pass the height requirements for military service. He returned to Florida and worked in the Tampa shipyard building Liberty Ships. After the war, he worked at various horse farms in Ocala and some horse racing tracks."

"Horses? Why horses?" Beaucharp asked.

Washbee said, "The way Olney tells it is that on one ranch he worked at, the owner noticed he had a gift, a natural acumen for working with horses. So, he mentored and nurtured Olney, hoping he'd develop the skills further, perhaps even becoming a professional jockey. But unfortunately, I think the war ended all that for him."

Washbee took a sip of tea and placed the cup on the edge of his plate. "Olney had tremendous skill with horses. Some believe he was an actual Horse Whisperer."

"Did he ever marry?" Fontaine asked.

Washbee smiled and touched Fontaine's wrist. "No. He loved everyone and advocated for issues pertaining to social justice and human dignity. Maybe that part of him grew out of what he learned in his travels. He respected other people's ideas and feelings and was open to them, even when they differed from his own. And, yes, he loved horses and his Boston Terriers."

"Boston Terriers?" said Beaucharp.

"Yes. Olney always had a Boston Terrier at his side. He also loved fishing and sharing from his garden."

Washbee took another small bite, chewed slowly, swallowed, and turned toward the blue urn. "He was especially proud of his tomatoes. He grew so many he would fill bins in a vegetable stand alongside US 301. Folks could take what they wanted for free. Some folks left change in a wooden box."

Stein slowly looked around the empty room, then at the simple blue urn. "I'm happy that I came today. Some people's lives just end. I've never met him, and I don't know if I am saying it correctly, but I feel people like Olney *complete* their lives."

Fontaine said, "I think I know what Wanda's saying. To people like Olney, life is the festival they share with others. Regardless of his tiny frame, Olney's character made him stand way above many others."

Beaucharp touched Washbee's elbow. "Everyone's existence is special, but not everyone is lucky enough to have made a difference before moving on. Olney must have impacted the lives of many people."

Washbee lowered his head and, as if exhibiting fatherly pride, reached across and gently touched Beaucharp's wrist, nodded, and said nothing.

They continued eating in silence. No one wanted to spoil the special moments that had grown out of Olney's story.

They finished and sat with empty dishes on their lap until Beaucharp collected the plates, cups, and napkins. Then Washbee directed her to a large plastic trash bin in a hallway closet. While Beaucharp performed the housecleaning, Fontaine pondered their next step. *How we going to transition into the interrogation ?*

Just as the last plate disappeared into the bin, four elderly women shuffled past Beaucharp and into the room.

Chapter 35

Two women walked with canes, and one leaned on an aluminum walker. Once in the room, they appeared confused, as if they had intruded into the wrong wake service.

Then the Aluminum Walker noticed Washbee waving them on. "You're at the right place, Etta. Please, come in."

Then Fontaine approached and said, "Thank you for coming. Mr. Washbee was just telling us about Olney."

Still mildly confused, Aluminum Walker looked at Washbee. "Cyrus, what's going on?"

"It's for real, Etta. They're visitors. Please come in."

Beaucharp moved the chairs back into rows and turned toward the women. "Mr. Washbee said Olney had a lot of wonderful friends."

Washbee struggled to his feet, walked over, and reached for Etta's hand. "I'm glad you all could make it." Then, turning to the three investigators, he said, "These are friends of mine who just stopped by." Touching Beaucharp on the elbow, he said, "This is Ms. Beaucharp," then looking at Fontaine, "This is Ms. Fontaine. They're Belenton Police Detectives." He then pointed to Stein. "That is Special Agent Stein. She's with the FBI."

Etta's eyebrows went up in surprise. "Oh my! Did Olney do something wrong?"

A murmur buzzed through the other three sisters.

Beaucharp said, "Oh no. We just stopped by to see Mr. Washbee. He told us about Olney, so we decided to visit for a while. And call me Michaela."

"Oh! I'm sorry," Washbee said, speaking to the detectives and Stein. "Let me introduce you." Shuffling next to the four women, Washbee started with the tallest lady using the walker. "This is Etta Casey. She's the bossy one." He pointed to another with a large blue ribbon, tied in a bow and attached to her hair like Daisy Duck. "This Gertrude Johnson."

"Call me, Gertie!" she interrupted, and smiling warmly, put a hand out to shake.

Washbee continued, "I'm sorry. Of course, Gertie."

Gertie smiled at Fontaine, tilted her head toward Washbee, and winked as he kept talking.

"Next to her is Bertha St. John, then Edith Story. They're all sisters."

Aside from the difference in the height of Etta, the four were unmistakable sisters. All wore wire-rimmed glasses, shared the same icy-blue eyes, and had small button noses that pointed up slightly. While Gertie had a large bow in her hair and Bertha wore a lime-green shawl draped over a shoulder, Edith, like Etta, were without extra accessories.

Three of the women stared at Etta, the apparent leader. Etta turned her head toward the urn, gathered some thoughts, then turned back toward her sisters, each with a grim face. Etta then rolled her eyes and nodded her head toward Fontaine and smiled. Two of the sisters seemed to understand the signal and nodded back.

Etta reached out and touched Fontaine's wrist. "Honey, where did all those beautiful freckles come from?"

Fontaine blushed. Beaucharp laughed and softly tapped her partner on the arm with a slow-moving fist. "Her mom's a 'Harp' from Londonderry."

Stein and Washbee chuckled, and Fontaine shook her head and pointed at Beaucharp. "Oh, good Lord! What am I going to do with her? Please call me Donna."

Once getting the humor, the sisters chuckled along with Stein and Washbee. In the meantime, Gertie got Etta's attention and also nodded toward Fontaine. Etta smiled back.

Fontaine said, "Yes. My mom's Irish, her family name is 'Billings' and my dad's family is French Canadian. Hence the name Fontaine—"

Beaucharp interrupted. "One story is that the Billings family was so notorious for being horse thieves in Ireland that they got a whole town named after them in Montana."

Gertie and Bertha laughed out loud and moved to either side of her. Then Gertie looped her arm around one of Fontaine's and said, "That's okay. We'll keep you."

"Keep me? Am I being Shanghaied?"

Bertha winked, "You are."

Etta looked at Washbee and grinned. "So, Cyrus, tell us why you got the cops here at Olney Hazelton's wake?"

Bertha stared at Stein and winked. "And the FBI?"

Stein smiled. "Yes, ma'am. We're working on a case together and have to discuss some matters with Mr. Washbee. Please call me Wanda."

Edith then asked if it had anything to do with the rigmarole taking place up the street. Stein assumed she was referring to the forensic tent on US 301.

Fontaine interrupted with a lie. "We're not sure. We were just there and, being close by, stopped to see Mr. Washbee."

"Then Mr. Washbee told us about Olney, so we spent some time with him," said Beaucharp.

Edith smiled and pointed to the luncheon table. "Looks like you had a few nibbles."

Washbee smiled. "You might say that I invited them to lunch."

Gertie winked at Fontaine. "Three cheap dates, Cyrus?"

Washbee placed his hand on Etta's as she clutched the top rail of her walker. "You'll have to excuse us. We were getting ready for a meeting just as you showed up. I'll be back later. Others may come along but enjoy your time with Olney and have some lunch. Remember, you got to take some food back home."

The detectives shook hands and then took turns at Olney's urn. Beaucharp and Fontaine stood in front of the vessel, side by side. Beaucharp made the sign of the cross, and Fontaine solemnly bowed her head.

They then turned and left. Stein approached, whispered something unintelligible, kissed the tips of her fingers, and gently touched the urn. She turned and held a hand up, gesturing a wave, and walked out to join her partners.

After waiting for everyone to leave, Etta gathered her sisters into a whispering parley. They agreed it had to be Fontaine and assigned Bertha to separate her from the others. Bertha would make her aware of a situation with Cyrus's niece, Hattie.

Chapter 36

Washbee waited in the hall for the detectives. He whispered, "We'll need a room larger than my office. Follow me."

They trekked behind Washbee. In her notes, Stein would later write: *We followed slowly, like ducklings, while along the walls, faces from the nineteenth century gazed out at us. Most were photos of men in various military uniforms sharing the walls with several twentieth-century Florida and national political figures.*

Stein recognized President Jimmy Carter, Bobby Kennedy, former governors Reubin Askew, and Lawton Chiles. She stopped at an old gray photograph. Behind the glass, and inside the frame on a faded piece of aged and faded yellow paper, was scribbling that looked like a handwritten poem. She stopped Washbee. "Is that Sydney Lanier's picture? There's a note stuffed inside the picture frame. It looks like he addressed to a Washbee."

"You have a good eye, Wanda. The poet was a friend and house guest of my family on numerous occasions."

"Is he related?" Beaucharp asked.

"No. But my family roots go all the way back to Colonial Georgia." He chuckled. "As you can see from the many photos, a grateful nation assured each generation could have a war to attend." He grinned. "Believe it or not, we've always been pacifists!"

"How about Lawton Chiles and Jimmy Carter?" Fontaine asked.

Washbee said, "They're family friends who visited while campaigning in the area. Chiles is from Lakeland and his son owns a restaurant on Anna Maria Island."

Beaucharp said, "The last time I was here, Mr. Washbee gave me a small tour while Donna played with Manfred in the bathroom. Somewhere else in this place are photos of Ted Kennedy and Jimmy Carter's Attorney General, Griffin Bell."

"We're in the presence of quite a celebrity. Ain't we, Mr. Washbee?" Fontaine joked and lightly punched Washbee's arm.

Manfred rushed to catch up and brushed his noisy face against Fontaine's leg. "Oh! There you are!" she said. "You here to trip me? Steal my wallet, maybe?"

Stein picked up Manfred, bringing him close to her face and, in baby talk, uttering, "Poor wittle boy. Is dat mean wady pickin' on you?"

Washbee smiled with his lips only. His compressed eyebrow spoke of a nervousness as he ushered them to a spacious, impeccably clean kitchen with up-to-date appliances.

Pointing to a white oak dining table capable of seating ten comfortably, he said, "Would someone like more snacks or something to drink? We got plenty of tea and lemonade. I can make some coffee."

The women shook their heads, no. Each kept an empty seat beside them. Washbee, beside Beaucharp, Fontaine, and Stein, faced them from across the table. Stein placed Manfred on the chair between her and Fontaine. The unsnapping of fasteners, and noisy searching through the leather bags for notepads and utensils competed with Manfred's loud purring.

Confident that everyone was ready, Beaucharp said, "You want to begin, Mr. Washbee?"

He spoke for fifteen minutes, uninterrupted, trying to describe pertinent incidents of the past three days. He explained again how the table scraps were gathered and delivered to Mr. Giovanelli's pig farm. Then in his undertaker's monotone he startled the investigators. "Beauregard was trying to deliver the scraps without knowing Ida Foote's leg was in the bag. It was placed there by mistake."

Beaucharp moved uneasily in her seat. "Wait a minute, Mr. Washbee. You know about the leg?"

"Yes, I'll explain that in a minute."

"What about the rest of the stuff in the sack?" Fontaine asked.

Washbee looked puzzled. "Food scraps?"

The detectives now realized Washbee knew nothing about the pieces of Rosa found in Wally Gaslight's truck. They were only unearthing a piece of a bad dream.

Beaucharp's attention was, again, drawn back to Washbee.

"I am worried that my nephews and niece might be in serious trouble." Washbee's eyes, a storm of worry, watered, and his voice trembled. Again, he dropped his face into his hands and rocked his head from side to side. "This is all my fault. They struggled and worked so hard. I have overburdened them. I've gone too far, assuming responsibilities way past their capabilities. I should be ashamed of myself."

Fontaine, speaking in almost a whisper, said, "Nobody move. I'm going to get us some cookies."

Stein said, "Yeah, we should take a few minutes here." She looked at Washbee. "That okay with you?" Washbee nodded and said, "Yes."

Beaucharp sensed something awry with her partner. Fontaine recognized Beaucharp's concern and pointed an index finger into the air signaling *I'll be right back*, pushed away from the table and left

Chapter 38

Once out into the hall Fontaine focused on her thoughts. What a nightmare this turned out to be! She took a deep breath, rushed into a bathroom, and splashed water on her face and stared into the mirror. *Get control right now! We gotta make this work.*

From her chair in the chapel, Etta spotted Fontaine searching for the restroom. Pointing her thumb toward the hallway, she signaled and mouthed to another woman, "Go after her." The woman nodded, then slipped away to wait at the bathroom door.

After regaining composure and drying her face, she slowly turned and opened the door. A gray-haired woman Fontaine hadn't met earlier waited on the other side. She was taller than the sisters by a couple of inches and had a soft, smooth face like a porcelain doll.

"Are you okay, dear?" she asked.

"Oh yeah," Fontaine lied, "it's been a busy two days, and I'm getting a migraine."

"I have some aspirin in my purse, honey," the woman said.

"Thank you. I'm okay for now. I just came to snatch up some of Olney's cookies. Are there any left?"

"There is. Better hurry. Etta's about ready to scoop them up to bring back to the community."

Unsure about the four sister's choice, the woman wanted to scrutinize Fontaine for herself. She approached cautiously and stared into the detective's face. *Look at all those pretty freckles. Can we trust her? Etta thinks so. There isn't any time. We gotta take the chance.* Nervous, she blurted out, "Me and Gertie want to speak to you about Hattie. We're worried about her."

Surprised, Fontaine squinted her eyebrows together and said, "Hattie? The niece?"

"Yes."

"Not sure I understand. What's going on with Hattie?" Then Fontaine's face reddened, uncomfortable with being caught off balance. She quickly said, "I'm sorry. Have we met?"

"Oh, I'm sorry, I'm Rachel Freeman." The lady shot her hand out. Fontaine smiled, and her long fingers wrapped around the warm, bony hand.

"I'm here with my husband to say goodbye to Olney. Are you one of the female police officers?"

Female Police Officers! She's an oldie! "Yes. I'm Detective Donna Fontaine, with Belenton, PD."

"Can we talk with you?"

"Mrs. Freeman—"

"Call me Rachel."

"Can it wait until we finish the meeting with Mr. Washbee? It won't be that long."

"Of course. If you want to stand by for a few minutes, I'll run back and get you a half dozen cookies."

"Mrs. Free-, I'm sorry, Rachel, I'm on my way in there now. I'll grab four. That'll be plenty."

"Are you sure?"

"I'm sure. My partner's starting to widen out; you know what I mean? I don't want to encourage her. It's all I can do to tote her around now. Is Etta still in the chapel?"

"Yes." Mrs. Freeman pointed to the bathroom. "I gotta get in there. We will meet up later?"

Fontaine pointed toward the chapel. "I'll look for you in there."

Mrs. Freeman smiled and threw her arms around Fontaine. "You're such a sweet girl. Your mother must be so proud of you." She released the embrace and walked through the bathroom door.

Fontaine smiled. *Girl! Someone is still calling us girls.*

In the chapel, Fontaine noticed three of the sisters gathered around a man she assumed was Mr. Freeman. Etta, seated alone, smiled, and waved her over.

Fontaine waved and raised an index finger, the universal signal for *wait a minute*, and started toward the gathering. Gertie rushed over quickly, snatched Fontaine by the arm, and dragged her into the group.

"This is Willy Freeman," Gertie said. "His wife just left for the ladies room."

Mr. Freeman reached out, and Fontaine shook his hand. "Donna Fontaine. Nice to meet you, sir. I just met Rachel in the hall. You're a lucky man, Mr. Freeman."

"Please, call me Willy," he said.

"I can't hang around right now, but I promised Rachel we'd all return in a little bit. I need to pick up some of these." She pointed at the cookies, grinned, and scooped up three chocolate chips and what looked like three macadamia nut and wrapped them in a napkin. "With any luck, I'll be able to put my partner into a sugar coma."

Everyone smiled.

Fontaine looked over her shoulder and noticed Etta waiting patiently. "Please excuse me. We can talk later, I promise, but right now, I gotta see to Etta for a minute."

Fontaine took the seat next to Etta. "How are you doing, Etta?"

Etta grinned, rocked her head back and forth slightly, and said, "Hanging in there. That's what the kids say these days."

Fontaine got to the point. "Etta, I just spoke with Mrs. Freeman. I promise we'll touch base with Hattie, but we have to know what's going on and why it concerns the police."

Etta's lower lip trembled, and her eyes widened and moistened. Fontaine recognized a troubled face typical of people frightened and near the end of hope. She placed her hand on top of Etta's. "Trust me. We'll do anything possible to help. But if Hattie is in some kind of trouble, we've got to know what it is."

Etta removed her glasses and dabbed her eyes and nose with a tattered, small section of tissue. Fontaine got up and fetched several large napkins from the buffet table. She placed them into Etta's hand. "Here, we usually use this type of fine Irish linen."

Etta smiled and, with one hand, brought a napkin up to her nose, the other snatched Fontaine's wrist. "There is something significant going on. We are all afraid for that girl right now. It may be hard for you to understand us not being relatives and all."

Fontaine, confused, squinted her eyebrows one more time.

Etta went on. "Do you know that Cyrus and his wife Rose rescued Hattie, Beauregard, and Winston from horrible conditions?"

Fontaine said, "I got a gist of something like that talking with Mr. Washbee."

Etta twisted in her chair and leaned forward with her hands on the aluminum walker. "They were living in poverty, struggling with mental illness, and heaven knows what kind of abuse they may have been subjected to. Yet, every one of them has become the most caring people one could ever imagine. Never does a holiday pass when all of them doesn't show up with cards and gifts."

"Why are you bringing this up?" Fontaine said. "Do you think we're here because of them?"

Etta motioned Fontaine closer. "Those kids are special. When Ida Foote was sick, one of them visited her every day."

The others noticed Etta weeping and started toward the detective. Fontaine held up a hand, signaling them to stop, and said, "We won't be much longer. Right now, I gotta get back to the meeting. In a few minutes, we'll all talk some more. I promise."

Fontaine patted the back of Etta's hand. "Be patient. It won't be long." Fontaine stood and started for the door.

"We'll be waiting right here," Etta said sternly.

Fontaine walked out and turned the corner just in time to hear Rachel's footsteps leaving the bathroom and approaching the chapel. She signaled Rachel to stop, then told her she would be back with her partners as soon as they finished meeting with Washbee.

Willy Freeman and the four sisters were still talking when Rachel returned.

She heard Bertha say, "We can trust them."

Willy looked around the room as if trying to find a secluded place to hide and think. The softness in his face faded into an empty stare. One hand allowed his chin to rest between his thumb and index finger. The other hand grasped the elbow.

Etta, watching, grinned inside. *It looks like Rodin's The Thinker.*

Chapter 39

Stein and Beaucharp filled the time while Fontaine was gone with questions about the kitchen appliances and meal preparations. Fontaine returned in time to hear Washbee finish the mournful saga of kitchen remodeling in an old home.

Beaucharp noticed Fontaine's wrinkled forehead and stoic stare, the face her partner exhibited when confronted with extreme concerns. "Everything okay, partner?" Beaucharp knew it wasn't.

"Doing good. Had to stop at the can, then I picked up some of these." She placed the folded napkin on the table.

Stein took a chocolate chip and noticed the same unease from Fontaine. She resumed the previous thread of their conversation before Fontaine left. "Cyrus, we don't see any malicious or unlawful acts trying to be covered up here."

Beaucharp added, "Mr. Washbee, we'll get this sorted out."

Fontaine pointed down the hall, trying to reassure Washbee's melancholy. "People in the chapel were just telling me what wonderful people your niece and nephews are. They say it's because you and your wife, Rosy, were exceptional parents and guardians."

Washbee removed his glasses to wipe the moisture from his eyes, then placed them back on, crookedly. "Oh, thank you. It is comforting to have you here. Rosy must have sent an angel to find all three of you."

Stein said, "The jury may still be out on these two." She pointed at Fontaine and Beaucharp. "I'm not sure how much they got in common with angels."

Washbee laughed and, again, had to remove his glasses to wipe his eyes. Manfred left Washbee, walked across the table, and nestled into Fontaine's lap. Fontaine, forgetting her previous days encounter in the bathroom, unconsciously caressed his fur. Manfred closed his eyes and resumed purring loudly.

Calmness settled back in Fontaine so Beaucharp tried to fracture what might have been left of the somberness. "Hey, let's eat these cookies. Unfortunately, my cheap-ass partner only brought six. Probably ate two on the way down the hall."

No one brought up Bunson Rosa's body parts. So far Washbee knew nothing about them. Good cop insight, along with training and experience, taught them that the less information floating around about a crime, the better the chances of tripping up perpetrators and making it less likely for investigators to end up chasing dead ends.

Suddenly, everyone stopped speaking and again the only sound in the room came from Manfred's drone and the psalms floating in from the hallway. Washbee, suspecting a problem, placed his cookie back onto a napkin and squinted nervously across the table at Stein.

It's so quiet! Did I say something wrong?" he asked.

Beaucharp answered, "No, Mr. Washbee, it's just that there is so much information. We have to take some time to process it."

Washbee bit his lower lip nervously. "Does it sound as if I'm fabricating things?"

Stein shot back. "Of course not. There are lots of moving pieces here, Cyrus."

Fontaine said, "You see, Mr. Washbee, these two have to work hard at processing things. If the truth is to be told, I'm here to help them think through difficult things. You'll notice that I didn't allow either of them to chew gum while this meeting was taking place."

Washbee smiled, once more deciding to trust his new acquaintances.

"We believe you're telling the truth, Mr. Washbee," Beaucharp continued. "You've provided some ample reasons for what's going on."

Stein said, "We'd like to speak to Winston and Hattie."

Of course, said Washbee. "How about later this afternoon?"

"That works," said Fontaine.

Washbee said, "If we're done here, I need to take a few minutes to do some administrative stuff. Can you tell everybody in the chapel I'll be there shortly?"

"Of course," said Beaucharp.

Fontaine said, "We all gotta get back to the chapel to say goodbye."

Beaucharp recognized Fontaine's tone and assumed something important awaited them in the chapel.

being off. You know, with Olney's passing and everything. Something men don't always understand."

Fontaine nodded. "Please go on."

"At first, I thought it was just me, but Etta, Edith, and Bertha agreed. We mentioned it to the Freemans, and they think something is off with her as well."

Fontaine looked down at the floor, searching for the right words. "We gotta talk to her later. I'll fish around some. But you think, whatever it is, it's serious enough for the police to know?"

"Well, probably not by just *any* police."

Fontaine's cheeks reddened again. "Gertie, I hope we can live up to the trust that you all are putting in us."

Gertie pulled another tissue out and handed it to Fontaine. "We've been around a long time." She winked at Fontaine. "Some of us have been downtown a few times, if you know what I mean."

Fontaine smiled slightly and shook her head. *Crazy old people!*

"We didn't just get dropped off by a turnip truck, and if there is anything that we do well, it is to pick out peoples' character. You three hit the character-meter out of the park."

Fontaine tilted her head and raised her eyebrows to leave no doubt it was a questionable look. She said, "What are you using to judge our character?"

Gertie shifted in her chair and said, "You're here now, aren't you? All of you are here. This has nothing to do with your work, and you're busy but still taking the time to sit with us."

Fontaine started to speak again but Gertie raised her hand to stop her. "Don't you think we saw how respectful you three were with Olney's urn?"

Fontaine took a deep breath, released it, and looked deeply into Gertie's eyes. Then, with her cop hat back on, she asked, "Wouldn't Mr. Washbee want to know if something was going on with his niece?"

Gertie looked down at her hands. Then, without lifting her head said, "Did you talk about things with your parents all the time? There is stuff you can only talk about with friends when you're young. She has never had problems discussing things with any of us. Now, suddenly, she is quiet and stand-offish. It ain't right."

Fontaine didn't take out her notepad. "Talk to me. What's her behavior been like before? Do you notice a drastic change in her personality?"

Gertie's eyes widened. "Yes! That's it! Everything about her has changed. It changed suddenly, and just in the past three days."

Gertie then commenced with a long narrative. Fontaine listened intently, and not far into the story, she feared that she recognized what had happened to Hattie.

Gertie finished talking, and Fontaine lifted her hands into her own. "I promise you. We'll examine everything we can to find out what's causing Hattie's behavior change."

Fontaine remained stoic throughout the conversation but knew something had to get done as soon as possible.

Chapter 41

S tein raised her eyebrows and tilted her head toward the stranger sitting alone.

"It's okay," Beaucharp whispered. "That's Mr. Gaslight. In a minute, I'll introduce you."

Stein then pointed at Fontaine huddled close to Gertie, each paying attention to the other. "What's going on with Donna? It's so somber over there, it looks like she and Gertie are planning another funeral."

Rachel appeared and abruptly took Stein's elbow commandingly. "Edith and I have to speak with you. It's important so let's find an empty chapel." She looked at Beaucharp. "Etta and Bertha want to talk with you."

Bertha approached Beaucharp and said, "We should do it now."

Stein looked at Rachel. "What about Willy? Shouldn't he be part of this too?

Rachel shook her head. "This is a girl thing."

Willy said, "She's right," alluding to Gaslight sitting alone. "I'm going to visit with Wally. He and Olney were friends, and I've never seen him this despondent."

Etta and Bertha led Beaucharp outside to a small tea table at the far corner of the massive oak porch. Upset by the intrusion, squadrons of scrub jays and black grackles pecking at the manicured lawn, suddenly rushed at the porch screeching in protest. But unfortunately, the racket's only value was in drowning out the whispers of the honeybees drifting amid the flower beds and rose trellises nestled against the porch railings.

Bertha took one of Beaucharp's hands into both of hers. "Something's wrong with Hattie."

"Something bad happened to her." Etta interrupted. "And it's significant. We can feel it."

Still angry at the uninvited guest for annexing a space considered their own, several brave grackles edged closer, scratching at the ground like defiant soldiers. Then, several yards behind, a chorus shouted with bursts of high-pitched screeches.

Etta, angry, stood and waved her arms. "Shoo! I've got a good mind to open the door and let the cat out."

Bertha said, "Sit down, Etta. They'll settle in a bit."

Beaucharp said, "I'm okay with them. But, if they become too bothersome, I've got a gun."

A stunned Etta and Bertha looked at each other, then back at Beaucharp. The first to realize it was a joke, Etta grinned and slapped Beaucharp's arm softly. "If it gets that bad, I can handle it." She pointed at Bertha. "But don't ever give a firearm to her."

All three grinned, then Beaucharp asked, "What's happened to Hattie that is so urgent that the police have to know about it?"

Bertha said, "That's it, Michaela. We feel that whatever happened is serious enough for a proper investigation."

"What the —" Beaucharp stopped herself before she let the word go. "Is she involved with drugs? Automobile accident?"

Etta raised her hand to silence Bertha just as she was about to speak. "Look, we don't know, and that's the problem. Hattie isn't capable of doing any of the things you just mentioned."

Bertha nodded.

Etta slid closer to Beaucharp. "She is a changed person, and it's happened within the last couple of days."

Beaucharp lifted one eyebrow higher than the other. "How do you mean?"

Bertha replied. "This may sound crazy, but she won't let us hug her."

Etta turned away and brought a tissue to her nose. "She was a huggy person before—"

Bertha interrupted. "Hattie would always greet us with a hug."

Etta nodded. "Now, she shrinks away as if she is afraid to be touched. There's something wrong. That's just not her," Bertha sternly added.

Beaucharp glanced down at the hand in Bertha's grip. "Tell me more."

Bertha noticed her fingers, now tightly wrapped around Beaucharp's. Embarrassed, she let go and said, "Oh! I'm sorry. I forgot myself. Am I hurting you?"

Beaucharp smiled and clasped Bertha's hand. "That's okay. You weren't hurting me. I just had to stop to think for a second."

Etta kept the conversation going. "She seems to be sick all the time now."

"What do you mean, sick?" Beaucharp asked.

Bertha said, "Stomach aches, headaches. She doesn't want to talk about it."

Now, upset with herself for taking so long to speak with the women, Beaucharp's face reddened. She closed her lips tightly, released Bertha's hand, and reached into an inside pocket for a pencil and notepad. Her police training and intuition sent hordes of images through her mind, all painful. If her assumptions were correct, Hattie might have experienced a terrible incident at the hands of someone.

Beaucharp flipped open the notepad and brushed past a dozen pages and stopped at a clean sheet. At the top, she wrote the date and time. She quickly assessed her thoughts, trying not to display her feelings to the already frightened and confused women.

Etta and Bertha were now confident that their feelings about the seriousness of Hattie's problem were being validated.

A storm of things flashed through Beaucharp's mind. Foremost was, if her assumptions were correct, how frightened, and confused Hattie must be. She then fretted about the responses of the anxious women sitting beside her if she tried to explain what she felt might have happened to Hattie. However, Beaucharp also sensed they had gained a sense of relief at being taken seriously about their feelings. Now, no one had to struggle with the gravity of losing Hattie's friendship for overreacting.

Beaucharp hid her feelings, but her mind shot far ahead of her note taking. *Each of them must be wondering if they were doing the right thing about the sudden change in Hattie's personality. They might wonder if it's drugs or latent mental illness emerging as Hattie's body chemicals change with her age. Washbee did mention Hattie struggled with mild autism. It must be horrible to have to confront a friend's dilemma and not have the wherewithal to understand it.*

Beaucharp allowed Etta and Bertha time for closure with the conversation, also noticing in their faces that they were comforted by discussing it with someone other than themselves. Finally, Beaucharp mentioned she would like to discuss the matter further with her partners, the other sisters, and Mr. and Mrs. Freeman.

Beaucharp said, "How about we all go back to Olney's wake? Does that work for you guys?" The women agreed.

***

After a slight tap on Washbee's office door, Willy Freeman pushed it open wide enough to shove his head in. Rachel, Edith and Stein were speaking softly.

Rachel spoke to her husband. "We're in the middle of something, Willy. It's going to have to wait."

"I'm sorry. This is serious. It's really serious."

"Can it wait a little bit?" Stein asked.

"I don't know? I think it is crucial," Willy said.

Stein said, "Can I go see what's happening? I'll be right back."

Edith and Rachel acquiesced.

Stein pushed away from Washbee's desk, edged around the side, and followed Willy down the hall and into Olney's Chapel. Now, close to a dozen new people occupied the room. More chairs had been secured for the room and Fontaine sat next to a melancholy Gaslight, his head hanging low to his chest. Stein started toward the two when Fontaine held up a hand, motioning Stein that she had the situation under control.

Stein, only now, noticed Willy Freeman's face. His eyes red and moist, one step away from tears, and his eyebrows bunched together in worry. She gently touched his arm and said, "Are you going to be okay, Mr. Freeman?"

He nodded and pointed to a row of chairs. "Tell Rachel I'll be waiting for her out here."

Stein escorted him to an empty seat, sat beside him, and touched his shoulder. "Sure you're going to be okay?"

Stein thought she noticed his eyes drying and some of the fear in his face fading. He exhibited a slight smile and said, "Yes. Thank you."

***

Stein paused in the hallway long enough to collect her thoughts and compose a narrative in her mind from what she heard and what she believed happened to Hattie. After moving on, she paused again at Washbee's office door. She stopped reaching for the doorknob when she heard a soft voice signaling from the end of the hall. It was Beaucharp, and she wanted to meet. Stein slowly opened the door and found both women whispering. Stein asked, "Are you guys okay?"

They nodded.

"I'll be back in a couple of minutes. You want to take a break or something?"

Rachel and Edith looked at each other. Edith answered. "Okay."

"Good. Let's meet back in fifteen minutes. Will that work?"

They agreed. Stein turned and walked to the end of the hall and found Beaucharp somber and rigid. "What's up, Michaela?"

"How is it going with you three?" Michaela asked.

"Oh, boy! Something happened to that kid."

Beaucharp looked at her feet. "Hattie?"

"Yes, Hattie. What did you find out?"

"Same thing. How are your two taking it?"

Stein shook her head. "I haven't told them what I think yet. I'm working on a way to explain it. We're taking a break right now."

Beaucharp glanced at her notepad and brought her eyes up to Stein's. "Did Donna talk to you?"

"No. Willy Freeman just asked me to speak with Mr. Gaslight. When I got there, Donna was talking with him. He looks down, and empty."

211

Beaucharp looked up and down the hall and shuffled Stein into an empty viewing chapel. "Wally Gaslight is overwhelmed. There has been too much thrown at him at one time, then add the death of his friend."

Stein said, "We got to wrap this Bunson Rosa crap up, and do it soon."

Beaucharp stared at an empty wall. "This stuff really pulls on Fontaine. She acts like a kick-ass cop, but she hates to see good people in pain. It really hurts her."

Hearing footsteps approaching, Stein and Beaucharp resumed the conversation with whispers. The footsteps stopped, and Fontaine stepped into the chapel. Her bag fell onto a chair with a thud. She took a deep breath and released it, then looked at Stein.

Chapter 42

S tein touched Fontaine's shoulder. "Sit down, Donna." She pointed to the empty chair beside her purse. Beaucharp dragged two chairs to the front of Fontaine.

"How'd it go with Gertie? What'd you find out about Hattie?" Beaucharp asked.

Fontaine looked down at her hands. "You brought her name up first. I take it that each of you got the same sense I did from the conversations."

Stein said, "We think someone hurt her."

Fontaine stared at her feet. "This is something else. It's 180 degrees from what we began with two days ago."

Stein scooted to the edge of her chair and leaned in toward Fontaine. "Hattie's problem is difficult news. I still don't know how I will explain this to Mrs. Freeman and Edith. They may come undone. But we still got to focus on that pile of bones and organs in the pit up the street. It's—"

"Wait a minute, Wanda," Beaucharp interrupted. "I know what you're saying." She pointed at Fontaine and then back at herself. "We both know what you're saying. But this freaking Bunson guy is just a piece of crap. I'm for running down whatever happened to him, but we gotta keep what happened to that young girl on the front burner too."

Stein slid back in her chair, stared at Beaucharp, then at Fontaine, and spoke. "Listen to me, now! It may sound preposterous but hear me out." Stein spoke continuously for fifteen minutes, describing possible scenarios, using numerous clues and solid reasoning.

The rundown consisted of pieces of evidence collected so far, what they knew about Gaslight, and what Beaucharp and Fontaine told her about the crowd at the Bucket of Blood. To Beaucharp, Stein's ideas were com-

Beaucharp tightened her jaw, lowered her head for a few seconds searching for the right words, then said, "None of you did anything wrong. You had no more control over this than Hattie did."

The Freemans flopped back in their chairs, and Rachel and Gertrude pressed their palms to their hearts.

Fontaine and Rachel then left to talk with Hattie. Within an hour Hattie, Rachel Freeman, and Fontaine left together. Two hours later, Stein and Beaucharp left. The sisters and Willy Freeman stayed with Washbee a while longer.

Chapter 44

The next day ADA Grover, speaking with Beaucharp said, "We don't want to mess this up. Is there a problem with interrogating this woman?" Grover stopped, looked down at the paperwork, and flipped over several pages, ". . . Hattie Winslow, at this time?"

Beaucharp said, "She should have counsel. She struggles with developmental issues."

Grover said, "She and her uncle don't want one. They feel no one has done anything wrong."

Stein said, "We don't believe she's done anything wrong." She stopped to gather more thoughts and went on. "So, with what I think we are going to hear from her, and all the horseshit going on with agencies trying to cover their asses, we don't want her or anyone in her family to become the scapegoats."

Beaucharp reiterated, "Ma'am, Wanda's right. It may be inappropriate, but we should insist she have a lawyer with her."

Again, Grover paused and turned toward the interrogation room. "Okay, I think you're right. How you going to address this with the family?"

"I'll talk to Washbee and see who he wants to hire," said Beaucharp.

Grover said, "Wait a minute. See if he would take Madeline Koch for counsel."

Beaucharp slapped her hand to her forehead and laughed.

Stein looked puzzled. "Who is Madeline Koch?"

Grover said, "She ran a law firm with a staff of progressive woman attorneys. She alone argued twelve cases in front of the Florida Supreme Court and four in front of the US Supreme Court."

"Never lost a single one," beamed Beaucharp.

"What happened to her law firm?" Stein asked.

"She is in her eighties. Gets around using elbow crutches and electric scooters," said Grover.

Beaucharp added, "She passed the law firm on to her partners when she turned seventy-five and joined the public defender's office."

"In her eighties, and still lucid?" Stein asked.

Beaucharp laughed. "Fontaine was a witness in a police case. She was the witness for Koch's client, even. Donna thought she should be kind to an old lady—"

Stein interrupted. "And Koch felt Fontaine was acting condescending?"

Grover added. "She tore a couple pounds off Fontaine."

Stein said, "I've heard about that happening to some cop. But I didn't think it was true."

Beaucharp then said to Grover, "Wanda and I will talk to Mr. Washbee now."

Chapter 45

Washbee, Hattie, and Fontaine sat quietly in the interrogation room. Hattie clutched Washbee's wrist like a rock climber, fearful of losing grip.

"Are you sure you are okay, honey?" Fontaine asked Hattie.

"I'm scared. I killed someone, and I don't know what's going to happen to me."

Fontaine touched Hattie's free hand and spoke, in a whisper. "Hattie, it appears you were defending yourself. Think about what could have happened if it were another person the man snatched. What if it were a child? Can you imagine how devastating that would have been?"

Hattie's eyes, circled with dark rings and sunken from lack of sleep, made her look much older than her eighteen years. She spoke, staring into the air like she was in a trance. "I'm still scared."

Beaucharp knocked twice, then she and Stein entered. When Washbee saw them, he smiled, shut his eyes momentarily, and whispered something to himself. His shoulders loosened and fell, and he stroked Hattie's hand. Later, he would tell Special Agent Stein how relieved he was seeing them show up like heroes coming to their rescue. He said he reckoned Hattie safer with Stein, Beaucharp, and Fontaine present.

At the sight of Beaucharp and Stein, Hattie's forehead wrinkled, and her lips quivered as she tried not to start crying again. Stein later commented that meeting Hattie for the first time was like coming across a captured and confused fawn.

Stein spoke first. "Cyrus, Hattie hasn't done anything wrong, but we think she should have legal representation from here on out."

Washbee started to speak, and Beaucharp raised her hand like a patrol leader stopping children from crossing a street. "Mr. Washbee, please let Wanda finish. We have a good plan."

Washbee looked at Fontaine and said, "I'm grateful for everything you three are doing. Are you going to get in trouble with all the help you're providing?"

Fontaine turning solemn and stone-faced, looked at Hattie, then at Washbee and spoke with sincerest confidence. "Don't worry about us. We can take care of ourselves."

Washbee looked at the frightened Hattie, then back at Stein, and nodded.

"We have a public defender in mind," said Stein.

"I can afford a lawyer," said Washbee.

Beaucharp intervened. "Mr. Washbee, you're gonna want this one."

"It's Madeline Koch, sir," Stein said.

"Madeline has been like family for over fifty years. I thought she retired. Are you sure she'd want to be part of this?"

"If she knows your family, she certainly will want Hattie to move on past this as successfully as possible," Fontaine said.

Beaucharp grinned and said, "Besides, she and Donna are old friends."

Fontaine frowned and squirmed. Washbee nodded in agreement to Stein. "I'd better call her right now—"

Beaucharp stopped him. "We'll get in touch with her."

Stein walked up to the mirror and nodded to Grover on the other side.

Chapter 46

On the third ring, she answered. "This is Maddie." The shoulder-length gray hair and the extra twenty-five pounds she had collected since retiring from her law firm made her look shorter than her five-foot-nine frame.

"Maddie, it's Grover."

"Assistant DA Grover? What's up?"

"I'm not talking to you right now. But I would like you to pick up a client."

"The guy owes you some gambling money, and you don't want him going to jail until he pays you?"

Grover smiled. "I'm not in this conversation right now, and the client is the niece of Cyrus Washbee."

"Hattie? What could she have possibly done wrong?"

"Where are you now, Maddie?"

"I'm at Corwin's Ice Cream."

"On River Walk?"

"Yup."

Grover looked at her watch. "The precinct is right around the corner. Can you get over here?"

"You're lucky. I took my scooter with me. Whoever she's with right now, from this second on, you tell them to leave her alone."

"She's safe, Maddie."

"I ain't shitting, Grover. This one's important to me!"

"She's safe, Maddie. I promise. She's with her uncle and a couple of good BPD detectives."

"Who are they?"

"Fontaine and Beaucharp."

Koch stared at what remained of her sundae and shook her head. *Son of a bitch!* It then clunked against the plastic trash bin walls, sending dozens of frightened flies scattering.

"Hold on," she said and groaned into her elbow crutches, then shuffled over to the handicapped electric scooter. Then, still talking to Grover, she shoved one end of an ear plug wire in, dropped the phone into a shirt pocket, and stuck the earpiece into her right ear. "Tell them I'll be there in ten minutes."

"I didn't have this conversation, but someone will meet you at the door. Look for Special Agent Wanda Stein."

"Freaking FBI, Grover? Are y'all crazy at County?"

"See you when I see you, Maddie."

Grover disconnected, mulled over some thoughts, and grinned. The moving parts of Grover's job were often filled with compromise and frustration.

She couldn't always push the legal system along in a straight line. Defense attorneys squeezed provisions out of existing laws that sometimes got tarnished by inept police work and bureaucratic red tape. Generally, the plea deal was the only way to acquire any semblance of justice.

The jails were full, and the courts crowded while the police got overwhelmed picking up all the human pain and suffering falling through the cracks of the under-funded social service systems. At this moment, though, Grover smiled. Everything is working! *One shit-bird eliminated, and Koch will kick someone's ass. There is a God.*

Chapter 47

Koch guided the scooter around a row of parked bicycles and swiftly shot across Bay Avenue and onto the Tenth Street's sidewalk. The ride to the police station gave Koch enough time to run a series of scenarios through her head.

Once in the building, she'd wave to the person behind the bulletproof glass in the reception area. Whoever it was, usually smiled once they recognized Koch. She'd then point to the scooter and where she wanted to park it. They'd say, okay. If it were Heather Killory, one of the civilians who worked at the desk, she'd give Koch a nod and a thumbs-up. Then Koch would smile, wave back, and ask how her twins are doing.

As she entered the building, the self-important Lieutenant Patroine, carrying a bundle of large manila envelopes, sashayed past. Held in low esteem by many of his fellow officers because of his arrogance and self-righteousness, Koch loathed how he always tried to wheedle himself into other's business. He stopped to watch without offering help as Koch struggled through the handicap door.

On seeing Patroine, Koch glanced at the reception desk and smiled. She turned right and slowly rode to the visitor's area, where several rows of empty chairs waited next to an umbrella stand and a coat rack. She parked behind the last row, out of the way and against the wall. Koch then grabbed her crutches and struggled to her feet. Balancing on one elbow crutch, she slung a strap from her backpack over a shoulder.

Patroine watched and waited until she stopped wrestling with everything before walking over. "Can I help you?"

Koch slid her free forearm into the crutch and, without looking at him, shouldered the other strap and said, "Get lost, Patroine. I'm not one of your ass-kissing lackeys."

"You can't just leave these things wherever you want to. This is a public building."

"I'm a member of the public. What's the problem?"

"For one thing, I'm a police lieutenant for the city of Belenton."

"That gives me cause for suspicion of the competency of Belenton Commissioners."

Patroine's lips tightened and turned white. He dropped the manila folders on an empty chair with a loud crash. "You can't talk to me like that."

"Like what, Patroine? Like an errant child."

"Do you think you can come here like you own the place and park your stuff anywhere you want?"

"Sue me."

Upon hearing a commotion, several officers joined Killory as she snickered behind the bulletproof glass area. She had to hush everyone in the booth to quiet the area long enough to turn on the microphone. "Attorney Koch. You have someone waiting for you. I'll send her right out."

Patroine scowled and bellowed. "We're talking over here."

"No, we're not," Koch said.

"Ms. Koch!" A voice rang out from the hallway door.

Without looking, Patroine bellowed, "I'm not through." Then turning toward the voice, he found a dark-haired woman in a handsome wool pantsuit pointing to her watch.

"We don't have a lot of time, Ms. Koch," Stein said.

Patroine remembered her as the woman he'd seen in a conference room the day before with detectives Beaucharp and Fontaine. Captain Bird came to their rescue. "We're talking here," Patroine shouted back.

Lapointe looked cautiously around the hallway one more time. "His name is Morris Labbe, and he's got history with Rodriquez. Probably figured he'd be able to work a plea deal with him for the charge we got against him. The Chief got a call during the break. We all gotta get down there right now. That includes you as well, Agent Stein."

***

All was quiet in the For Police Use Only elevator until the door opened on the first floor. Lapointe led the way, turning right into a wide hallway and stopping abruptly in front of a small alcove. A young officer behind a bulletproof window said, "Unload here, Detectives, and I'm afraid you as well, Agent Stein."

Stein nodded. One at a time, sidearms snapped and clicked from waist belts. The officers released magazines and verified the chambers were empty. They traded their weapons, ammo magazines and handcuffs for a hardened-steel safe key with a number etched into the end.

Lapointe turned toward the officer behind the glass and said, "John, can you tell Rodriquez we're here? He's waiting."

"Go on in. I'll tell him."

The officer touched a button under the counter, and an alarm notified them they could pass through the glass door with Interrogation Rooms lettered in black across the front. Once everyone got through, Lapointe stopped abruptly and turned to the detectives.

"Rodriquez wants to talk to Beaucharp first. After that, we'll go behind the mirror in the watch room."

Each of the Belenton PD interrogation rooms was equipped with video and audio equipment. The data is transmitted to separate viewing rooms and stored. Some, along with the audio/video equipment, use an adjacent room with a large one-way mirror as well.

"Where's Rodriquez?" Beaucharp asked.

"Should be here in a minute," Lapointe said.

"You're pretty quiet, Agent Stein," said Fontaine.

Beaucharp and Stein had wide smiles.

"You can call me Wanda. We're friends now," Stein said.

"Don't start trouble, Fontaine," Beaucharp said.

Stein responded, "I'm trying to be respectful, Donna. It's like a little chapel. Everyone's quiet, no guns, no billy clubs."

Fontaine laughed and softly fisted Stein's arm. "Billy clubs! Think we're still doing it the Brooklyn way?"

"Okay, let's get serious here, you guys," said Beaucharp.

As they walked along the hall, Lapointe stopped, turned to them, and said, "Beaucharp's right. Get squared away."

Lapointe resumed the lead. Fontaine's face wrinkled, and she stuck her tongue out at Lapointe's back.

Beaucharp whispered to Stein, "She's maturing nicely."

Then Lapointe said, "The rubber hose is better. It doesn't make as much noise, and if it's used right, there won't be any marks. If you're lucky, you'll get a chance to see how it works today."

All three paused, their mood sobered, each wondering if Lapointe actually said what they thought they heard.

Queries ran through each of the women's minds.

Fontaine: *He is one of the most respected police officers in the state. How could he think like that?*

Beaucharp: *Do we know this man?*

Stein: *Guy's got to be kidding.*

Rodriquez came around a corner and moved toward them from the end of the hall. Lapointe turned his head back toward them again, winked, and smiled.

Fontaine tapped her fist against his shoulder and said, "Sergeant, you scared Wanda. Don't joke like that."

"I knew he was kidding all the time," said Beaucharp.

They both looked at Stein. "I'm staying out of this. In Brooklyn, a rubber hose seems quite humane."

"Okay, shape up. Rodriquez is almost here," Lapointe said.

Detective Angel Rodriquez, a native of Puerto Rico, lived in the continental United States his whole life, yet he still spoke with a hint of a Latin accent. His six-foot-three frame, and broad shoulders conflicted with his soft voice.

"Thanks for coming. I'm Detective Angel Rodriquez."

Lapointe introduced them. "Angel, meet Detectives Beaucharp, Fontaine, and Special Agent Stein."

"So, what are we doing here?" Beaucharp said.

Puzzled, Rodriquez looked at Lapointe.

"I haven't said anything yet. I didn't know how you wanted to work it."

Rodriquez moved them into an empty interrogation room, suggesting each take a seat at a long table. Seeing only four chairs, Lapointe stepped into an adjacent room and returned with two more. With everyone seated, Rodriquez tipped forward onto his elbows and said, "First, Detectives Beaucharp and Fontaine, that was a good bust this morning."

Lapointe said, "Fill them in, Angel. They've been up since early morning."

Rodriquez looked at Lapointe and nodded. "Okay, sorry. The victim, who this guy was punching around, is in critical condition. If she dies, the ADA wants Murder One. Because of that, they did a rush on the results of the bloodstains on his clothes to be sure that they belonged to the woman. They found three sets of DNA: his, the battered woman, and some belonging to Bunson Rosa."

"What the fuck"—Beaucharp rose out of her chair—"can this get any nuttier?"

"Crazy enough for your partner to swear, Fontaine," Stein said.

Lapointe laughed loudly. "Wow, can you believe it? Miss Prissy Boston using profanity."

"Sounds like a South Boston Street cop," said Fontaine.

"Wash her mouth out with cheap vodka," said Stein.

Rodriquez wrinkled his brow. "Did I miss something here?"

Everyone chuckled while Beaucharp and Rodriquez kept silent.

Lapointe smiled. "It's a private thing, Angel. So please keep going, and I'll fill you in later."

Fontaine threw her hands in the air, "I'm just appalled."

Stein and Lapointe smiled.

"Okay, let's move on," said Beaucharp sternly.

Rodriquez looked down at his notes. "So, this Rosa guy is a notable perp with more luck than an Irish bookie."—He pointed with his thumb in

Labee's direction—"The Bozo in there, must have had some connection to Rosa."

Stein squinted impatiently and asked Rodriquez, "So what's the problem, Detective? What do you need from us?"

Lapointe said, "When they found Rosa's DNA on this guy's clothing, someone in the lab called the Chief while we were still in the meeting. So now, he wants someone to connect the dots."

"So, what are we supposed to do?" Beaucharp asked.

Fontaine smiled, "Stop using profanity, for one. You're shaming us."

Rodriquez leaned back and rocked his chair, "The guy's been nailed a few times and knows the drill. He's a jerk and is having trouble with being arrested by a woman cop. We haven't brought up the Bunson Rosa situation, and he doesn't know how much of a world of shit he's in yet—"

Lapointe intervened. "It's an old interrogation thing. We bring in Beaucharp, and she acts like Little Miss Entitled. That will irritate him, piss him off, and if we're lucky he'll get callous. Then we'll pull Beaucharp out, and I replace her."

Rodriquez jumped in, "It won't look good for him in lock-up when they find out he was taken out by, no disrespect, Detective, a woman cop, with a small frame. If Sarge can get on Labbe's good side by dumping on you"—he pointed to Beaucharp—"for being an entitled, undeserving female, the perp will act the tough guy and might begin singing."

Fontaine jumped in. "I get it. You see, Rosa was supposed to be a mean bastard. Maybe we can get him to show how tough he is by bragging about kicking Bunson Rosa's ass. He might think that story will endear him in jail better than being busted by a tiny woman cop. We'll pull out what we can from him as to where to find what's left of Rosa."

Lapointe looked at the detectives and Stein. "That's the Reader's Digest version. Then you guys take it from there."

"What do you want me to do?" Beaucharp asked.

Stein said, "Act prissy. You know, little Ivy League Debutante stuff. Act like you were entitled to the job because daddy was a friend of the governor. Stuff like that."

Fontaine smiled. "That should be easy for you. It does mean watching your language. None of the nasty 'F' words from your dirty mouth."

"We know you've been in a fight with him," Rodriquez said.

With both hands clutching the soda can, and eyes blinking nervously, Labbe said, "Why you so upset about Rosa and me? Is the pussy filing charges?"

Lapointe took a sip and held onto the can. "That piece of shit might be your trump card for easier jail time." Lapointe went on. "He's been up and down the systems in Florida and throughout the East Coast. Knowing who he is, I don't think he could've made too many friends." Lapointe stopped long enough for another sip. "Kicking his ass gotta get you some points inside."

Lapointe looked at Rodriquez, got a nod, then exhaled loudly. "Morris, we're going to tell you something, and we'll deny it later if you try to quote us. Are you following me?"

Labbe leaned forward attentively, and nodded, *yes*.

Rodriquez said, "We know you had a fight with Rosa, and neither one of us gives a shit about him. If it were up to us, you'd get a medal for kicking his ass—"

Lapointe interrupted, "It doesn't bother us if you come up with a self-defense plea. Use the Florida Stand Your Ground law if you want."

"Is he filing assault charges against me? What's this all about?"

Rodriquez, while looking at the top of his soda can, said, "Never mind what he wants. We found his blood on your clothes."

Lapointe said, "Are we clear on what we're looking for here?"

"What is it you want? I kicked his ass, and that's all there is to it. Whatever else he says is a fuckin' lie," said Labbe.

Lapointe propped his elbow on the table and leaned into Labbe, whiffed his odor and pulled back. "Okay, Morris, if you want some help, you gotta to be straight with us right now."

Rodriquez said, "We mean, *right now*, Labbe! They pulled me and my partner off something because you said you wanted to talk to me. We can't spend any more time screwing around on this without getting something. Once we finish our drinks, it's over. The ADA will be the next one you see. She's new on the job and hungry for some headlines."

Labbe's face lost color, he squirmed in the chair, and his hands shook so hard he had to place the can on the table to keep the contents from splashing around. "What the fuck do you want from me? Want me to say he attacked me?"

"We don't care how you word it. Did you have a fight with Bunson Rosa?" Lapointe asked.

"You know I did. He's the piece of shit that attacked me. It was self-defense. I don't care what the asshole says."

Suddenly the room grew silent, again, Lapointe, again, hoping the thirty seconds would seem longer for Labbe. Staring at him all the while, Rodriquez then asked, "Okay. Where'd you dump him, Morris?"

"Dump who? That asshole was crying like a baby when I left him." Then, turning toward Lapointe, he said, "Go see for yourself. He's camping in a storm culvert in Ellenton."

Rodriquez asked, "Where in Ellenton?"

"Not too far from the place where a guy's always butchering pigs and hanging them in the dooryard."

"So, when you left him, he was awake?" Lapointe said.

"The asshole limped away."

"Did he say anything to you?" Rodriquez asked.

"Anything about what? All he did was pick his ass up and get out of my sight."

Labbe turned to Lapointe who was staring at himself in the mirror, his eyebrows raised with the right hand supporting his chin. Ignoring the stare, Lapointe spoke to Angel's reflection. "Look, Angel, something's got to happen here." Then, turning to Labbe, he said, "This isn't even my case. I'm just sitting here for Dione because you were having trouble with Detective Beaucharp."

Rodriquez looked at Labbe. "So, what are we gonna do here—"

Lapointe's chair scratched loudly against the floor as he stood and looked at Rodriquez. "Dione will be back in a minute or so." Then to Labbe, "Morris, why don't you just lawyer up? Maybe you can get a better deal."

"Wait a minute, Sergeant." Labbe continued. "What kinda deal?"

Lapointe said, "Where's Rosa now?"

"I'll show you where I saw him last. I ain't going with those bitches, though."

"We'll do it today?" Rodriquez asked. Labbe nodded and said, "Okay."

Lapointe looked at Labbe and said, "I'll find someone to take you back to your cell, Morris."

Already anticipating the move, Grover arranged for someone to escort Labbe. After two knocks on the door, Lapointe said, "It's okay. Come on in."

A beefy, sunburned deputy with a GI haircut entered and pointed at Labbe. "He coming with me?"

"Yes." Then he turned to Labbe. "You probably want something to eat?"

Everything that happened so far was too much for Labbe's mind to get wrapped around. He nodded, looked down at the table, and shook his head from side to side.

Rodriquez said, "Tom, take Mr. Labbe back to his cell. They're still serving. I'll get a tray for him."

"No need, detective. I'll call and get his meal released," said the deputy.

Lapointe unlocked the handcuffs and helped Labbe out of the chair. Then, leaning close, he whispered. "We'll talk again, Morris."

Lapointe, Labbe, and the deputy barely reached the metal door when Rodriquez said, "Dion and I will take him to Rosa's campsite. I know you've been working all night, Sarge."

"Thanks, Angel. This is supposed to be my night off, so I gotta get home and get some sleep."

Rodriquez looked at Labbe. "It's almost six o'clock. We still got a few hours of daylight. How about you show us the place after you eat?"

"Yeah," Labbe said. "But I gotta be sure you're gonna tell the judge how much I'm cooperating."

Rodriquez said, "We'll certainly do that, Morris."

The deputy said, "If you want to move this along, bring him to Holding, and I'll go and get his tray."

"That okay with you, Morris?" Rodriquez asked.

"Yes," Labbe said.

With the doorknob still in his hand, Lapointe stopped and turned to Rodriquez once more. "Make sure they call me if anything big comes up."

***

Behind the two-way mirror Grover removed her glasses and pinched the bridge of her nose while she turned to face everyone. "Those guys did a good job. But he's not the one who killed Rosa."

Detective Dione shuffled his feet. "Nothing I can do here. I gotta start on our report." After shaking hands with everyone, he quietly slipped out.

Grover said, "Someone chopped off a couple of pieces of fingers, took a few chunks of Rosa's vital organs, and tossed them in a bag with what looked like left-over food scraps and a tiny human leg and foot."

"Crime lab says the leg and foot is an elderly woman's," Beaucharp said. "That rules out a missing child."

"Eighty to ninety years old." Fontaine added, "if it were a man's limb, it could have been one of my partner's boyfriends."

Agent Stein smiled, slowly shook her head, then said, "What's this all about? We got random bits of DNA and fragments of human remains like you might find scattered from a plane crash."

The room went silent.

Engrossed in thought, Fontaine looked to the ceiling for a moment, then at the wall in front of her, as if answers might be written in either place. She spoke first. "Yeah, but the discrepancies here are too varied. The lab said there is also blood DNA from another female. That's another victim."

Grover spoke without turning away from her gaze into the interrogation room one-way window. "Let's check the DNA of Labbe's victim again. She may have taken part in an incident along with Rosa." She turned and waited for a signal, acknowledging they were all still on the same page. Then, while jotting something into her notebook, she said, "You guys see if we can find any female crime victims, aside from the woman Labbe put in the hospital. We got to check for missing persons, things like that."

Beaucharp and Agent Stein, already on that wavelength, signaled each other with quick nods. Stein mentioned she was waiting for replies to messages she placed with the FBI National Crime Lab for anything she called Regional. "They'll automatically search the serial killer databases, and we might find parallels to give us some leads," she said.

go to waste. He said he'd take it, even gave us burlap bags to toss the stuff in."

"I know all about that, Duff. What about Miss Ida's leg?"

"I think it got stuffed into a bag for Mr. Giovanelli's pigs."

Washbee's crooked frame tensed. Manfred moved over to his lap and rubbed his face against Washbee's chest. "Okay. So, what was the leg doing in the bag of scraps for Mr. Giovanelli? How could that have happened?"

Bleiu whispered. "I found Katie wrapping scraps in the refrigerator. She had stuff wrapped in what looked like an old rag that she tried to cover with butcher paper. She wanted to know when Winston would be taking everything to Mr. Giovanelli's. She must've thought everything in the sack with Miss Ida's leg was for the pigs and tossed the scraps she was discarding into the same sack."

"Okay. Get Miss Ida's leg, and we'll fire up the crematory right now."

"I can't do that, Uncle Cyrus. Winston went into the refrigerator with a bunch of food scraps and found the sack too full. So, he must have started a new one and took both bags. Miss Ida's leg is in one of the bags he brought to Mr. Giovanelli's."

Chapter 27

At home, Beaucharp sipped a large cup of tea and munched on an overstuffed turkey breast and mayo sandwich. She watched Mischief, her aloof and lazy, white-footed black cat, try to stay awake on the chair directly across the table. His eyes flickered like a sleepy child trying to outwit bedtime. The loud purring was the only challenge to the crumpling of Beaucharp flipping through the daily newspaper.

Fifteen minutes after finishing the sandwich, Beaucharp struggled to keep from nodding off and abandoned the idea of reading further. She looked at Mischief. "I got to fold up, buddy, and get some sleep. Picking up Aunt Donna early tomorrow."

Once in bed, she tried to shut her mind down, but the day's events kept rushing through her head like a slow-motion movie segment that kept repeating itself in an endless loop. Concerns for the welfare of Wally Gaslight and Cyrus Washbee kept poking at her and creating foggy narratives. Her last thoughts before sleep were what Stein will think of Gaslight and how her visit with Washbee will go tomorrow?

Beaucharp drifted away into sleep and soon dreamt about illusionary patches of crushed oyster shells, scents of stale beer, and images of the frightened eyes of some of the lost folks at the Bucket of Blood. Washbee's voice was in the room as she listened to Manfred speak in a confusing French dialect. The cat complained about Donna Fontaine, and Beaucharp tried to intervene, defending her partner. Washbee gently raised his hand, signaling Beaucharp to allow Manfred to complete his line of thoughts.

Manfred ceased momentarily, and as Beaucharp tried to speak, he would wink at her and go off on a new rant. First, it was Fontaine's choice of perfume, then the slow Southern drawl when she spoke, and he didn't like her choice of shoes. Finally, Manfred said he was upset with how she tried to ma-nipulate situations on the job to push most of the hard work onto Beaucharp. In the dream, Beaucharp smiled, bent down, and lifted Manfred onto her lap. His ranting ceased.

Beaucharp said to Washbee, "He speaks French! How many people know about this special gift?" Manfred pushed up close, rubbed against her chin, and whispered, "I can get away with it. I'm a Canadian."

Suddenly, Manfred was Carroll's Cheshire Cat. A toothy feline face filled most of the room, the purring replaced with the rare bird-like trill unique to Beaucharp's cell phone.

"Tweedle-tweedle-tweedle, Tweedle-tweedle . . ." Lunging at the night-stand, she snatched the phone, fumbling to silence the warble.

"Beaucharp. This you, Fontaine?" she asked.

"It's Captain Bargiel, detective."

"What's up, sir?"

"You and your partner get in here as soon as you can. We had some new developments in the Gaslight case last night. I waited to give you guys some extra sleep. Y'all had a big day yesterday."

"Anyone called Fontaine?"

"No. Wake her up."

"Yes, sir, we'll be there in less than an hour."

"See you then." Bargiel hung up.

Beaucharp hit the speed dial for Fontaine's phone.

***

Fontaine groped and cursed, then finally, grabbing the phone, shouted, "Hello! Fontaine."

"Well, good morning, grouchy pants. Are we a little testy today? Did you run out of gin last night?"

"What's up, Beauchy?"

"We gotta get in right now."

"Shit. It's 6:05. Did Lapointe call again?"

"Bargiel called. Something happened last night with the Gaslight thing."

"Why didn't Birdy call me? He plays golf with my dad every week. He and Virginia used to babysit me when I was a kid."

"That's why. They're probably way over being sick of you. I'm coming right now. Be ready!" Beaucharp hung up.

Beaucharp's phone immediately went off again. It was Fontaine. "Did someone call Stein?"

"I don't know. We'll call her on the way in so she'll get a little extra sleep."

"Okay, you better hustle prima-donna lady," Fontaine smiled, "that's the name Labbe gave you. Let's keep it around for a while."

"You better be wearing suitable clothing and have a couple of black coffees in your hands when I get there."

"Suitable clothing?"

"That's right. We're not going out to pick up sailors."

Fontaine smiled and hung up.

Lapointe continued. "I got something to show you. Something that the department isn't supposed to have. It was passed to us by someone in the Florida Bureau of Prisons and possibly sent by mistake. However, Birdy thinks they may have sent it on purpose, as a heads up, by somebody who once worked here."

"What's going on, Sarge?"

"Detective, this is a serious avenue we're about to go down. We could all take early retirements if this hits the Westinghouse from the wrong direction."

"What do you need?"

Lapointe looked around the hallway. "Okay. This gotta be quick. I'm off duty in twenty-five minutes. Let's go back in and get your partner and Stein."

Along with Stein and Fontaine, several others hung around, drinking coffee, and chatting. Lapointe got Stein and Fontaine's attention and tilted his head toward the door, and mouthed, "Let's go next door."

They followed Lapointe out and into the empty conference room across the hall. Lapointe hung a Meeting Taking Place sign on the door and directed each to a seat at the conference table.

He produced a manila folder and took a deep breath. "All right sometimes cops come up with things we gotta keep quiet about. What I am about to say, and show you, is not illegal. There are no statutes we'll be violating once we look at this. However, it is full of unprincipled boogiemen that could be considered breaches. I'm not going to disclose who else has seen this. As far as we're concerned, I'm the only one."

"Sarge, what's going on?" Fontaine asked. "If there is nothing slimy going on here, why all the mystery?"

Beaucharp tapped Fontaine's arm. "Donna, there are things we are not supposed to know about others while they're passing through the judicial systems—"

Stein interrupted. "She's right. Sometimes cases are processed incorrectly, and that information is kept out of the public eye because it could be detrimental to jurisprudence."

Lapointe bounced in his seat. "You know about this, Agent Stein?"

"This morning, I got something. It may be what you're talking about."

Lapointe surmised out loud. "Oh boy! Maybe someone wants to wrap this up and bring you back to Tampa for another, even bigger case."

Stein looked at Fontaine and Beaucharp and said, "I think what Sergeant Lapointe is trying to get to is both of you have promising careers. Others, higher than the sergeant in the food chain, think the same way. So, he might be allowing us to step back from this."

Lapointe said, "She's right. This goes a long way up. You two are the fine detectives. Maybe the best in the department. You're the most respected and have the most to lose. Stein's superiors must feel the same way about her. Everyone else involved can draw their pensions early if it all heads south."

Fontaine wriggled in her chair. "I didn't become a cop to settle into something cozy. So, I'm in. Let's see what you got, sergeant."

"I'm with my partner," Beaucharp said. Then, feeling hurt and thinking Stein held information back from them, she turned to her. "You got some explaining to do, Stein."

Stein nodded.

Lapointe picked up the package. "I think Stein was covering for you two just in case this sensitive material didn't come out right away. If neither of you knew about it, you both were safe." He quickly unsnapped a brown folder and dumped documents stamped with Florida Bureau of Prisons at the top and the bottom. Pulling out the first page, he read the name, Bursor Rose.

"This was the guy that was supposed to be paroled instead of Bunson Rosa," Lapointe said.

"How the hell did that happen?" asked Beaucharp.

"I know how," Fontaine said, lifting another sheet out of the pile. "Just read Rose's file. He's in for writing rubber checks and served two and one-half years of a five-year sentence. A model prisoner who earned a GED and worked the difficult jobs in the prison system, particularly with elderly inmates. The prisons are full of sick, broken-down inmates these days."

Stein said, "American prisons reflect society. Inmates are aging, forcing some prisons to turn whole wings into geriatric centers. So now, they're trying to unload non-violent offenders to make room."

Beaucharp turned to Fontaine. "Prison nursing homes! I bet you wouldn't have trouble finding a boyfriend there, Donna."

Lapointe, suppressing a laugh, smiled momentarily. "That's about it. But we're not here to talk about old inmates. It's about how Bunson Rosa got parole and its significance to the powers that be."

Beaucharp added her perspectives. "Let me guess. This Bursor Rose guy is going up for parole, and his file gets mixed up with Bunson Rosa. In the meantime, Rosa's shyster lawyer is working on a technicality with the trial transcripts—"

Fontaine interrupted. "Things go haywire, and before you know it, Rosa is out the door, and Rose is back to square one. One massive clusterfuck. A field day for a shyster lawyer, the news media, and political adversaries as far away as the Moon."

Lapointe went on. "Rose's lawyer recognizes the discrepancies and starts to blow the whistle. The Attorney General gets wind of the mistake and tells Rose's lawyer that they will make the problem right. The AG then talks to the Governor's office. Now, in an election year, everyone is trying to put the pin back in the grenade."

Fontaine turned to Stein. "Let's go back a little here. How'd you find out about this, and when?"

Stein said, "I got a memo around four this morning from a Confidential-Encoded Bureau email system. We sometimes get a special note with a unique Bureau fingerprint. It directs us to an encoded email system. I almost fell off the toilet when I read it."

Fontaine laughed. "Toilet! You check email from the toilet?"

Beaucharp said, "So there was a screw-up with the parole. Why not just bite the bullet, pick up Rosa and make things right?"

Lapointe said, "The problem isn't just because the names got mixed up in the file. Number one, Rosa disappeared. Let me read the names of the people who wrote the letters of recommendations for Bursor Rose."

Lapointe read off names as he dropped sheets of paper onto the desk. "The prison warden, someone in the Attorney General's office, the prison hospital, and geriatric division," he went on, "the prison shrink, several prominent clergy leaders, one letter from a former governor, and a letter from the Florida State Senate president."

"Those endorsements make it sound like they had Mahatma Gandhi in there," Stein said.

Lapointe took over the conversation again. "These recommendations were supposed to be for Rose. Can you see why so many people at the state level are nervous? The file is full of fingerprints of prominent Florida people. Everyone is, pissed off at the Bureau of Prisons."

"All these accommodations ended up in Rosa's file?" Beaucharp asked.

Stein said, "That's exactly what happened. The boys, and I do mean the boys, in the prison system are rushing, elbows to asshole, trying to fix this as fast as they can."

Fontaine rolled her eyes and tapped her knuckles against the table. "Then, suddenly, Rosa's organs show up in a bag of food scraps, with an old foot attached to a leg and some bloody DNA belonging to a woman who no one has a record of. Holy Batshit!"

Lapointe needed to bring the meeting to an end. "The brass in the prison system are crapping themselves! So now you know why so many agencies are showing up for meetings and why only a few are getting involved, aside from expediting lab work."

Beaucharp looked at Stein. "How come the Bureau sent you a copy, Wanda?"

Lapointe pointed to the Belenton PD emblem on the door. "I think I can answer that. There has to be a few shit-birds somewhere along the food chain, especially among federal judges, who are getting their asses kissed by important people. They want this moved along and are nudging the Bureau to get this done as soon as possible. The FBI probably have more pressing business and want this to be over with as well."

Stein added, "The Bureau, sometimes, does contribute anonymously."

Lapointe chuckled. "We love our brothers and sisters at the Bureau. But—"

Stein interrupted. "But, is the big word that often means, sometimes we may ask too much. We hear that all the time. You guys are lucky. Belenton PD is pretty much squared away. There are dozens of departments, not just in Florida, that are so messed up that agencies like the FDLE or the FBI need to take their hand and lead them through cases. Often, neither the Bureau nor the FDLE takes credit for them."

Dione swung his arm in an arc. "He's running around in the corner of that hayfield. It looks like he's playing with a small soccer ball. First, we needed to wait for someone to pick up Labbe, then we were going to see if we could entice the dog to come to us."

Beaucharp pointed to several large rolls of fresh hay. "In the meantime, how about we take a walk out there and see if we can roust him up? It shouldn't be too hard. It looks like the field's been mowed."

The sirens were getting closer when Stein looked out into the field and said, "Hey! Who knows? The way things go around here, we might even come across a gremlin or two out there."

Fontaine warned, "Just look out for snakes."

Chapter 31

Donning latex gloves and carrying large evidence bags, Stein, Beaucharp, and Fontaine spread out fifty feet apart and began combing the hayfield. At a couple hundred feet from the car Fontaine let out two shrill whistles. Almost immediately, a sharp yelp returned. "It sounds like a puppy," she said, then whistled again.

A young puppy, smaller than a beagle and barely able to hold his head up with the weight of the skull in his jaws, raced toward Fontaine. He stopped twenty feet away, dropped on his front legs, and spit out the head. His tail wagged so rapidly his rear quarters nearly toppled him over.

"That's a blue tick," Beaucharp shouted. "My Uncle Dan had one once. Get ready for some excitement. They're friggin clowns."

"He just wants to play," Stein said. "He'll run us ragged if we chase after him."

Beaucharp took a step forward. "What the heck is that sticking out of the front of the skull?"

"Looks like a billy club," said Stein.

Fontaine joked. "Billy club! Leave it to a New York cop to see that. That's a Rorschach ink blot image for them." She continued, "Let's try to work with him a bit to avoid getting him too antsy. We want him to ease up closer to us."

They all stopped moving.

Beaucharp said, "The more we chase him, the more he'll think we're playing. So, let's try talking to him, one at a time."

"You two keep him occupied. I got an idea," Stein said. She raced back to the car, trusting that Beaucharp and Fontaine could keep the dog's attention.

They clapped their hands and spoke in high-pitched cheery tones, as if they were playing with a toddler. It worked. He ran from one detective to the other, playfully dropping the skull and picking it back up in front of each one.

"He's a cute little shit, ain't he?" Fontaine said.

"Certainly is. Where the heck is Stein?" Beaucharp blurted.

Fontaine looked at her and bellowed. "Hell! Beauchy. Can't you say hell? Where the hell is Stein? Swear once in a while. It's good for you."

Beaucharp laughed, then Stein's voice shot out from behind them. "I'm right here. How's it going with our new friend?"

Beaucharp turned to Stein. "He's having a great time. Did you come back with a secret weapon?"

"Sure did." Stein clapped her hands together and got the dog's attention. He rushed playfully over, still clutching the skull. Stein produced a bright yellow tennis ball, juggled it from one hand to the other, and tossed it to Fontaine. "Here, catch." Fontaine caught it, and the puppy ran to her, still clamping the skull.

Fontaine threw it to Beaucharp. "Catch." The puppy dropped the skull and looked at Beaucharp. Beaucharp juggled the ball from one hand to the other, keeping the puppy's focus, then tossed it back to Stein. The puppy picked up the skull and ran to Stein.

Stein tossed the ball up and down in her hand and said, "Here, puppy!" and purposely tossed it over Fontaine's head. Fontaine feigned an attempt to rush for it. The dog dropped the skull and raced ahead of Fontaine to scoop it up. With the ball securely in his mouth, the playful toying resumed. Stein scooped up the head and dropped it into the large evidence bag Beaucharp produced.

Once secured, they gathered around to view what looked like a small lopsided ball covered with maggots. They estimated only about forty percent of the body tissue remained. Dark green slime oozed out of the base of the skull and the eye sockets. The ears and nose were gone, but patches of hair remained connected to the cranial bone tissue.

"We got it," Beaucharp said.

The dog frolicked up to Fontaine, still carrying the orange tennis ball. She clapped her hands playfully, and he ran past her and stopped. She grinned and looked at the other two. "He wants to play some more."

"We got the head, and he seems to have taken a liking to you," Stein said.

Fontaine walked over and stared at the contents in the bag. "Looks pretty bad. How long do you think it's been hanging around? What the hell is that sticking out of its mouth?"

Beaucharp said, "It looks like the shin bone of some kind of animal. Something my mother used for a soup bone. We don't know how long it's been here either."

Stein said, "This place is full of coyotes and feral hogs. Then there are the scavenger sets, like vultures and tissue-eating insects. We don't know how long they take to work the carcass clean." She hefted the evidence bag. "Seems pretty light."

"It's light. Empty-headed, huh? Gotta belong to a guy," Fontaine said.

All three chuckled.

The puppy ran up to Fontaine and dropped the ball at her feet. She picked it up and tossed it back into the field as far as she could. He shot out. "That'll take care of him for a while." She then pointed to a tent at the roadside. "It looks like the forensic people. We'd better get over there."

"Want to toss your gloves in here?" Beaucharp asked, pointing to the evidence bag where she and Stein had deposited theirs.

"Oh yeah, I almost forgot."

Still walking, Fontaine started to remove her gloves, then stopped. As they neared the forensic tent, the dog returned to Fontaine, still with the ball in his mouth. She said, "I'll keep the gloves on for now. We can't let our little cannibal go anywhere near the corpse. He might snatch another body part and take off again."

Stein spoke. "My car is still running, and the air is on. Can we get him inside until some animal control people show up?"

"She's right," Beaucharp continued, "he's been helpful. We want to make sure he gets taken care of."

The puppy clung to the trio as they trekked toward Stein's car. "This little guy thinks he's part of the team now," Fontaine said. She stopped,

Manfred rushed over, purred loudly, and rubbed forcefully against Stein's leg. She turned to Fontaine. "So, this is the notorious cat!"

"That's Manfred," said Washbee. "He has a special place here as family and, almost, an employee."

Stein lifted Manfred into her arms, and the purring grew louder. "He's beautiful. A little on the chunky side, though."

Washbee said, "That's because he enjoys an over indulgence in treats. I'm afraid he can be a little mischievous," he pointed at Fontaine, "the detective can tell you that."

Fontaine brought her face close to Manfred's, waved an index finger at him, and said, "Naughty boy!" Then turned to Washbee. "Oh, I'm sorry! This is Special Agent Stein from the FBI."

"Oh my! An FBI agent. I'm delighted to meet you." He reached out to shake hands, "Agent Stein—"

Stein stopped him abruptly. "Please call me Wanda."

"Wanda, it is. Please call me Cyrus."

Stein balanced Manfred on her left arm and shook Washbee's hand.

Beaucharp said, "We had to leave in a hurry last time. I think you were in the middle of telling us something. You said it was important. You got some time for us now?"

A grandfather clock chimed, reminding Washbee of the half-hour. "Hey, it's eleven-thirty. Have you eaten yet?"

Beaucharp said, "Actually, we just left a crime scene and—"

Fontaine barged in. "We're starving. What you got hanging around?"

Washbee lit up with a glowing smile, clapped his hands together and said, "Oh, my! Follow me. We have a buffet set up in a chapel." He wriggled off, inchworm-like, with his back close to a wall, in his usual sideways gait.

Fontaine and Beaucharp hesitated, looked at Stein, shrugged, and started out. Washbee waited for them to catch up. Then, he turned to Stein. "Come walk with me, Wanda."

Stein scooted past the detectives, and all four proceeded at Washbee's clumsy pace of three steps, pause, and then three steps again.

"So, tell me, Wanda, are those two so troublesome that the FBI has to send agents to keep an eye on them?" He turned his head and winked at the detectives.

Stein grinned and flicked her thumb over her shoulder. "We just met yesterday. You'd be surprised. It's a little bit like hanging out with Laurel and Hardy."

Washbee said, "An FBI agent, here! I am so honored."

Suddenly, he stopped and turned toward the detectives. His forehead creased with worry. The missing eyebrow made his blue eyes appear more distressed. "We have some things to talk about. I hope you won't become cross with me."

Something's wrong! Fontaine thought. "Mr. Washbee, we're here if you need help. We're not trying to get anyone in trouble."

"She's right," Beaucharp said. "We got a lot of loose ends, and some pieces seem to unravel in this direction. You can help us clear up parts of a puzzle." *I hope I'm not lying.*

Washbee turned and resumed the tortuous march.

Stein, still clutching Manfred, touched Washbee's elbow, and he paused again. "Don't worry, Cyrus. The cat's been whispering in my ear." Then, turning to her partners, she smiled. "The FBI's got your back."

Washbee nodded, sadly thinking, *oh, dear Lord, I hope they're being truthful.* He stopped at an empty room, still, except for the angelic hymns softly flowing from hidden wireless speakers. "We call all our viewing rooms chapels," he said.

White oak panels made the room look cool, and the floor, massive, polished pine planks, gave it the appearance of a small country chapel. There were sixteen empty folding chairs with soft red cushioned seats, four rows deep. Along the west wall sat a table with an assortment of tiny sandwiches and tubs of potato salad and coleslaw, all with Publix food store stickers on the lids.

Alongside were various plastic packages of mayonnaise and ketchup, small bags of potato chips, and at least three dozen multiple types of cookies. An assortment of pickles filled a silver-colored plastic tray tightly sealed in plastic wrap. Two plastic one-half gallon containers of room temperature iced tea sat at the end of the table. In front, were stacks of plastic cups and white plates designed to keep foods separated with three concave sections. Several piles of white napkins and plastic dinnerware sat at the beginning of the array.

Seeing the women were confused, Washbee pointed to a blue nylon urn on the marble-topped table in the front. He explained. "That's Olney Hazelton. He was a member of the Ellenton Masonic Temple. It's one of the oldest lodges in Florida, its charter beginning soon after the Civil War. There are not many members today, and those remaining, God bless them, are quite elderly."

Washbee revealed that his family has been performing burial services for the lodge since the funeral home opened. Traditionally, the lodge sends visitors a small, complimentary buffet whenever a member passes away. Olney had no living family but many friends. His Masonic brothers brought the food earlier, paid their respects briefly, and would return later for a short Masonic ceremony.

Washbee said, "We're expecting others to show up as well. Right now, as you can see, it's relatively slow."

Stein placed Manfred on an empty chair and looked around the room. "Poor Olney. No one is here to say goodbye. Are you sure we should take some of this food? Does this often happen, Cyrus?"

"Quite a bit. Even if no one shows up, we come and sit with the deceased. Everyone should be missed by somebody."

"We?" interrupted Fontaine.

"My nephews Duff and Winston and my niece, Hattie. We visit and spend some time."

Stein reached across and tapped Washbee's wrist. "That is a wonderful gesture by your family. You're honoring Olney's life accomplishments."

Fontaine said, "We'll just sit her for a while with Olney, but let's leave the sandwiches for anyone who comes in."

Beaucharp turned to Stein and grinned. "Works for me, but I can't believe my partner is passing up food."

"Please," Washbee said. "Let's all have something to eat. We usually toss most of it in a sack and bring it to Mr. Giovanelli's pig farm."

Fontaine said. "Pig farm, Mr. Washbee?"

"Yes," Washbee giggled. "The kids have been saving leftovers for Mr. Giovanelli's pigs for a long time."

"Kids?" Beaucharp asked.

"Oh, my two nephews and a niece. They've lived with us since they were toddlers."

Fontaine changed the subject. "Okay. I'm not going to insult people by refusing their food. I'm gonna eat. Gotta wash up a little first." Her partners concurred.

"You know where the washrooms are," Washbee said and began clearing plastic wrappings from the trays.

Everyone returned in ten minutes and began filling plates with small sandwiches, little scoops of potato salad, coleslaw, and pickles. Washbee circled four chairs.

Fontaine, silent, and pondering something mentioned earlier, went last doubling the amount the others took. She then joined the circle, each sitting with a plate on their lap with a Styrofoam cup of room temperature iced tea balanced on the edge.

They ate in silence until Fontaine said, "Wait a minute! Mr. Washbee, what kind of bag do you pack these leftovers in?"

"Mr. Giovanelli gives us some old canvas bags. We stick them in the forensic refrigerator with the cadavers until someone can bring them to his farm." He placed his sandwich on the plate, one small bite taken out of it. "I know why you're asking me that. Let's eat first and pay our respects to Olney. I'll try to explain it all later. Is that okay?"

Beaucharp and Stein, puzzled at first by Fontaine's inquiries, decided to trust that there were valid reasons for the direction she was going in.

Beaucharp said, "That'll work, Mr. Washbee."

Fontaine and Stein agreed with nods.

Stein, wanting to lighten the air said, "Cyrus, please tell us more about Olney."

They learned that Olney left the area as a teenager, at the height of the Great Depression in 1933. Like many of his cohorts at that time, he felt that leaving would unburden his family from having another mouth to feed.

Chapter 37

S tein, Fontaine and Beaucharp remained focused, trying to gather everything as accurately as possible.

Later, when reviewed by prosecutors, judges and public defenders, everyone decided that the team produced the most significant set of written briefs of the entire case.

Washbee waited silently for three minutes while the detectives finished writing. He grinned, "With all the concentration taking place, I think I'm starting to smell rubber burning."

Without lifting her head from writing, Fontaine got a smile from everyone saying, "That odor is probably because my partner took her shoes off."

Washbee assumed the detectives were only investigating how Ida Foote's leg ended up in Gaslight's truck. He informed them about the letter from the hospital and the conversation he had had two days earlier with his nephew, Duff Bleiu. Now he needed to do his best to explain how it got mixed into the bag of food scraps.

To avoid time-consuming questions Washbee provided each a copy of the letter from Doctor Burns apologizing for the hospital mishap. The detectives read the letter several times.

When she was sure everyone finished reading, Beaucharp looked at her peers. "So, the leg and foot were sent to you after the body was removed from the hospital?"

"Yes," Washbee continued, "and the cremation had already taken place before the leg was delivered."

"Does that happen often?" Stein asked.

Washbee dropped his face into his hands. "I couldn't say, Wanda, it was a terrible mistake. I shudder at the difficulties it must have brought down on

Mr. Gaslight. It had to have placed him under severe and undue suspicion. There is nothing untoward about him. He is the kindest person you'll ever find."

Washbee explained that when he got the letter from the hospital, he contacted Bleiu right away. He then learned that Bleiu didn't want to overwork the crematory equipment, so he decided to add the leg to the next funeral pyre, leave it at that, and eventually explain it all after.

Washbee then described the conditions of the old crematory equipment. "Bleiu's concern for me drove him to do what he did with the leg."

Fontaine wanting to reassure Washbee said, "Although he knew the procedure was irregular, he felt it was the best thing to do at the time."

Washbee said, "I asked about getting the leg from the refrigerator and incinerating it immediately. That's when Bleiu told me it was missing and that it must have, somehow, got mixed in with the food scraps that go to the pig farm."

Beaucharp asked, "So you think that is how the leg got mixed up with the food scraps?"

Washbee nodded and said, "Yes, there must have been two bags, the leg being in one. Whoever took them thought both bags were food scraps."

Stein asked, "How did they get into Gaslight's truck?"

Beaucharp said, "There was only one bag in the truck. What could have happened to the other?"

Washbee said, "I don't know. My nephew, Winston, was taking the scraps to Mr. Giovanelli's. He stopped at the Bucket of Blood to get a soft drink. My niece Hattie commandeered the van from him. Unbeknown to her, Winston snatched one sack out before she drove off, never realizing that what he thought were just food scraps had Ida Foote's leg as well."

Fontaine began to say something but decided to let Washbee resume.

He told them a that a careless cigarette tossed out of a car window caused a small brush fire a mile away. Winston smelled the smoke and being a member of the Manatee County volunteer fire auxiliary, he tossed the sack into the bed of Gaslight's truck, planning to return for it later. Then he rushed to the firehouse, several hundred yards away.

He continued, "That part of the episode I learned the following morning. Winston didn't realize that the leg was in the bag. He still doesn't know."

He finished the narrative then Beaucharp looked at her partners and noticed they were struggling with what they heard and trying to tie together some loose ends.

Fontaine tapped her pencil on the table. Stein shook her head, "no", signaling Beaucharp. She and Fontaine knew what Stein was implying. Washbee had no idea that Rosa's body parts and the DNA of an unidentified woman were accompanying Ida Foote's leg.

Each pondered who the female DNA could belong to and how do they tell Washbee about Rosa's body parts?

Stein said, "Cyrus, how did Gaslight's truck end up on Manatee Avenue, almost ten miles away?"

Washbee said, "When Winston returned from the fire a couple of hours later, he found Mr. Gaslight just leaving the bar. The best answer I can come up with is that while approaching the truck, Gaslight noticed Winston and, for some reason, he crawled into the passenger seat and fell asleep."

Fontaine and Beaucharp were now making sense of their notes from the previous day at The Bucket of Blood. Several patrons noted Gaslight asleep in the passenger seat and "*. . . the Beauregard kid was driving.*" They had both written the same sentence.

Stein tapped Fontaine's shoulder. "You getting this?" Fontaine said, "Review our notes from yesterday."

Stein said. "Oh yeah. It's sounding familiar now. I'm sorry, Cyrus. Can you go on?"

Washbee said, "Winston was going to borrow Gaslight's truck while he was asleep to take the food scraps to Giovanelli's, then drop Gaslight and his truck off at his house and walk home from there."

Fontaine raised her hand, signaling Washbee to stop talking. "Do you know how the truck end up on Manatee Avenue?"

Washbee went on, "Winston made a wrong turn, got confused and ended up crossing Green Bridge. Once across he turned onto Manatee Avenue driving in the wrong direction. It was fortunate that it was early in the morning with little traffic. He panicked and left the truck with Gaslight still sleeping in the cab."

The detectives scribbled in notepads.

When everyone stopped writing, Stein asked, "What did you do next, Cyrus?"

Washbee said, "After hearing Winston's side of the story, I was still unsure if Ida Foote's leg was actually in the bag, so I went back into the refrigerator and closely re-examined every shelf and nook."

When Washbee finished speaking, Manfred walked across the table and climbed onto his lap.

The detectives kept writing furiously, each taking extreme care not to mention the other contents in the sack, leaving out the pieces of Rosa's body and the separate blood deposits with DNA belonging to a female. As far as Washbee knew, the police visits were due only to the discovery of Ida Foote's leg.

Hymns from Olney's wake softly crept into the kitchen without disturbing the soundless scrapings across the detectives' notepads. Everyone stopped writing and the room grew silent except for Manfred's purring and the soft music.

Beaucharp spoke first. "Cyrus, where else did you think the leg could have gone if it weren't in the cadaver refrigerator? Could something else have happened to it?"

"I can see you are looking for some loose ends," Washbee said.

"Is it possible," Fontaine asked, "that the leg could have gotten mixed in with Olney's remains?" She, Stein, and Beaucharp already knew the answer. It was an instinctual investigative question used to find out if the interviewee was on the level. They all knew Washbee was being truthful, but Fontaine wanted all the bases covered in case a follow-up investigation had to take place.

Washbee shook his head. "That's not possible. Olney's remains were cremated two days before Ida's."

Beaucharp started to speak, then suddenly stopped and pondered in worry with her thoughts.

This is a family of angels. How does stuff like this happen to them? That's okay! We'll pile everything on Bunson Rosa.

Chapter 40

S tein, Fontaine, and Beaucharp went back to the chapel. Bertha, Etta, and Gertrude were sitting together. Having met earlier, Stein and Beaucharp just nodded, then walked over to the Freemans and introduced themselves.

Stein said, "So how well did you know Olney, Mr. Freeman?"

He stretched his hand out. "Please, call me Willy. Olney was one of the first people we met when we moved to Florida over forty years ago. After that, we spent nearly every holiday event with him."

Mrs. Freeman said, "Please call me Rachel. Olney was a family friend. During difficult times the community could always count on him to be there for folks."

Stein said, "He had to have been a wonderful person to have such loyal friends."

Bertha, noticing the detectives, left Etta and Gertrude and limped over, her cane tapping out each step. "You're back," she said.

"We said we'd come back." Beaucharp then stabbed her thumb at Fontaine. Besides did you think my partner would walk out of this place without pinching a few more cookies?"

Bertha, delighted with the newly gained friendships, looked at the Freemans, and pointed with her free hand. "These two women are Belenton Police detectives, and the other is an FBI agent." She looked at Willy and winked. "You'd better behave yourself."

While looking at the detectives, Rachel rolled her eyes, tilted her head in Willy's direction, and smiled. "I'm asking for your cards just in case he tries to get smart with me."

Stein, Beaucharp and Fontaine reflected on their training relating to human behavior. Seldom had they encountered a community of so many warm people. It caused each of them to ponder the paradox of this gruesome investigation. One of the cruelest, most sadistic criminals Florida ever produced is leading them into this gentle community and the Washbee's Funeral Home and Crematorium.

Stein quickly glanced around the room and mulled. *Amid this whole mess, how is it possible? None of these people are liars or cons.*

Beaucharp said, "It's nice to meet you all. Is everyone from Ellenton?"

Willy said, "We aren't. Originally, we're from Ohio."

Fontaine excused herself. "I promised Gertrude I'd connect with her and Etta when we came back."

As Fontaine started out, Rachel stopped her. "Don't let her hear you call her Gertrude."

Fontaine stopped. "Oops. You're right. It's Gertie."

Gertrude, now sitting alone, watched Fontaine approach, and signaled to the seat next to her.

"Where's Etta?" Fontaine asked as she dropped into the seat. "She was sitting here a minute ago?"

"She just went to the ladies room. Don't worry, she'll be back. She doesn't want to miss anything."

Fontaine then noticed a man in a blue suit sitting alone in a chair detached from the row. *He wasn't here when I came to get the cookies. Why does he look so familiar? He's staring at me.*

Fontaine waved. He waved back. She asked Gertie who the person was when she heard Beaucharp call out, "Hello Mr. Gaslight?"

Fontaine looked at him again. "Oh! So, it's you, Mr. Gaslight! I didn't even recognize you."

Gaslight offered a sad smile and looked down at his boots. Fontaine smiled back.

Beaucharp took the seat next to him and said, "Mr. Gaslight, I almost didn't recognize you. Are you doing okay?"

Gaslight nodded. Beaucharp gently rubbed the back of his shoulder, said something, then got up. He went back to staring at his feet.

Gertrude said, "I would have gotten up to join you all, except that my hip is giving me trouble. I think it might rain." She pointed at Gaslight. "Wally seems quite despondent over Olney's death."

Fontaine nodded. The gesture was part of a lie since she knew Gaslight's world had already been turned upside down.

Fontaine said, "We'll be around for a while. Are you going to need some help getting to your car?" As Fontaine spoke, Gertie glanced at the group talking to Stein and Beaucharp. She made eye contact with the Freemans, signaled by raising her eyebrows, then tipped her head back quickly looking for a reaction from someone. Mrs. Freeman acknowledged her with a nod.

Fontaine looked at the group, then back to Gertie. *What's going on?*

"Thank you, but I'm sure I won't have any problems getting to the car." Then, trying to change the subject, she said, "You're such a pretty girl. You got someone special out there?"

"I think I got something going with a young guy I picked up this morning." Fontaine didn't mention that it was the puppy.

"Good for you. You are a policewoman, and I'm sure that sometimes you must ask questions you don't want to."

"It happens."

"Can you keep a secret if a stranger tells you one?"

"Of course. Well, I say of course, but it depends on what I'm hearing. If it is about something unlawful, I'm compelled to tell someone."

Suddenly, Gertie grimaced when a sharp pain shot through her side. She moved to reposition herself in the chair and was again at ease. Looking at Fontaine and smiling, she whispered, "Olney and I were lovers."

Lovers! Holly shit! "That is so sweet, Gertie. Olney was a lucky man. How long have you two been an item?"

"An item! That's what they call it these days?"

Fontaine's eyes lit up and a grinned broadly flashing a mouthful of perfect teeth.

"For the last three years."

"Thank you for sharing that, Gertie. Why is it a secret?"

"You know how people can talk in these little towns. I don't want anyone tarnishing Olney's name."

"There is no way someone can blemish Olney's name for being with someone as nice as you."

Gertie's eyes rolled upward and released an enormous sigh of relief. "Oh! You don't know how special those words are for me right now. If I could get up, I'd give you a hug you'd never forget."

Fontaine's eyes moistened. Gertie touched her cheek. "You are such a sweet child. Am I upsetting you?"

Fontaine looked into Gertie's face. "No! No, you are not upsetting me. On the contrary, the genuineness of all these people here is touching. In my line of work, we rarely see such a gathering of angels."

Gertie pulled a tissue from a plastic package and dabbed her eyes.

Fontaine said, "Gertie, we're gonna finish our work here soon. Where do you usually hang out in Ellenton?"

"We're living at the Fair Creek Apartments. It's an independent living facility on Twenty-Seventh Street."

"Whenever my partner and I are in the neighborhood, would you mind if we stopped by to say hello to you folks?"

"Oh! That would be nice. Please, stop by anytime. Can I tell the others about this?"

"Of course. I'm not promising when we'll get a chance, but we'll visit if we're around. My partner would like this as well."

"How about the pretty FBI lady?"

Fontaine said, "She works out of the Tampa Office. We'll let her know the invitation is open to her. In the meantime, we really have to get moving here. What did you and Etta need to talk about?"

"I got something important to tell you. Did you meet Hattie? She's Mr. Washbee's niece."

"No, we were hoping to see her later today. Why?"

"Something's happened to her. She isn't the same."

"How do you mean?"

Gertie examined Fontaine's face for several seconds before going on. "She stops by at least once a week with cookies or cupcakes. All of us"—she pointed to the four still speaking with Beaucharp and Stein—"have coffee and snacks in the community dayroom. The past two times that she stopped by something was upsetting her. I thought that it was just me plex, yet so were the workings of a Swiss watch. Fontaine could envision Stein's ideas rolling into place like the complicated gears in the automatic transmission of a semi.

When Stein finished, Beaucharp gently tapped Stein's bony shoulder. "That's why you guys at the Bureau make the big bucks."

Fontaine looked at her two comrades, her eyes icy and determined. "How we gonna work this? First, we gotta talk to the women again, then Mr. Washbee. Everyone's gotta know what we think happened to Hattie."

"Let's ask Cyrus if we can use the kitchen again." Stein went on, "We'll get everyone together in there."

Fontaine stood and tugged the bottom of her jacket flat. "I'll see to Mr. Washbee. Somebody gather the women and Mr. Freeman. He's gotta be part of this now."

Stein said, "What was the story with Gaslight, Donna?"

"He was coming undone. Too much happening to the old guy along with his friend dying and such. I think he's okay now," Fontaine said.

Beaucharp interrupted trying to lighten up the mood. "Besides I think he's got a thing for her."

Stein and Fontaine grinned.

***

Beaucharp said, "I'll get Bertha and Etta. I sensed some relief for them after talking about it. But they're still pretty upset."

Fontaine took a deep breath and let it out. "I imagine that once they hear what we tell them, they'll go through the usual business of blaming themselves for not catching on sooner."

"We can deal with that after we get them settled somewhat," Beaucharp said.

Stein stuffed her notepad into her bag. "Okay. I'll get the Freemans and whoever I can, Beauchy gets the rest. That how it's going to go?"

Fontaine said, "Whoa! Agent Stein. Way to go."

Beaucharp and Stein looked puzzled.

She pointed at Beaucharp. "Calling my partner Beauchy. Oh yeah. You're there now."

Stein chuckled. Beaucharp smiled and said, "Fontaine, partner, you're a freaking nutcase. One of these days, I'm going to have to sneak you out of an institution, I'm sure."

Stein and Fontaine started for the door. After several steps, Fontaine stopped, and turned to Beaucharp. "Way to go, partner. You're getting pretty good with those *copulation* words. Freaking! C'mon! It's a good start though—"

Beaucharp blushed, then realigned the chairs back into a straight row. Before leaving she uttered under her breath. "Freaking is not a dirty word."

Unlike her first visit to Olney's Chapel, Beaucharp found the room alive with chatter. The serenity of the earlier mourners gave way to speaking loud enough to compensate for the volume of the other voices in the room. The noise boiled out into the hallway.

The sisters, Rachel and Willy Freeman simmered together in discussion while a nervous Bertha and Etta tried to explain what they learned from the conversation with Beaucharp.

An ashen Gertie held a hand to her mouth. Willy Freeman wrapped his arm over Rachel's shoulders and she leaned into him listening to every sentence.

Beaucharp approached. "We are going to ask Mr. Washbee to let us meet in the kitchen. Is that okay with everyone?"

"I don't understand any of this," said Gertie.

Beaucharp said, "We hope we can bring everyone up to speed at the same time. You must have a lot of questions."

"We have to do something," Rachel Freeman said.

Edith spoke. "Do what? We're lost here."

"We'll talk about it," Beaucharp said.

Chapter 43

Cyrus Washbee walked into the kitchen with red, swollen eyes, Fontaine and Stein close behind. Everyone stood, and Bertha rushed to his side, grabbing his hand like a child claiming a missing parent.

Edith and Gertie approached, their eyes swollen and teary. Washbee wrapped his arms around as many of them as possible, then he sat and buried his face into his hands with his elbows resting on the table. Etta gently stroked the top of his shoulders.

The cruel expressions of grief lingered over everyone in the room like an odorless toxic gas. The detectives remained stoic. Stein wrote in her notes; *Sorrow was having a celebration.*

Fontaine touched Washbee's arm. "I'd like to meet Hattie."

Washbee wiped his eyes and turned to Fontaine. "She should be in her room. I haven't seen her since breakfast."

He then closed his eyes again and spoke softly, almost in a whisper behind his teeth, his jaw closed tightly. "I should have known something was wrong. She's been too quiet. I thought she might be experiencing growing sensations, and I didn't want to butt in. How insensitive can a parent be?" He buried his face back into his hands again, his head bobbing to a rhythm of sobs. "What am I going to do? I let her down! I should've been there for her."

Fontaine gently pulled his hands away from his face and moved closer. "Mr. Washbee, you didn't let anyone down. None of this is your fault." Then, surveying the despondency around the table, she said, "Nobody in this room is at fault. If what we think happened is true, it's terrible and unfortunate. We can't change it, but we can help fix whatever damage may have come to Hattie."

Beaucharp said, "Hattie's gonna need every one of you to help her work through this."

Etta said, "She's right. We'd better pull this together."

Washbee reached across and clutched Etta's hand. "Thank you. I feel so helpless. I'm frightened."

Willy Freeman, silent through it all, finally spoke. "Cyrus, for as long as I've known you, your family has been there for others. I feel that Hattie, Winston, and Duff are as much our children as yours—"

Rachel Freeman interrupted. "He's right, Cyrus. We're part of this with you. The important thing is that Hattie gets better, no matter what it takes."

The detectives sat quietly and allowed the painful dialogues to ensue. When the venting and hugs subsided, Stein spoke. "We can see you all get the information you'll need to help understand the problems that can surface for Hattie." She looked at Fontaine and asked. "There are resources in the community to help as well?"

Fontaine nodded.

Beaucharp said, "We're still not sure what happened. All we have are ideas that stem from our professional training and experiences."

"One of us will have to meet with Hattie," said Stein.

Fontaine looked at Washbee. "Where can I find Hattie? I'd like to be the one to talk with her."

Washbee said, "If she's not in her room, you'll find her at Olney's wake."

"I know where her room is," said Rachel. "We're very close, so I'd like to go with you."

Fontaine thought for a moment and nodded. "Okay. She'll probably feel safer with you there."

"This is unbelievable," Washbee said.

Stein said, "The shock of hearing about this can knock folks off balance and the first thing they do is blame themselves. They feel that they needed to be there protecting someone or feel guilty for not seeing the signs."

"No, we're not," Koch said. Then she turned and pointed at Patroine. "Stay out of my way."

"Is that a threat, Madeline Koch?"

Koch laughed, shook her head, and slowly hobbled toward Stein.

Before Patroine could utter another word, Stein approached Koch, stuck out her hand and said, "I'm Special Agent Wanda Stein, Ms. Koch."

Patroine stared coldly.

Koch's elbow crutch lifted off the floor as she shook Stein's hand. "I know who you are." She winked. "I'm a Brandeis brat as well."

Stein pointed to the Police Only elevator. "It's important that we get you to your client." They walked away, Stein keeping with Koch's slow gait.

The elevator dinged, the door opened, and Patroine wailed in the empty hall. "This ain't over, Koch!"

Before stepping into the cage, Koch leaned back over her shoulder and smiled. "Yeah! And the dish ran away with the spoon!"

Stein edged Koch through the door, trying not to display a smile.

Koch tapped the side of Stein's leg with the crutch. "Don't worry. He's a bozo. In my line of work, if it weren't for stupid cops like him, I wouldn't have any laughs."

Stein turned and faced Koch. "I think you're right, ma'am."

"Ma'am! Ma'am! My Aunt Becca's name is ma'am. Call me Maddie. Do I call you Agent Stein?"

"Okay, Maddie. Please call me Wanda."

"Wanda, I'm not shitting you. I'm Brandeis, 1969. We were the ones pushing back, along with Howard Zinn, when Maurice Silber tried to take down BU. Silber thought being a college president entitled him the power of a czar."

Stein said, "Yeah, if there is any place you cannot pull that stuff, it's in Boston." Koch nodded, then Stein asked, "So, how do you know about me? I've only been here three days."

The elevator stopped, and the door opened. Before Stein could step out, Koch grabbed her elbow. "Belenton is a little big town. News travels as fast as a fart in church. Something's going on, and it's overwhelming the political community like scentless smoke. You guys are in the middle of it, and I want you to know that you also got a lot of friends here." They stepped out of the elevator and started down the hall. Koch stopped again. "And Wanda, the detectives you're working with are the best."

"I agree."

"I don't have any idea what's going on. I take it you three are responsible for my client being here?"

Stein nodded, looked at Koch, and shook her head. "There is a term that everyone's been using since I got here. This is a real shitstorm, Maddie."

Koch resumed her slow gait, then stopped again, looked at Stein, and grinned. "We'll see about that."

Stein smiled. *Should I ask her? Screw it!* "I'd like to ask you something before I leave you with the Washbees."

"Go ahead."

"What's the story with you and Detective Fontaine? She was your star witness. The story is you slammed her, bad."

Koch stopped again, smiled, and leaned against the wall. "Fontaine was the star witness. However, it was a police incompetence case, and she stepped up when she didn't have to. I got word that, although most of the Belenton Police Officers agreed with her, some of her brothers and sisters in blue were upset that she was testifying. Also, it was a real tight jury and—"

Stein interrupted. "Yeah, Manatee County isn't known for its progressive thinking."

Koch continued. "While on the stand Fontaine tried to handle me gingerly."

Stein rolled her eyes and said, "Oh shit! I can see that. Fontaine is such a softy."

Koch smiled back and said, "Oh shit is right. I'm not a feeble old lady that she needed to worry about making look bad."

"Juries can see that stuff," said Stein.

"Yes, after I got the statements I needed from her, I led her into a verbal trap concerning some foolish police procedures. I chastised her a little in front of the jury so that they, and her fellow officers, wouldn't think she was a Public Defender's stooge."

Stein nodded. "I guess it worked, huh?"

Koch said, "I saved her ass with the department and many folks in the judicial system. I don't know if you know it, but her dad was a police captain in Tampa. Well-liked and well-respected, a real cop." Koch chuckled. "The judge even sent him a note saying how proud he should be of his daughter for demonstrating such courage."

Stein pointed to the end of the hall. "You'll get to see her in a second. Whenever you're ready, Fontaine will be the one interviewing your client."

They resumed down the hall with Stein keeping pace as Koch waddled along, leaning into each elbow crutch. Stein stopped in front of the interrogation room and grabbed the doorknob. "Maddie, can I get you anything? A soda, water?"

"You know, some water would be nice. If it's in plastic bottles, can you bring a couple, dear?"

"Of course." Stein knocked twice, opened the door and Koch stepped through.

Washbee attempted to stand, but Koch signaled for him to stay seated. Upon seeing her, Hattie smiled and got weepy. "Aunt Maddie," she said.

Koch rested her elbows on the crutches, grasped Hattie's cheeks with both hands, softly kissed her forehead and said, "I'm here honey." She moved around the back of Hattie's chair and touched Washbee on the shoulder. "How are you doing, Cyrus?"

Washbee's eyes watered. "I'm fine. Thank you for coming, Maddie."

Hattie said, "I'm really scared."

Koch patted the back of her hand. "Don't worry, honey. Things are going to work out." She then turned and acknowledged Fontaine. "How are you, detective?"

"I'm fine, counselor. I'm sure you want some time alone with your client."

Koch nodded.

Fontaine started out of her chair, and Koch stopped her. "Detective Fontaine, you're one of the best police officers I've ever known. You understand the reasons behind our encounter that day in the courtroom."

"I was angry at first, but afterward, a few of my colleagues went to bat for me. Then I realized you were letting everyone know I wasn't a rat."

Koch said, "I've been around the system for a long time, detective. Regardless of what is said, if you carry a badge and do the right thing, you will get respect from the real cops around you."

"Thank you for saying that. I learned that lesson as well."

Koch nodded, and Fontaine slid away from the table.

Stein rapped two times, then opened the door. She noticed Hattie's frightened face staring at her as she placed four bottles of water and two cans of soft drinks on the table. She smiled and winked. Hattie returned a shy grin, and Stein left with Fontaine.

Still standing, Koch moved over to the one-way mirror and rattled it with two taps of a crutch. "You guys can get out of there and turn the lights on." The background lights in the viewing room showed if there were any occupants.

that her mind wasn't clear at the time, but she could hear words in her head but didn't know where they were coming from.

From their training and experiences, Fontaine and Koch knew that horrific trauma could ignite voices inside a victim's head.

Later, Fontaine shared parts of the recorded narrative with Beaucharp and Stein before turning it over to Captains Bargiel and Bird. ADA Grover kept her own copy.

At one point, Beaucharp paused the video to speak. "She's terrified!"

She then restarted the video in time to hear Hattie say, "The scariest thing was not being able to use my voice. Not being able to scream for help! I should have screamed for help."

Beaucharp clenched her jaw and internally surmised the setting. *Rosa knew that would happen. He's familiar with terrorizing other's and understood its impact on people.*

She doesn't know what made her do it. But the last time Rosa leaned into her face, Hattie jammed the soup bone into his mouth like a sword swallower, shoving it deeper and deeper into his throat. Her hands shook, and her eyes fluttered side to side as she described Rosa's gagging and convulsing and how his hands frantically tried to dislodge the bone.

"His throat bulged like a snake swallowing rabbit, blood and broken teeth shot all over my face and clothes," Hattie said she tried closing her eyes, hoping to block the visions. It didn't work. Like a never-ending scary video, it kept returning and rolling inside her head.

While trying not to disturb the narrative, Koch laid her hand on Hattie's.

"If I try to shut my mind off from everything, I still see a picture of eyes bulging like big grapes with tiny blood vessels swelling and getting ready to burst like a cheap garden hose put under too much water pressure. The white of his eyes turned as red as checkerboard squares."

Hattie said she didn't remember how long it took to crawl out from under him, nor why once free, picking up the cleaver and with both hands chopping away at his carcass.

The culvert was sticky with blood, human entrails, and organs when it was all over. Flies and insects had already begun to accumulate. It is assumed that because she was still in shock, Hattie, unknowingly scooped up various pieces of his organs and body parts and wrapped them in Rosa's dirty shirt. When Hattie finally stood, she found her whole upper torso covered in blood and sticky matter.

Still in shock, Hattie tried to square away her bloody torn shirt and bra, then without thinking, picked up the cleaver and grabbed Rosa's shirt with his body parts wrapped inside. Using her foot, she pushed the remains of the carcass further down into the bottom of the culvert.

Ashamed, and not wanting to draw attention to herself, Hattie followed the drainage culvert to Wally Gaslight's house. Once there, she rushed to the rear and found the water spigot. Not thinking, she tossed the cleaver in the brush on the side of his gravel driveway.

Then, with the garden hose, she rinsed away pieces of skin tissue and what seemed like bone fragments from her hair and shirt. Next, she rinsed her clothes the best she could and wrung them out. Shaking and confused, she put the wet clothes back on, then she noticed Rosa's shirt, and the pieces of his body spread out on the damp grass. At the sight of them, more fear and confusion stunned her as she didn't know why she had taken them.

It was later concluded that Hattie was still overwhelmed and in shock at the time.

Hattie's narrative lasted nearly an hour. When she finished, Koch dropped her pencil on the legal pad, removed her glasses, and pinched the bridge of her nose again. Hattie stared lifelessly at the table. Beaucharp, Stein, and Grover watched behind the mirror.

Chapter 50

Everyone behind the mirror quietly masked their thoughts. Then Stein broke the stillness. "If we could dig him up and put the pieces back together, I'd show you a way to kill the bastard."

Beaucharp stroked Stein's arm, just below the shoulder. "Wanda, from time to time, we got to deal with shit-birds whose behavior is too evil for decent people to stomach. Their wickedness will eat you up if you allow yourself to carry the rage for too long. If that happens, you'll have difficulty finding enjoyment, and people like this Rosa character wins."

Stein nodded. "You're right. Just got to let go of some steam, I guess."

Grover and Beaucharp nodded and kept staring into the room and listening to Hattie describe more of the horror.

Once her mind settled, she began to focus on the pieces of Rosa that she unconsciously chopped up and took with her during the escape panic. There were portions of something that looked like it belonged to a heart, pieces of fingers, and various undistinguishable intestinal parts. There were pieces of a rotten tooth and a chunk of tissue with parts of a faded jailhouse tattoo of a cross. Everything reminded her of the slaughtered fowl and food scraps that went to Giovanelli's pigs each week. That's what gave Hattie the idea.

***

She edged her way home, walking the brush line behind the homes and businesses. Evading passing vehicles, she remained unnoticed.

The door buzzer alarm went off, signaling someone entering through the back door. Washbee called out, "Is that you, Winston?"

"No, it's me, Uncle Cyrus," Hattie said trying to sound as routine as possible.

"What are you doing coming in the back way?" Washbee grinned and kiddingly said, "Are you running from the law or something?"

Hattie hated to lie. "I went for a walk and picked up a couple of McDonald's lunch bags someone must have tossed in front of the house. I was putting them in the trash, and I found a couple of loose lids. You know that the raccoons would have loved that." That was the truth.

Washbee, still at his desk, looked at his watch and yelled, "Hattie, Winston said he would make supper. Should be ready in about twenty minutes."

"I'm going to wash up now."

Hattie rushed to the refrigerators in the embalming section, praying that there would be a sack with table scraps. She found one nearly full, so she grabbed another for Rosa's body parts, removed some refuse from the overstuffed one, and placed it into Rosa's bag, making them both appear equal. Because there were two bags, it meant that someone would go to the pig farm that evening or early the next morning.

She grabbed a plastic garbage bag from the hallway pantry, rushed upstairs to her room and tossed the damp, torn, and bloody clothes into it. She, then, jumped into her bathroom shower. Although it was an unusually long shower, Hattie still felt soiled. As she toweled off, she looked at the bruises on her chest, upper arms, stomach, and thighs. She began to shake with fear again. *I got to get control of this. Uncle Cyrus, Bleiu, or Winston have enough to worry about.*

To hide most of her bruises Hattie wore dark cotton slacks and a shirt with three-quarter-length sleeves at supper. She struggled to maintain her composure all through the meal.

Winston said, "I'm going to bring the scraps to Mr. Giovanelli's tonight after supper. The bag is nearly full, so if I don't do it now, we'll have to start a new one tomorrow."

Chapter 48

Koch pulled a yellow legal pad and several pencils out of her back-pack. She placed the pad in front, took one pencil, and placed the others to her right. Hattie, Koch, and Washbee then spent almost an hour discussing everything that had transpired over the past three days. Hattie summarized some of the things she talked about with Detective Fontaine and Rachel Freeman late in the afternoon the day before.

"Where did they meet with you, Hattie?" Koch asked.

"In my room."

"In your room?" She looked at Washbee. "Why'd they come to your room?"

Washbee explained, "Rachel Freeman, and the sisters"—Koch new who *the sisters* were—"felt something bad had happened to Hattie. They pulled the detectives and agent Stein aside seeking their assessments. Upon hearing what the sisters had to say, the detectives and Stein surmised something serious was going on and someone needed to talk to Hattie right away. Rachel Freeman and Detective Fontaine opted to do it."

Koch, familiar with the plight of people who had been abused, understood where this was leading.

Hattie wept and squeezed Washbee's wrist. Koch draped an arm around her and kissed her temple. "Have you been to see a doctor?"

Hattie said, "Detective Fontaine and Mrs. Freeman took me to the ER at Manatee Memorial. I saw Doctor Gouin."

Koch jotted on the pad as she spoke. "I know her, she's a wonderful person and a good doctor. That's who I would have advised, as well. Someone must have the report."

Washbee, uneasy, wiggled uncomfortably, and the feet of his chair squeaked against the cement floor. "The police and the hospital have them. Detective Beaucharp is going to get you an official copy—"

Koch lifted the palm of her free hand, signaling Washbee to pause. She flipped over to a new page and wrote the number twenty-two on the upper right-hand corner, then signaled for Washbee to go on and resumed writing.

Washbee rubbed tears from his eyes and sniffled loudly. Hattie released the pressure on his wrist and touched his cheek with the back of her hand. "I'm sorry, Uncle Cyrus."

Koch reached into her backpack, pulled out two traveler's packets of tissues, and dropped them on the table between Washbee and Hattie. "I'll get all the information about that from the detectives," she said.

Washbee said, "I'm sorry it took someone else to make me aware that something had happened. I wasn't there for you, Hattie."

Koch lifted the pencil, pointed it to the ceiling, and said, "The one to blame is the state of Florida. They let a monster out of jail. We don't know, and may never know, how many others he's hurt since being released."

Koch removed her glasses, dropped them on the table, and pinched the bridge of her nose. *How many times have I defended innocent people? Some judges even shook their heads and scowled at prosecutors when they overlooked evidence, sometimes extremely apparent, of a person's innocence. Some of the innocent spend over a year in jail waiting for trial. An absurdity is, although everyone in the criminal justice system knew of this Rosa guy, some lazy bastard couldn't take the time to follow up on paperwork.*

The room grew still again, except for the sniffles of Hattie and Washbee. Koch reached into her backpack, fumbled around, and fetched a cloth. She used it to wipe her glasses and placed them back on her face. She then turned to Hattie. "I can talk with the detectives about doing this interview a little later if you want."

Washbee kissed the top of Hattie's head and patted the back of her hand and looked toward Koch. "What's going to happen now?"

Koch stared down at her notepad, flipped through several pages of notes, read them, and said, "Nothing is going to happen to Hattie. I promise you that."

Washbee said, "Are you sure, Maddie? I think there is a lot of people trying to run for cover."

Koch removed her glasses again and placed them on the yellow pad. She stared at the tabletop for a few seconds searching for the right words, and then at Washbee. This time, he noticed how different she looked without glasses.

"If it doesn't end today," Koch paused, "by this afternoon, even. I promise you, there'll be mushroom-shaped clouds all over the state. The largest will appear above Tallahassee."

Hattie twisted in her seat, faced Koch, and said, "I want to tell the detectives what happened now. I want to get this over with."

Koch looked into Hattie's face and patted her hand. "Are you sure, honey?"

Hattie said, "Yes." Then turned to Washbee, her lips trembling. "Uncle Cyrus, can I do this without you?"

Washbee said, "Okay. I won't be far away if you need me." He started out of his seat, stopped, sat back down, and looked at Koch. "Take care of her, Maddie."

Koch nodded. "We'll be okay, Cyrus."

Washbee looked one more time at Hattie. "Are you sure you're okay, honey?" Hattie's nod and his confidence in Koch put Washbee at ease.

Koch said, "Wait a minute, Cyrus. I'll get someone to come to get you." She punched in Grover's cell number. In two rings she got a response. "ADA Grover."

"It's Maddie, Grover. We're ready. Send someone to get Cyrus and bring Detective Fontaine back."

Stein was using an extra desk in Grover's office filling out her reports. Grover spoke a little louder than a whisper. "Agent Stein, can you notify Fontaine that they're ready?"

Stein folded the laptop and said, "I got it."

***

Fontaine and Beaucharp were at separate computers working on reports when Stein saw Washbee and an officer about to rap on their door. Officer Moquin stopped when he heard Stein hailing.

Upon noticing who it was, Washbee said, "Wanda."

Stein approached and said, "Cyrus, how's Hattie doing?"

Washbee rubbed his forehead with the tips of his fingers and stared into his palm. "As well as can be expected, I guess. They're fetching Detective Fontaine because she's ready to make a statement."

"I'll take it from here, Officer," Stein said.

Moquin nodded and looked at Washbee. "I didn't get a chance to thank you personally for the services for my Uncle Armand. He lived in Florida for only a year and most of the people he knew were either dead or still living in Vermont and too weak to travel. My small family, some members of the department, along with several nurses from the hospital, stopped by for his wake. One of your nephews or your niece was always there with him just in case nobody showed up. Thank them for me, Mr. Washbee."

"I will, Officer, . . ." Washbee stopped to look at the nameplate. "*Moe-quinn?* Is that French? Am I pronouncing it correctly?"

Moquin nodded then turned to Stein. "He's all yours, Agent." He then gave Washbee a thumbs-up signal and left.

Stein moved close enough to place an arm over his shoulder. "I'm so sorry about all this." She pointed at the room behind the door. "Everyone in there feels the same. Everyone, including ADA Grover, want to make this as easy for Hattie as possible."

Washbee tissued his eyes. "I know. It frightens me to think how this might have turned out if none of you were around."

Stein pushed the door open and escorted Washbee into the room.

Beaucharp, startled by the sight of him, would later add to her notes: *. . . Mr. Washbee looked fragile, pale, and feeble. His gate, more wobbly than usual; his hand trembled when he brought it up to his forehead. He was at a loss and stared at the office wall as if he were trying to see right through it.*

Beaucharp folded her laptop and started out of her chair while at the same time Fontaine closed out her document, got up and pulled a chair into the table. "Sit here, Mr. Washbee."

He said, "You people have been wonderful."

Fontaine moved closer. "One day at a time, Mr. Washbee. The worst may be over, and the healing can begin."

"I know what you're saying," he continued. "But I still think I let Hattie down, somehow."

Beaucharp slid her chair next to him. "You didn't let anyone down. Unfortunately, this whole episode was because of someone else's incompetence. Not yours, not Hattie's."

Washbee looked down at the floor and shook his head from side to side. "I'm at such a loss here. Such terrible things have happened in the lives of those children. We've always been able to move past them. However, something like this? I don't know?"

Beaucharp said, "There's resources available. We've notified some agencies so people will contact you and Hattie."

Fontaine said, "She's right, there's no reason to face this alone."

There was a tap on the open door and Grover stood at the threshold. "Detective Fontaine, we're ready for the statement."

Fontaine touched Washbee's shoulder and said, "Things will work out." Then left with Grover. The echoes of their footsteps against the empty corridor walls overpowered their whispering.

Stein and Beaucharp escorted Washbee to a visitor center with commercial vending machines, comfortable chairs and a substantial magazine library. Before leaving to join the team behind the mirror in the viewing room, Beaucharp said, "Mr. Gaslight, you want something other than what's in the vending machines? The coffee here is pretty good, but we got a bigger assortment of snacks in the patrolman's lounge."

"No, this will be fine."

Stein said, "We'll come get you when the interview is over. Koch will probably want to talk to you in private."

Beaucharp nudged Stein's elbow. "We got to get moving, Wanda."

Chapter 49

Sometimes, events in life make us feel as if we've been shattered like crystal sugar bowls knocked onto a tile floor. Yet we find the strength to endure. Other times, things as simple as forgetting a purchase from the grocery list can make us come undone.

Two days earlier, Hattie thought it would be a quick walk to Mr. Jache's to visit his new blue-tick puppies. She brought a large soup bone for the parents, Sadie and Sammy. It was the choice of Mr. Kanopolous, a butcher at Detweiler's Market.

His last words to her were, "It's about a foot long, Hattie. If you can wait around for a little while, I'll chop it in half for you."

Hattie was running late. "It's okay, Mr. Kanopolous. I'll do it."

Knowing she would have to walk past Wally Gaslight's house, Hattie planned to use the rusty cleaver he always kept stabbed into the oak block at the end of the dooryard. She'd get it as she walked by and chop the bone in half when she got to Jache's then give the two pieces to the parents. They'd gnaw at them for hours and eventually, like Silas Marner, bury what's left in secret spots. On her way home she'd put the cleaver back.

As she proceeded past Gaslight's house with the cleaver in one hand and soup bone in the other, she noticed the man on the side of the road. The Washbee family championed the concept of helping others, especially strangers. It was only natural that Hattie reached out to aid the older, shabby-looking man as he struggled with a sheet of paper. As she approached, she noticed it was a map.

In Hattie's early life she struggled with learning difficulties and the family's overwhelming problems brought on by poverty, ignorance, and substance abuse. Uncle Cyrus and Aunt Rosie rescued her. However, as traumatic as her earlier years were, nothing in that arduous past could have prepared Hattie for the horrors that were about to unfold.

Detective Fontaine listened intently, all the time knowing that Hattie would exhibit the common traits found among victims of similar acts of violence. Their recollections of the events were often imperfect, unable to recall some details. However, they remember being frightened and overwhelmed with panic.

The panic usually makes them angry with themselves for losing control. It creates self-doubt and causes them to think that they could have done things differently. This doubt, induced by second-guessing, caused Hattie to feel as if she allowed it to happen and part of it was her own fault.

In Fontaine's notes, she wrote: *She was immobilized, her forehead wrinkled, pushing her eyebrows toward the hairline. Both eyes were glassy, focusing on nothing, as if staring at a demon in disbelief. Her lips quivered like a child that had seen a cat get struck by a speeding car.*

Hattie began, "He said he was lost and asked if I could look at his map and show him where he was."

Fontaine remained stoic outside using her training to control the thoughts going through her mind.

Her eyes displayed the fear that spurred him on. His sense of power fed on it. These bastards gain pleasure from seeing that fear in another person. That's their control and their control over a victim is what lifts them up.

***

First, his hands and fingers probed and rubbed, and then he knocked her to the ground. His laughter grew the more frightened she became. Rosa tore Hattie's shirt open, sat on her stomach, and began rocking forward and backward like a child on a playground toy. His sweat and spittle dripped onto her face and bare chest.

Hattie's hands shook uncontrollably while she told the story. "He pressed and rubbed his hands across me like he was seasoning a roast."

Fontaine and Koch sat quietly. From time to time throughout the narrative Hattie grew pale and deathlike, and the blue veins at her temples bulged like streets on a roadmap. Sometimes she'd stop, sit motionless and stare into the wall, then suddenly lapse into uncontrollable shaking. Alarmed, twice Fontaine gently rousted Hattie out of the trance.

Throughout her career, Koch had become familiar with the pain of those who experienced Hattie's assault. She remained quiet and took notes. She and Fontaine knew that a part of her healing journey would begin with Hattie telling her story in a safe place.

Anger engulfed Fontaine to a point where only her professionalism and training controlled her composure. She had to keep reminding herself of the FBI instructors' words and techniques at the Rape Debriefing seminars.

"Along with collecting all the facts of the event, we're there as part of the healing process for the victim. Our anger can disrupt the apple cart and jeopardize everything. After the interview, there is plenty of time to yell or kick at walls if you must. But, for now, *'Weep Inside'*."

It happened quickly, like tripping a mousetrap. Rosa snatched her shirt collar and dragged her into the overgrown drainage culvert next to the road. The same storm culvert where police later found the pieces of his body scattered about. At the bottom was a small clearing of flattened brush and weeds with empty beer cans and an assortment of discarded food wrappings spread about. He had been living there.

Fontaine listened, her thoughts kept in camouflage and hidden from Hattie and Koch. *It wasn't the guy's first shot at this.* Rosa knew and enjoyed the fact that he wouldn't even have to place his hand over her mouth to keep her quiet. She'd be in shock, paralyzed, frightened, and easy to wrestle to the ground once he pulled her into the gulley.

***

Sitting on her stomach, Rosa pulled off his rancid shirt and laid it alongside, flattening it with one hand as if the dirty rag was about to be ironed. It was then that he noticed the rusty meat cleaver. Hattie was too overwhelmed to remember it was still in her hand. First, he snickers, then laughed loudly and yanked it out of her hand.

"What are you going to do with this, sweetheart? You gonna chop me up?" he teased, gesturing with it as if it was a trophy. Then, he picked up the soup bone that dropped out of her other hand and held it in front of her face, laughing and taunting. "Maybe we can find a use for this later."

Hattie remembered him waving the cleaver, like a flag, across his face and chest. "You gonna kill me with this?" He mocked her fear and stuck the soup bone into her hand like a dagger. "Here! Stab me with this." He laughed and rocked more violently and tore at was left of her bra.

His giddiness swelled into convulsive fits of laughter as he kept rocking forward and backwards on her stomach like a child sashaying in a dance. Piercing pain drove into Hattie's ribs, and her chest felt like she was being kicked and stomped on. She struggled to breathe.

The sight of Hattie's terror and fruitless struggle was a narcotic for Rosa. First, throwing his head back and wailing in wild pleasure, then tipping to within an inch of her face, drooling spittle and dripping sweat that stank like garbage in a landfill. Her cries of pain only made him laugh and rock with more ferocity.

Each rock forward and fit of laughter exposed the gaping, foul-smelling, and dripping mouth. "A hole in his face," Hattie told Detective Fontaine and Madeline Koch.

Everything went blurry for her after that. She remembered being slapped and struck in the face whenever she struggled, and his clothes stunk like moldy, sweaty rags. He was filthy, and his unshaven face was almost as greasy as his hair. He had extensive black and blue injuries on the right side of his jaw, evident even through the unshaven and dirty face.

When it ended, her shirt, torn and buttonless, was spattered with blood, saliva, and what looked like pieces of a rotten tooth.

***

Hattie said she remembered struggling to catch her breath and that her temples "...pounded like the speeding train that flashed by the Avon Park Amtrak station when Uncle Washbee took me, Winston, and Beauregard to Jacaranda Hotel for the Christmas Buffet." She told Koch and Fontaine

Hattie, trying to act a little uninterested, sliced a piece of meatloaf, placed it on a fork, and lifted it to her mouth and said, "You know, I can do that, Winston. I was going to go out to visit the sisters, a little later."

"I want to see Mr. Jache's blue-tick puppies as well," Winston said.

Hattie struggled to suppress the tremble of her hand after hearing mention of the puppies.

She just nodded casually and started running a plan through her mind.

Chapter 51

Winston was surprised to find two canvas bags in the refrigerator. While he loaded the van, Hattie rushed to the Bucket of Blood and waited. He always made a ceremonial stop there for a soft drink. She watched him back into a parking spot next to Gaslight's truck then hailed Winston from across the lot.

After getting close enough, and before Winston could react, she said, "I gotta take the van, Winston. I got some bingo things to bring to the community center. I'll bring it right back."

Hattie jumped in, started it, and the van began to move. It happened quickly, leaving Winston no time to process what was going on. In his mind, he saw the table scraps getting rancid and reeking in the van. *Better keep them here*, he thought. He popped open the rear door as Hattie began to drive away. Unfortunately, he was only able to pull one sack out.

Then Winston smelled the smoke. A careless cigarette tossed out of a car window started a brush fire close by. As a member of the Manatee County volunteer fire auxiliary, Winston needed to respond. He tossed the sack into the bed of Gaslight's truck planning to return for it later. He then rushed to the firehouse a half-mile away.

Winston returned three hours later, and Gaslight still hadn't come out of the Bucket of Blood. Assuming it wouldn't be much longer, and that Gaslight more than likely would be drunk, Winston decided to wait for him in the truck. Then when Gaslight showed up, he'd drive to pig farm, leave the scraps in the refrigerator in Giovanelli's barn, then take Gaslight home and walk back to the funeral home.

Chapter 52

After she'd taken the van Hattie felt alone and confused and began second-guessing her own behavior. *Did I lure him on? Did do something that enticed him? I should have screamed. Not doing so may have sent him the message that I didn't care. Why did I have to kill him? Why did I have to chop him up? Only a crazy person would do that. I'm so ashamed. How am I ever going to tell Uncle Cyrus? I didn't even know who the man was. Maybe I overreacted? Perhaps he was drunk and about to stop when I rammed the bone into his mouth. I'll probably go to jail. How can anyone believe me when I killed someone and chopped them up? What will I do when they discover the body in the ditch? What if the pigs don't eat all the pieces in the bag and Mr. Giovanelli finds them?*

Then another thought rushed into her mind. *The sea life will eat everything, and his bones will settle to the bottom. Still thinking she had Rosa's remains, Hattie decided to dump the contents, sack and all, into Palma Sola Bay. I'll throw them off the De Soto Bridge.*

She tossed the sack and drove back to the Bucket of Blood. Winston wasn't outside, but several vehicles were still in the parking lot including Gaslight's truck. Nervous and confused, she assumed Winston had left so she didn't stop, instead she drove back home.

Epilogue

The Florida judicial system agreed to quash any charges against Hattie when Madeline Koch threatened the state with massive lawsuits. First on the list was the Bureau of Prisons, then every state and local person with a signature on Bunson Rosa's release.

Unfortunately, one incompetent member of the Attorney General's office, trying to acquire notoriety, threatened charges against Cyrus Washbee for the loss of Ida Foote's leg. Koch then drew a petition to depose the Governor, seven members of his staff, and sixteen prominent Florida legislators. The charges against Washbee were quickly quashed and the Attorney General's Office fired the individual. However, Koch, now angry, demanded that Hattie receive a massive, undisclosed, cash settlement due to the negligence of the state of Florida.

***

Although Washbee tried to discourage her, Hattie used a portion of the cash to install modern, efficient crematory apparatus. Duff Bleiu still runs the new crematorium after spending three weeks at the Ohio school sponsored by the company that manufactured and installed the new equipment.

Winston is still a volunteer with the fire district and, along with two other volunteers, completed three months of search and rescue training from Florida Fire Marshals. He still cares for the Washbee Funeral Home and its extensive grounds and performs minor building maintenance.

Hattie still performs administrative duties for Washbee and is enrolled at USF as a literary major hoping to become a writer.

The sisters, Etta, Gertie, Bertha, and Edith along with Rachel and Will Freeman still celebrate their friendship with Washbee, Hattie, Bleiu, and Winston. To supplement everyone's joy, Wally Gaslight delivered a spayed feral cat to the adult community where she is shared and spoiled by everybody.

Cyrus Washbee still coordinates the happenings at the funeral home. He tries to, once a month, set an afternoon aside for a picnic lunch on the porch with the Washbee family, the sisters, and the Freemans. Fontaine and Beaucharp attend the event periodically, and often are only there long enough for Fontaine to grab a sandwich and a soft drink.

Detectives Fontaine and Beaucharp were awarded commendations for their work on the Bunson Rosa case. They're still a team and from time to time are presented with the most sensitive cases.

Sargent Lapointe's canny and below the radar police instinct for sniffing out the unsuspected is still held in high esteem by police agencies throughout Florida. Lapointe, also, keeps turning down The Florida Department of Law Enforcement's request to recruit him.

Special Agent Stein returned to the Tampa Office but maintains the strong camaraderie developed with Beaucharp and Fontaine. From time to time their professional careers bring them back together on cases that intertwined. Stein, Fontaine, and Beaucharp have become a powerful investigative unit sharing resources and their networks of law enforcement connections. Stein also tries to visit the Washbee family and the sisters in the senior community.

Mr. Jache gave the blue-tick puppy to Fontaine. After naming him Bumper, she passed him on to the lap of luxury at her parents' home in Tampa. Several days a week, he can be spotted at the bow of Fontaine's dad's Boston Whaler.

Manfred is still gaining weight and, when no funeral services are taking place, lends most of his time to sleeping.

Acknowledgements

I must thank many for their help with this book. My wife, Sue, and son Sean for their encouragement and patience, and a brilliant niece for providing the inspiration of a character. Special thanks go to lifelong friends from whom only the wholesome personalities and character traits in the story spring from. They will know who they are. I'm extremely grateful to my dear friends and fellow writers at the Dream Center Writers in Bradenton, Florida. Their patient readings and kind critiques of my work were especially encouraging. This work would not have been possible without the help of editor, Mark Mathes. His encouragement, patience, and honest critique helped me to create order out of the scattered pages of ideas. Any flaws noted in this work are solely due to my stubbornness. I take full responsibility for all things wrong.

About the Author

Dan Brady was born and raised in New Hampshire and currently lives on the West Coast of Florida. Palmetto Crossing is his first novel. Before writing, he was a telephone construction lineman and cable splicer. Upon retirement he became a community organizer for a New Hampshire consumer advocacy group, then a learning coordinator for the homeless continuum in the state's largest city. He was a member of the NH AFL/CIO Committee on Political Education (COPE) and served on the New Hampshire Public Employee Labor Relation Board. He was associate professor at Hesser College in Manchester, N.H.. In Florida he joined the adjunct faculty of St. Petersburg College. Dan and his wife of fifty-one years are dog and cat people. Trust that his work will be witty, sincere, crude at times, and full of plot twists.

Afterword

TO MY DEAR READERS

I love to hear from my readers. If you enjoyed Palmetto Crossing please leave me a note at danbradyauthor1946@gmail.com. I will respond. However, please don't send me lengthy texts files that need downloading.